DARK WATERS

A DS KATE HAMILTON CRIME THRILLER

GAYE MAGUIRE

INKUBATOR
BOOKS

Published by Inkubator Books
www.inkubatorbooks.com

ISBN (eBook): 978-1-83756-208-4
ISBN (Paperback): 978-1-83756-209-1
ISBN (Hardback): 978-1-83756-210-7

PROLOGUE
TUESDAY APRIL 5, 2011

As dawn broke the young man sat in his car, looking eastwards out to sea. By eight o'clock the joggers, cyclists and dog-walkers began to arrive, breathing in the promise of spring in the bright April morning. Still he remained, eyes on the horizon, where a lumbering container ship awaited its tug-boat, looking for all the world like it was suspended in mid-air over the unusually calm waters of Dublin Bay.

Soon the car park began to fill up as drivers vied for the few spaces available. Children spilled out of cars and ran towards the shore and the teeming rock pools ripe for exploring. After parking up, a stressed dad, vainly trying to hold on to two small kids and a dog, noticed the figure in the car. He envied the man his serenity, and his top of the range BMW. An hour later, as he strapped a wriggling child into her car-seat, he noticed that the figure was too still, too serene. *No one could sit that still for so long. Unless...*

1

TEN WEEKS EARLIER - SUNDAY JANUARY 23,
2011 - MIDNIGHT

"There's a girl! I think she's going to kill herself."
The voice was shrill and panicky.
"Do you require police, fire brigade or ambulance, caller?"

"Oh God, I don't know! Send them all. Send the coastguard as well; she's going to do it."

"Can you give me your name and address, caller? And the nature and location of the incident?"

"My name is Lucy Piper. I live in Bray. There's a girl online, an Irish girl. She posted a video on YouTube. She's really upset. I think she's going to kill herself. She said she was going to the sea to do it. It's somewhere in the Dublin area. Please, you have to do something. I think she's serious."

"I'm dispatching units right now, Lucy. Please stay on the line. Do you know the person involved? Are you with her now? Has she told you she's going to take her own life?"

"She's told the whole world! She posted a video on YouTube."

Alerting the Gardai, fire brigade and coastguard simultaneously, the emergency operator watched as the screens of her colleagues lit up, all at the same time. She realised there were multiple callers for the same incident. Standing up, she shouted over the other voices.

"If it's the girl who posted on YouTube, the Guards, coastguard and fire brigade are checking out all the main beaches in the Dublin area."

The room filled with the hubbub of voices reassuring multiple callers. The woman sat down, her face dark with worry, took out her mobile phone and logged on to YouTube. *Maybe it's a hoax. Social media is full of pranks, isn't it? Please God, let it be a sick joke.*

———

Two hours earlier

THE VODKA TASTES nasty on its own but she can stomach it with orange juice. Over the course of the evening she downs more than half of the litre bottle she'd bought on the way home from college. She has the house to herself. Her parents and younger brother are on an activity weekend in Connemara. She had cried off the trip, citing exam revision.

She surveys her wardrobe with intensity. *It has to be something special... the red gown she wore to her Deb's Ball.* It cost more than all the rest of her clothes put together. Mum had taken endless photos on the night of the ball, and invited friends round for prosecco to see her off. She'd felt like a supermodel as the full silk skirt swished around her. Everyone loved it, even the handsome but dull neighbour's son who was her date for the night. He'd been a mistake, expecting her to sleep with him even though they'd barely spoken all evening and he'd gotten stupidly drunk in front of her friends. He looked good in the photos though, and that kind of mattered, back then. At two a.m. she'd gone home, leaving him asleep, head on the table, snoring softly among the empty glasses and discarded food.

NOW SHE APPLIES her makeup at the dressing table. Her hand isn't steady but it looks OK. Lots of waterproof mascara and a bright lip stain, the exact shade of her dress, a little blush on her slightly hollow cheeks. She'd lost weight in the last few months. Her mum had noticed and started prepping healthy packed lunches for her to take to uni. Mostly she couldn't eat, but there was always someone around who'd gladly take the food off her hands. She brushes her strawberry-blonde hair until it falls into place just as she likes it, framing her face. Almost ready, she takes a dozen selfies, pouting for the flash. Picking the best one, she posts it to her Facebook page without a caption. The likes are swift, the compliments lavish, but she doesn't feel the usual buzz. Gently she eases bare feet out from under her sleeping dog, but he wakes anyway, stretching and coming to rest with his nose on her knee. She bends and kisses the top of his soft warm head.

"Oh Moo, best boy in the whole wide world."

A tear creeps down her cheek. The dog puts his two paws on her thigh and moves to lick her face, his big brown eyes full of love.

"From now on you can sleep on my bed every night," the girl whispers.

Then she lets the dog climb onto her lap and allows her tears to flow.

After a few minutes she lifts a sleeping Moo onto the bed and tucks him under a throw. The dog sighs contentedly at this rare treat. She tidies up her makeup, checks her phone is fully charged, and puts on her best trainers. *She can't wear the strappy silver heels that go with the dress. As Ashling would say, they're standing, sitting, or posing shoes, not walking shoes.*

The thought of her best friend makes her pause. It would be so easy to call her... it's been hard keeping secrets from her all these months. So many times she'd wanted to pour out her heart. But Ashling would only blame herself, and she has enough to deal with.

Sitting on the end of her bed, she turns on the camera on her laptop and sets it to record video. The room is dimly lit so her face is in deep shadow. She makes sure to keep it that way.

"Gonna keep this short and sweet. Sweet as sugar... LOL. Get it? Sweet as sugar – that's me. Hello, world, and goodbye world. Look at me. I'm wearing my favourite red dress, and I'm going to my favourite place in the world, the seashore. But this will be my last swim."

She gives a soft laugh, bitter and hollow.

"You see, I've messed up. Like *really* messed up. My life is fucked and I can't fix it. It's gone too far. Mam, Dad, little brother... please don't hate me. I love you all to bits... I just can't fuck up your lives too. I have to do this. There's no other way. I can't seem to be happy anymore. I can't be me. I'm not that girl, the happy one... She's all used up... The truth is... she's dead already. Please don't try to stop me. I'll be at peace, for the first time in ages."

She uploads the video to YouTube and closes the laptop. Downstairs the house is quiet. She's never liked being home alone, and tonight it's grave-still and mid-winter dark. She jumps at a noise behind her.

"Silly boy. You should have stayed asleep."

The dog bounces up and down excitedly as the girl puts on her coat.

"Sorry, Moo, you can't come with me. Not this time."

She bends down for another hug, feeling more than a little unsteady as the vodka takes hold. Then she makes herself walk out the front door and closes it quickly. The dog whimpers behind her and scratches at the door.

"Don't worry, Mum and Dad will be back in the morning. You'll be OK."

She can still hear him howling as she closes the garden gate. *You always know when something's going on, don't you, Moo?*

It's dry and bright with moonlight but there's not a soul out on the street. Most of the houses are in darkness. It takes just ten minutes, the walk to the shore, the walk she's done a thousand times before. At first holding her mother's hand, then cajoled into holding her little brother's grubby one as they half-skipped half-ran, with buckets and spades swinging and the promise of ice cream spurring them on.

The crunch of her feet on the stones gives way to the rhythmic sound of gentle waves breaking on the shore. A full moon hangs low in the sky over the calm glassy sea. The moonlight paints a pathway across the windless waves. Minutes pass. The girl sits on the sand, crying quietly as the waves lap at her feet. She stands awkwardly and walks forward into the dark waters, the long dress flapping against her legs, threatening to trip her. She struggles to continue upright, and her breathing is quick and laboured. Her teeth begin to chatter, but she keeps walking.

2

THE NEXT DAY - MONDAY JANUARY 24, 2011

"Have you seen this?"

Rory Gardiner met Kate at the door of the squad room, holding his laptop. A video was playing on the screen, but she couldn't quite make out what it was.

"Morning to you too, Rory. Exactly what am I looking at?"

"You'd better sit down. Here, take this and just play it from the start. Oh, and listen to the audio too," he said.

Ten minutes later she'd watched it through twice. She found Rory in the tiny kitchen down the hall, making coffee.

"Is it a hoax?"

"I don't think so. Whoever she is, she posted that just after midnight. It went viral in minutes. Hundreds of people dialled 999. The service was jammed with calls, and not just from Ireland – from all over the world," he said, stirring his cup. "Your usual?" he asked.

"Yes. Make it good and strong. Tell me more. Did they

find this girl? How did they know where to go? She sounds Irish but she could be anywhere."

"The Guards, the coastguard, ambulance, lifeboat service, everyone basically, they checked out every major beach in the Dublin area. They never found her. They found a coat though, on Killiney Beach, so they're taking it seriously."

"Do we know her name?"

"No ID yet; she managed to hide her face quite well. Though we've had a few calls from people claiming to know her."

"And..."

"Uniforms are fielding the calls. Nothing definite yet."

"Poor kid. If it's genuine it's bloody awful. How old do you think she is? Or was?"

"Eighteen or nineteen maybe."

"They share their entire lives, but this is a new one on me. Making a video of your suicide note. I hate social media," said Kate.

"You realise you sound about eighty there, Hamilton," said Rory handing her a brimming cup of black coffee.

"I know I do, and I don't give a shit. I can't imagine anything worse than sharing my every move with the world."

They walked back to the squad room together.

"Mostly it's harmless stuff, you know."

"It's shark-infested waters, Rory. You know that well."

"Unfortunate choice of words," he said.

Detective Inspector Jim Corcoran was calling the team together. Kate and Rory slipped in at the back of the group.

"Right, all of you, this is an odd one for us but the Commissioner herself called me first thing to take it on.

We've got nothing on the books at the moment except the usual gangland feuds," he said as all eyes fixed on him.

"If you've had the morning news on, you'll know about The Girl In The Red Dress," he continued.

One or two officers looked puzzled but most nodded.

"A young Irish girl posted a video online saying she was going to commit suicide by going into the sea in the middle of the night."

"Was it for real?" asked a voice.

"We don't know yet. There's no body, and we haven't identified her. But it's practically melted the internet, here and globally. The suicide helplines are hopping, and there's a very real fear of copycats. The whole thing won't go away until we identify the girl, find out if she's dead or alive, or if there's foul play involved. The site took down the video this morning but it's too late; it's been shared already and there's no way of deleting it. The Minister for Justice is involved. He was straight onto the Commissioner at six o'clock this morning. The government has been taking a hammering from the public about unregulated social media. Parents are up in arms about what it's doing to their kids. It's a political sore point because most of the big social media firms have their European HQs here in Dublin. The bosses want this to go away as quietly as possible, and they want us to make that happen."

"But it's not a murder enquiry, boss, is it?" said Lawless.

"No it's not, but the Garda Commissioner feels we're best placed to look into it, and I'm not in a position to argue with her. Would you rather be running twenty-four-hour protection on some lowlife with a contract on his head in Finglas? It can be arranged, you know."

The DI's voice dripped sarcasm and Richie Lawless had the good sense to shut up.

"Right. We'll give this a day or two. Let's hope it's a quick job. I'll hand out assignments in a moment. In the meantime, if you haven't seen it, watch the video. It's been dubbed The Girl In The Red Dress and it's been shared a million times. You can't miss it."

Corcoran's first assignment went to Kate and Rory.

"We've apparently been flooded with tips as to the girl's identity. They have to be checked out. Take over the lists from uniforms. They've enough on their plate without chasing down every teenage girl who didn't come home last night. Find the most promising and pursue them."

"Can the techies do anything to enhance the video so we can see more of her face?" asked Kate.

"Already on it. No joy yet, though."

"It's a strange one for us, sir," she said.

"I know, and I'm not comfortable being at the beck and call of our political masters, but that's just the way it is. At heart it's a possible tragic death, or a fucking cruel hoax. Either way, we should be able to get to the bottom of it fairly quickly, and if something else comes our way, like a real case, I'll have a good reason to lob this straight back to the local Guards, and to hell with the minister."

Rory Gardiner logged into the Pulse system and set about gathering together all the tips that had been submitted to the Gardai overnight. Kate went online. #reddressgirl was trending on Twitter in Ireland, but slipping down the lists worldwide. *How quickly people moved on.* She found the video again and clicked on it, making a transcript of the audio and some notes on what could be seen in the picture. Soon she had two columns on her page, headed Words and Pictures, then she sat back.

What do I know now that I hadn't known before?

The Girl in the Red Dress was definitely Irish, her accent made her almost certainly a Dubliner, and probably from a middle-class family. The dress was interesting. It didn't look like a chain-store buy, but something more expensive. Kate spent a few minutes trying to match it online and finally found it in a boutique called DeeDee's which specialised in Debs' dresses. The Debs, or Debutantes' Ball, an Irish tradition a bit like the American Prom, is an event to celebrate leaving Secondary or High School, with the girls wearing evening dresses and the boys in smart suits or tuxedos. It was usually held a few months after the Leaving Cert exams, just as many students were starting college or university courses. This put the girl's age at eighteen plus. On DeeDee's website the dress was priced at 450 euro.

Not cheap. More evidence of a privileged background perhaps?

The coat, which was evidently retrieved from the seashore, was more generic, a grey puffer jacket with a fur-lined hood. Kate made a note to find it in the evidence store and take a closer look. No one over twelve had name-tags sewn into their coats, but the brand might provide a clue.

"Right, I've narrowed it down to a few names," said Rory, scooting his chair over to her, laptop in hand.

"How did you narrow it down?" asked Kate.

"I've listed the names that have been tipped to us by more than one caller, which gives us around nine in the Dublin area. I've ruled out anyone over thirty, and under sixteen, and I've a separate list for girls from outside Dublin, based on her accent."

"That could be misleading, Rory. You know kids nowadays all have that mid-Atlantic drawl. I blame kids' TV. It's all *Hannah Montana* and *Barney*."

"Not anymore, Kate. I grew up with those ones. I think there might be a new batch by now," said Rory, smiling.

It was a bit of a running gag between them, Rory a mere twenty-eight versus her great age of forty-three. Kate didn't feel that different, but certain things brought the age gap into sharp relief. She'd grown up in the 70's and 80's, with no mobile phones, no internet.

"I'll keep any other names that show promise on hand. I've never really worked missing persons before. Who knew how many young women leave home or run away? It's crazy the number we have. People have called in their droves, but some of their daughters have been missing for months or even years. We could make a start on these. What do you think?"

"We'll need phone numbers and home addresses for the informants. And did anyone give us a home address for Red Dress Girl?"

"I don't think so. I'll email you the list, with details, such as they are. My top pick had three tip-offs, but two of them were hang-ups. A young female said it's a girl called Emily, but wouldn't leave her own name," said Rory, his fingers flying over the keyboard.

"Is it worth going after a hang-up?"

"Well, the Garda who took it said the caller sounded genuinely upset. We had two more who offered the same name – a tutor in UCD who thinks it might be one of his students, and an anonymous young male, the second hang-up."

"So, three calls suggesting the same name. OK, let's find the tutor," said Kate.

"Will I ring him?"

Kate glanced at her watch; it was almost 9 a.m.

"Do, and see if he'll meet us. We can go out to the campus if he's at work. I want to get this sorted as soon as possible, and if it's the right ID, that'll be a good start."

Minutes later the two officers were en route to the UCD campus, just a few miles south of the city centre. Ireland's biggest university, it stretched over a vast greenfield site, a sprawl of mainly glass and concrete blocks, some dating from the 60's. The hotch-potch of buildings, new and old, was softened by landscaping and an abundance of trees and shrubs. There was a running track, some sports fields, and a man-made pond in the centre of the site. Rory drove and, after he'd parked up, Kate followed his lead. It was a warren of twists and turns but he seemed to know where he was going. She had an idea he had done his Master's degree in Criminology on this campus.

"You're quiet, Kate. Everything OK?"

Kate and Rory had grown close in the previous few months. Both were outsiders in a very traditional organisation still largely dominated by conservative, straight men. Garda HQ was a hotbed of gossip and speculation, so they kept their personal friendship quiet.

"Is it this case?" he asked.

Rory knew Kate had gone through dark times in the months since the violent events that had left her close to death. Now her hand went to the scar that ran across the base of her neck. He'd noticed how often her fingers moved to the now faint white line, especially if she was stressed.

"No, I'm fine, just tired."

"Bad night?"

"Something like that."

"Anything I can do?"

Kate hesitated. She couldn't remember when last she'd slept well, and it was beginning to take its toll. It was only a few months since her mother had died, and though it was a relief to let her go after years of watching her mind destroyed by Alzheimer's, it was still a raw pain. Kate's boyfriend Greg was busy in London, where he worked as Europe correspondent for the Washington Post. They barely managed to see each other every few weeks. She hated the travelling, the Saturday morning flights when one or other of them could get a weekend off, the forced cheerfulness on Sunday night as they parted. Sometimes, alone in the small dark hours, she was beginning to question the wisdom of being in any relationship, much less a long-distance one.

"Will you come over tonight?" she said. "We can order in food. There's something I have to do and I don't want to do it on my own."

"Of course I will. Sounds intriguing. Will I bring a bottle?" said Rory.

"Bring two. I think we're going to need them."

They'd finally reached their destination on the fourth floor of the arts block. The sign outside the door read A. QUINN with a string of letters after, and underneath: Senior Lecturer, School of Languages, Cultures and Linguistics.

The door opened quickly after a single knock from Rory. A man of about sixty introduced himself as Andrew Grant and ushered them into a long, narrow office. He retreated behind his desk with his back to the window.

"Help yourself to chairs," he said.

Rory removed two of the moulded plastic chairs so beloved of academic institutions from a stack, and the two officers sat opposite.

"Apologies for the state of my room. You wouldn't believe I take tutorials with up to ten students in here, would you?" said the lecturer with a smile.

Kate left it to Rory to ask the questions.

"I believe you telephoned your local Garda station in the early hours, sir?" he asked.

"Yes, I did indeed. I must tell you this whole business is very upsetting. I just hope I'm wrong, I really do."

"How did you come to see the video online, sir?"

"I'm a terrible sleeper. I read a lot or sometimes I scroll through Twitter, though to be honest the latter rarely puts me to sleep – quite the opposite. The video popped up in my feed and I played it, the first time without the sound. Then I got curious. I could see people were tweeting frantically about it so I played it again with the sound. Very disturbing, don't you think?"

Andrew Grant took off his glasses and began to polish them with the end of his tie.

"We're investigating the source of the video, sir. At this point we can't be sure it's not a fake, a prank of some sort."

"Oh, really? Well, that's a comfort. I hope it is a prank."

"You told the officer who took your call that you know who the girl is..." said Kate.

"I think so, though I could be entirely wrong. There was just something about her face that seemed familiar, but it's not a very clear picture, as you know. It was when I played the audio that a name sprang to mind. I recognised her voice. I don't want to send you off on a wild goose chase, but I think that girl is one of my students, though I truly hope it's not her."

He opened his laptop.

"She's one of my Second Years in the French class. Her

name is Emily Sweetman. I should be able to pull up her registration record here, though I'm not sure if I'm allowed to share it with you," said the tutor, "confidentiality and all that."

"Professor Grant, anything you can do to help us identify the girl in the video would be helpful. Prank or not, this is a Garda investigation and your co-operation is vital," said Rory. "We'll need any contact details you have including mobile number, home address, next of kin..."

For a brief moment the tutor seemed to be considering his options. Then he took a pen and started writing on a sticky note.

"Thank you, sir, we really appreciate your assistance," said Rory.

Kate was anxious to speed things up.

"Before we leave you, may I ask you about this girl, Emily? How well do you know her?"

Passing the note to Rory, Andrew Grant went back to scrolling on his laptop.

"Let me see what my records say... She's been in my tutorials since she was a Fresher, so I would see her twice a week during term. Emily is a gifted student. I think I recognised her voice because she always speaks up in tutorials, which is more than can be said for some of them. She's so enthusiastic, and she hands in her assignments on time. Well, she used to..." He paused.

Kate and Rory waited. The tutor soon filled the silence.

"If I'm honest, she hasn't been herself lately." Again Andrew Grant turned to his laptop. "Her grades have been slipping and her last assignment was a week late. I called her in for a one-to-one."

"You met her alone?"

"Yes, we had a chat over coffee in the restaurant. I don't have one-to-ones with my students in here; college protocol. I find a chat over coffee works better anyway, particularly if I need to be a little... critical," he said.

"And you were critical of Emily?" asked Kate.

The academic looked offended.

"No, not critical, that was the wrong word. I merely told her I was concerned her work was not up to her usual standard. I'm not the stern type. This isn't school. The students have to take responsibility for their own work. We don't do much hand-holding. I did ask if I could do anything to help her get over the slump."

"How did she take it?"

"She was quiet, didn't say much. She apologised and promised to re-focus. She knew her work was not up to scratch, nothing I said was a surprise, but she didn't offer any explanation for the dip. To be honest, I put it down to something personal, an affair of the heart perhaps? She's been underperforming for quite a while, and I did suggest she could see our Pastoral Care Department if she needed help."

"She seemed unhappy to you?"

"Yes, that was my impression these last few months. God, I hope I didn't miss something. Maybe I should have seen the warning signs..." Andrew Grant's voice tailed off.

"And do you know if she followed your suggestion? The Pastoral Care?" asked Rory.

"I wouldn't know that, Officer. All of those things are handled confidentially. All I know is that Emily's work continued to be below par. Don't get me wrong – she wasn't going to fail, but the promise she'd shown in First Year had all but disappeared. It was almost as if she was treading water..."

Kate and Rory exchanged a look.

"Good Lord, my apologies; an unfortunate choice of words."

The tutor stood up then, signalling an end to the interview. Kate and Rory left, promising to keep him informed of developments, if at all possible.

"What do you think?' said Kate.

"He reminds me of every lecturer I ever had."

"Me too. He seems kind enough, though. Let's hope we don't have to give him bad news," she said. "What's her address, this Emily Sweetman?"

"Hillcrest Drive, Killiney."

It took just twenty minutes to reach No. 35 Hillcrest Drive. The houses were well kept, typical of those built during the property boom, three-bed, semi-detached, with room for two cars in the driveway and small gardens. The estate was quiet. It was ten thirty and there was no one out on the street. A gust of wind whipped their faces. The still night had been followed by a blustery day, with dark skies threatening rain. Kate thought she could detect a faint scent of the sea as she pulled her collar up against the January cold.

"No car," said Rory, nodding towards the driveway of No. 35.

"Let's see if there's anyone in," she said.

Before they got to the door a flurry of loud barks reached them from inside. Rory rang the doorbell, and the barks became even more frantic. They waited, listening. They could hear the dog scratching at the door. The barking gave way to a whimper. Kate bent and peered through the letterbox, quickly moving back as a cold doggy nose poked its way towards her face.

Another ring on the bell brought no human response, though from the sound of it the dog had positioned itself just inside, whining softly.

"What now?" said Rory.

"Let's have a look around the side."

The wooden side gate opened easily and they made their way past wheelie bins and plant pots to the back. French doors led to a wooden deck the full width of the house. Some outdoor furniture was shrouded in waterproof coverings, but they could make out the shape of a table and chairs and a barbecue. The garden was mainly lawn with a small, neglected-looking vegetable patch, and some lacklustre flower beds.

They peered in through the French doors. Inside there was a modern kitchen diner, with sleek and shiny dark grey cupboards. The room was tidy, the wooden worktops free of clutter. The dog had followed their move to the back of the house. He was medium sized, golden and fluffy, probably a labradoodle, thought Kate. He had plonked himself in a big furry dog bed just inside the patio doors, from where he watched the two detectives with doleful eyes, still giving the occasional whine.

"Well, this tells us nothing. I imagine someone will be home soon. There's no food in the dog's bowl but he seems well looked after. I can't imagine the family would leave him like this for long," said Kate.

"Will we wait around a bit, canvas the neighbours? Or move on to the next name on the list?" asked Rory.

Before Kate could reply they both heard the sound of a car pulling into the driveway out front.

"Someone's home," said Rory, and the two made their way through the side gate.

A man and woman were just getting out of a Volvo estate, and seemed startled to see two strangers rounding the corner of their house. Kate and Rory showed their Garda IDs. A teenage boy got out of the back seat. All three looked blankly at the detectives.

"Can I help you?" said the man.

"Is something wrong?" said the woman, cutting across him.

"I'm Detective Sergeant Hamilton. This is Detective Gardiner. Are you Mr. and Mrs Sweetman?"

The man answered 'yes'.

"We'd like to ask you some questions, please. Can we go inside?" said Kate.

"I'd just like to see those IDs again," said the man, "if you don't mind?"

Kate and Rory handed over their warrant cards. He made a show of examining them carefully, then handed them back. The woman looked embarrassed.

"You can never be too careful," she said with a half-smile.

"Absolutely," said Rory.

"Can I have the keys? I need my phone and my tablet," said the boy, his face sullen. His father locked the car and handed over the keys.

"You'd better come inside then," he said.

"I warn you, we have a rescue dog. Impossible to train but harmless. He can be a bit excitable," said the woman.

She was talking a little too fast.

These people are not used to visits from the police.

"Oh, we heard him alright," said Kate, hoping fervently that this was not the right family. Not the family of The Girl in The Red Dress.

The boy had disappeared upstairs, leaving the front door

open. The dog raced out and jumped excitedly up on each of the Sweetmans, then came to sniff at Kate and Rory's feet. The father calmed him with a pat on the head and a quick hug. Then he sent the animal into the house, where it ran upstairs.

"You'll have to excuse my son. We've been on one of those Outward Bound weekends in the wilds of Galway. You know the kind – no phones, no internet, no TV. Finn found it a bit tough. He's never without his phone," said the woman.

Kate and Rory exchanged a look.

They haven't seen the video.

3

The couple led them into a comfortable sitting room. There were tasteful abstract prints on the walls, amid lots of family photos. Kate found herself studying the pictures of Emily Sweetman, including a professional portrait more formal than the family snaps around it.

It was her Debs picture... in a red dress.

"What's this all about?" asked the man.

"We need to ask you about your daughter Emily," said Kate, her heart sinking.

"Is she OK? Has something happened?" The woman's voice rose with fear.

"We're investigating a video posted online overnight. We don't know for sure that anything untoward has happened but we would like to speak to her. Do you know where she is at the moment? Mrs Sweetman, when were you last in contact with Emily?" asked Rory, keeping his voice even and calm.

Before the woman could answer, running footsteps could

be heard on the wooden stairs and the boy they'd seen earlier burst into the room, seemingly upset, his face more animated than earlier.

"Mum, Dad, it's Em! She posted something really weird."

Ignoring the two detectives, he pushed his way between his parents on the sofa.

His mother started to speak but he cut her off.

"Please, just look at this. It's definitely Emily and she's really upset," said the boy, his voice shaky with emotion.

Rory looked at Kate in horror. She had to do something quickly.

"Don't play the video, please," she said firmly.

All three looked at her in surprise.

"Not yet. Let me talk to you first, just for a moment."

The boy looked mutinous, but pressed pause on the tablet.

"What you're about to see was posted last night, and it seems to suggest that the person in the video, who may or may not be your daughter, has done themselves some harm. That's why we're here this morning, to look into the identity and check on the welfare of that person. I want to warn you that the content is distressing, and also to say that we have no proof as yet that anything bad has happened."

Shock had drained any colour from the faces of the Sweetman adults. The boy was flushed and tearful.

"Now can I play it," he said, his voice catching in his throat.

Kate nodded. The little family leaned inward, with the boy holding the tablet between his parents.

The girl's voice filled the room. Kate felt she knew the words by heart now, and the pictures that accompanied them. She sat back down beside Rory, her heart aching as she listened.

"It's Em, isn't it, Mum?" said the boy.

Mrs. Sweetman seemed unable to speak. Her husband nodded.

"What's this all about, Finn? What's she playing at?"

"Just watch, Dad," said the boy, now openly crying.

Kate and Rory sat silently as the family watched the video through, both believing now that The Girl In The Red Dress was indeed Emily Sweetman. When it was over, all three were crying. The father jumped up.

"What are you doing about this? What are the Gardai doing? It's only five minutes away." He headed towards the door.

Rory headed him off. Kate put a hand on his arm.

"Mr Sweetman, emergency services and the coastguard were alerted to the video within minutes. Gardai were on every main beach in Dublin by 12.30, including your local one. The coastguard helicopter was in the air soon afterwards. As of now they've found no trace of your daughter."

"That's good though, isn't it? Surely if she... if she went through with it they'd have spotted her?"

"That's our hope, sir, that she didn't actually go in the water. We're still searching."

"Sir, there's nothing you can do at the spot where the incident occurred. A thorough search is continuing both on shore and at sea," said Kate. "For now, I really need your co-operation."

Finn Sweetman huddled in the corner of the sofa, his skinny knees drawn up to his chest, his head bowed. Hugh Sweetman sat back down beside his wife.

"It's some stupid joke, isn't it, Hugh? Something to scare her friends," said Susan Sweetman shakily.

He didn't answer, just gripped her hand.

"May I ask again when you last spoke to your daughter?" asked Rory.

"We left here around five o'clock on Friday. That was the last time," said Hugh.

"And you had no contact when you were away?" asked Kate.

"No. We were doing this Outward Bound thing for families; you weren't allowed to have a phone, and there wasn't one in the Centre either. They call it a digital detox. We all left our devices at home," said Susan.

Finn raised his head long enough to give his mother a resentful glare.

"So none of the three of you heard from her in the last three days; is that correct?" said Rory, making notes.

They all agreed.

"She was supposed to come with us, but she cried off at the last moment..."

Hugh's voice tailed off, then Susan spoke up.

"Emily has exams coming she had to revise... That's what she said..."

Kate was getting impatient. Fearing the worst, she still had a faint hope that The Girl in The Red Dress was alive somewhere, either regretting a stupid impulse or laughing with her friends about the storm she'd created.

"We need the names and numbers of Emily's closest friends," said Rory.

Hugh and Susan looked helplessly at one another.

"Emily's nearly twenty. She's got a whole new set of friends since she went to UCD. I don't think I have numbers for any of them. There's Ashling and Max – those are the names I know. They don't hang out here. Those two live in a student house, I think. That's where they spend all their time... When she was little I knew every one of her friends, and their parents," said Susan.

Finn spoke up.

"They're all on social media. I can show you."

"That's brilliant. Thanks, Finn," said Rory. "Let's pop out to the kitchen and we can go through those. Bring your tablet."

The boy unfolded from his position on the sofa and followed Rory out of the room.

"I need to ask you a few more questions," said Kate, anxious to get moving on the investigation, and to get away from this house and this terrified family. It was all written on their stricken faces – the shock, the disbelief, the fragile hope.

"Has Emily ever had mental health issues?"

Both parents chorused a shocked 'no'.

"Nothing? No exam stress, depression or relationship issues?"

"Emily's a straight-A student. She's never failed an exam. She doesn't even have to try very hard; it seems to come easily to her," said Hugh, a hint of pride cutting through the worry in his voice.

"And she's not in a relationship," said his wife. "There have been boys in the past, but no one serious, and no one at the moment. At least I don't think so."

"Has there been a change in her mood lately?"

"She's been a bit quiet."

"And she lost a bit of weight," said Hugh.

"Just a few pounds, but girls her age are always dieting."

"You say she was quiet?" said Kate.

"A bit... just recently. I thought maybe she was just growing up, losing that bubbly teenage thing, taking life seriously," said the father.

"Have there been any incidents like this one? Any talk of self-harm?"

"God no! Nothing like that," said Susan. "Emily's a rock of good sense, the kind of daughter you dream of having."

"Do you think this could be some sort of prank she's playing?" asked Kate.

The Sweetmans looked at each other. Written on their faces was the hope that this was indeed a bad joke, and equally, the certainty that their daughter wouldn't do such a thing.

"I don't know what to say... I'd never believe this of Emily... not as a joke, and not as a real thing. It has to be some kind of social media stunt," said Hugh.

"I can't believe she'd do this to us... not on purpose. Emily is the most loving... sweet girl..." Susan Sweetman broke down again.

Rory returned to the sitting room alone.

"Your son has gone to his room for a bit," he said.

"We'll be in touch as soon as we have news," said Kate, making ready to leave.

"But what do we do?" said Hugh, standing up suddenly. "What should we do?"

"The best thing is to stay put, here in the house. Contact your close friends and relatives to see if they've heard from Emily – anyone you think she might turn to. Here's my card. You can call me at any time," said Kate. " If you hear from Emily or anything happens, let me know."

Rory handed over his card too.

Back in the car, they both shared a sigh of relief.

"Christ, that was tough. I've always hated the death knock," said Kate.

"At least you're used to it," said Rory.

"You never get used to it, and this wasn't strictly speaking even a death knock. It just felt like it."

"So you think she's dead?"

Kate rubbed a hand across her eyes.

"I don't want to believe the smiley girl in all those photos committed suicide... but a hoax seems out of character... I hate to say it but I think we're looking for a body now," said Kate.

The two sat in silence until finally Rory started the engine and put the car in gear.

"So what did you get from the boy?"

"Two friends that stand out, both class mates, and they seem to be in constant contact, always together. Ashling Byrne, and Max Egan."

"And how are we going to track them down? I presume they haven't put their phone numbers on their Facebook profiles?" said Kate.

"Listen to you, all clued in to social media!"

Glad of a moment's lightness, Kate gently punched his shoulder.

"I do know how these things work. I'm not a complete dinosaur. How are we going to get to these two, and bloody fast?"

"Our old friend, the professor. I texted him to say that we believe it was Emily in the video, and asked him for contact numbers for the two pals."

"Good thinking. I hope you told him to keep schtum."

"I did. He was pretty upset, but promised to keep it under

his hat. The other two were not in his lecture this morning, and he said the three of them are usually joined at the hip."

"So where do you reckon we'll find them?"

"I phoned Ashling Byrne, and she picked up. I've told her and her friend Max to meet us at the restaurant block in UCD in half an hour."

"How did she sound?"

"Freaked out. And she wasn't all that surprised to get the call," said Rory.

"Well, these kids live and die by social media."

"I wouldn't quite put it that way," he said.

"You know what I mean, Rory. They're never off their phones, day or night. I imagine they saw the video as soon as it went up. The question is why did we have to find them? Why didn't they come forward?"

"Good question. If our friendly prof recognised Emily Sweetman, why didn't they? They're supposed to be her besties," said Rory.

"They must have recognised her..."

"The hang-ups!" he said, slapping the steering wheel. "One young female, very upset, one young male, also agitated, according to the guys who took the calls."

"Sounds plausible, so why didn't they leave their names?"

"Maybe they've got something to hide?"

"What, though? If this is anything, it's a tragic death by suicide. If it's a prank and they're involved, the most they'll get is a slap on the wrist. I'm not even sure it breaks the law," said Kate.

"I know, I know, but aren't you curious? This girl seems to have everything going for her. If she's ended her own life, there must be a serious reason," said Rory.

"Agreed, but that's for the coroner to determine, not us. We're just involved because the minister is pissing his pants that this might blow back on him. The truth is, unless you're a celebrity, suicides tend to go unreported and unmarked except by the families. There's still a massive stigma; even the death notices say 'so-and-so died tragically' – that's pretty much code for 'died by suicide'," said Kate.

"But why did she share it online? Why be so public about it? Isn't this usually a solitary thing?" said Rory.

"Maybe it was a way of justifying herself? A sort of video suicide note?"

"I've seen her social media pages. She just doesn't seem the type... There's lots of photos, mostly of her dog and these two friends. There's the usual chit-chat, but nothing overly personal or confessional, nothing serious, you know what I mean?" said Rory, pulling the car into a parking space outside the restaurant block on the UCD campus.

"Right. How shall we play it?" he asked.

"Just keep in mind these two are not suspects, not even witnesses. They're just friends of someone who, for now at least, is a missing person," said Kate.

4

TEN MONTHS EARLIER - MONDAY MARCH
1, 2010

"Did you get your assignment in?" asked Emily.
Max plonked his backpack on the floor and slumped down beside her.

"Do they deliberately make these seats uncomfortable? Seriously, I could sue for back pain," he said.

"So that's a no, is it?" said Ashling.

"More of a not exactly..." Max grinned.

"You didn't..."

"I did..."

"You got another extension?"

"Yep. Only three days, mind you. I'll really have to motor on this one."

"I don't know how you do it, I really don't," said Emily.

"It's my irresistible charm, and I play the 'parents divorcing, child of a broken home' card," he said.

"You're such a jammy dodger, Max," said Ashling. "I sweated blood and tears to get the bloody thing in on time."

"Me too," said Emily.

Max and Ashling looked at their friend and burst out laughing.

"No you didn't, ya big swot! I bet you submitted yours early, way before the deadline," said Max.

Emily blushed.

"I might have... just a few days... It was interesting," she said.

"Are you mad? Intellectual Movements in France in the Post-War Years. Discuss. Feckin' Sartre does my head in," said Max.

"Enough of this work stuff," said Ashling. "I'm in the shits and I don't know what to do."

"Seriously?" said Emily.

"Yep. I'm late with the rent and I can't ask my folks again. They don't have it anyway. My grant is dried up already. I only got a few shifts this month behind the bar. I'd swear that poxy manager hates me since I told him where to go with his gropey hands. He only puts my name on the roster when they're desperate. I need to make some dosh or I'm out on my ear."

"I could lend you some cash," said Emily. "I've still got some birthday money left."

"Thanks, Ems, you're the best, but it's two months' rent. That's nearly 800 euro. No offence but your birthday cash would go nowhere. I wouldn't take it off you anyway. I need to sort this out myself, or I'll be in the same fucking mess again next month," said Ashling.

"What we need is a get-rich-quick scheme," said Max.

"You're not exactly desperate, Max, and neither are you, Ems," said Ashling ruefully.

"My asshole father keeps me on a pittance. I swear to

God I think he believes you can live on fresh air," said Max, "not that *he* goes without."

"My parents are pretty good, but they're a bit pinched at the moment. I've heard them talking about the mortgage. Interest rates are going up apparently and there's something called negative equity which seems to worry them. Plus Finn's bleeding them dry. They're so afraid he'll have one of his meltdowns, they give him everything he wants, between that and the fees for his therapy sessions, the little shit," said Emily vehemently.

Ashling and Max exchanged a surprised look. Emily rarely talked about her home life, although they knew it could be difficult. Her younger brother had issues, and she'd hinted it made for problems at home.

"So that's all three of us, skint. It's like I said, we need a get-rich-quick scheme," said Max.

"No, what we need is a sponsor," said Ashling, "or three sponsors maybe."

The other two looked puzzled.

"Someone to pay us just for being us?" said Max doubtfully.

"A sponsor? For college? Like a bursary?" said Emily.

"Not exactly," said Ashling.

"But what's in it for them?" said Max. "These hypothetical sponsors? Would we have to wear a t-shirt with their logo on or something? Ooooh, maybe they'd give us a car, you know, one of those nifty little ones with branding all over it, or a giant beer can stuck on the roof, or a banana!"

He was warming to the subject.

"Not a corporate sponsor, dope," said Ashling, "a personal one."

"Like a rich uncle who funds you just for the sake of it?"

"Something like that..."

"But what's in it for them?" asked Max.

"Look, it's just a thought, OK? There's this girl I follow on Twitter, I think she's at UCLA, and she has what she calls Pay Pigs," said Ashling.

The other two looked blankly at her.

"I know, awful name, but apparently it's big in the States. Anyhow, these Pay Pigs send her money all the time. She just says 'I need new shoes,' or 'I want to go away for the weekend,' and hey presto the Pigs send her the money."

"But what do they get in return?" asked Emily.

"Nothing, just the pleasure of being 'rinsed'," said Ashling.

"Say what now?" said Max.

"It's called financial rinsing or financial domination."

"You're going to have to explain that one, Ash. I just don't get it," said Emily.

"Well, you know how some people like to be hurt, you know, physically? Like slapping and whipping and all that stuff?" said Ashling.

Max and Emily nodded.

"BDSM – it's quite popular among my people," said Max archly.

"Ewww! TMI – Maxie, too much information," said Ashling.

"Don't worry, Ash, not my cup of tea," he said.

"Never mind the true confessions, do you want to hear this or not?" she said.

"We do, we do," said Emily.

"Instead of getting beaten, these Pay Pigs like to be taken for a ride. No, that's not it – there's no riding involved."

They all laughed.

"Pay Pigs want you to take money from them, to enslave them financially. It's called financial domination. You send them a message like 'HEY, PIG, SEND ME 5O EURO, YOU TIGHT BASTARD' and they do. It's as simple as that."

They laughed again.

"Is this really a thing?" said Emily.

"According to the girl on Twitter, it is. She gets money from loads of Pay Pigs – sometimes only like $20 here, $50 there, but it all adds up. She says she wants to try out a new restaurant, and they send her the cash, or she's stuck for rent money, and *chi-ching*, more money!"

"But how? Wouldn't she have to give them her bank details? That's a bit dodgy," said Emily, ever practical.

"She's got a special digital account online, with a credit card. It's all secure, apparently. They transfer it directly in. She never meets them. They just give her free money," said Ashling.

"And you believe her?" said Max.

"I do. This Pay Pig malarkey – it's a thing, honest to God. Google it."

That was the beginning. Max and Ashling were the most enthusiastic, Emily less so, but they all agreed finding Pay Pigs was worth a try. Emily lent Ashling all 150 euro of her birthday money. Max faked a toothache and got a few hundred from his father for emergency dental treatment. This meant Ashling could pay off one month of what she owed. That left her just four weeks to get the rest of the arrears, plus another four hundred that would then fall due. This deadline meant they worked fast. Max was into computers, so he set up a digital bank account online in the name A Byrne, and a shiny new credit card arrived to Ashling's address within a week.

"I know I'm the brokest of us, but why my name?" she asked.

"It's the most common surname in Ireland. There must be thousands of A Byrnes – this way you're anonymous, pretty much," said Max.

"Common and anonymous. Gee, thanks, you say the nicest things, Maxie!"

"I thought we were all going to get a Pay Pig," said Emily.

"We are. Well, that's the plan," said Max, "but if it's one account it'll keep it simple and minimise the risks."

"So we'll share whatever cash we make three ways, right?" said Ashling. "I owe you two anyway. If this works out, I'll pay you back as soon as the money starts rolling in."

Emily laughed.

"You're hilarious, you two. You actually think there are all these men – I presume they're men – all these men out there just waiting to shower us with cash to fund our glamorous lifestyles! This is mad!"

"This is a sound business model, Ems," said Max. "It's what my father would call entrepreneurship!"

"And my dad would say there's no such thing as a free lunch," she said.

"According to my Twitter source, that's exactly what it is," said Ashling. "I sent her a private message and she gave me some tips on getting the ball rolling."

"Amazing. So, what do we do next?" said Max.

"Simple. We start with three brand new Twitter accounts. Not in our own names; we'll make up some. Then we follow my Twitter friend, so her guys see our accounts, and we tweet that we're in the market for a Pay Pig. She reckons there's more than enough of these guys out there."

"Just like that?" said Emily.

"Yep, just like that. It's how she started. We're bound to get a few freaks and weirdos, but my contact says it's easy to weed out the nutjobs; they're obvious. All we need is a couple of legit ones to get started," said Ashling.

"I'll set up the accounts. Just send me a picture you like," said Max.

Ashling, who had bright red hair, freckles and a curvy figure, sent Max a picture of herself stretched out on a Spanish sun lounger in a bikini and sunglasses.

"My tummy looks flat when I'm lying down, but it does make my boobs flat too... It's a bit of a trade-off," she said. Max used a shot he liked from a black-tie family wedding.

"The name is Egan, Max Egan," he said in his best James Bond voice.

Emily insisted on using a long shot with her dog Moo, walking along Dun Laoghaire Pier.

"Dog-lovers are the nicest people; that's a given. I only want nice Pay Pigs, and Moo is adorable."

It took a couple of months to take off, but soon the three students were seeing a steady cash flow. They decided firstly to clear Ashling's rent arrears, then as the money and the number of Pay Pigs grew, Max got his 'dental emergency' money back, and Emily her birthday cash. Soon they were making enough, together with her bar work, to keep a roof over Ashling's head. For Max and Emily it was extra spending money, a few nights' clubbing, meals out, new clothes. It wasn't all that easy. Some of the Pigs wanted more than they were prepared to offer. These were swiftly blocked. Some were just plain creepy, and they too got the cold shoulder. The three students, who laughingly called themselves the Sugar Babies, used what Max called 'burner phones', pay-as-you-go mobiles with untraceable numbers. The Pigs often wanted private texts, not just online chat. That was fine, just as long as they kept track of who was who, and what elicited the most money. They soon learned what would glean the most cash. Max called it creative writing. Ashling said it was fantasy role-playing. It became a shared experience they all had fun with. The three set aside a couple of hours a week spent together, 'stoking the fires' as Max called it, keeping their enterprise on the go.

"My Pay Pigs are sweethearts. I can't believe I didn't get into this sooner," said Ashling.

"But are they really?" asked Max. "Mine are a bit on the raunchy side. If I have to send one more dick pic, it'll drop off."

"Oh my God, you're not, are you?" said Emily with a squeal.

"Yes, darling, of course I am. How do you think I keep them sweet?" Max continued eating his crisps and swigging Coca Cola.

The three friends were in the UCD coffee shop, their usual haunt. Ashling giggled at Max's revelation.

"Some of my Pigs want pictures too," she said.

"Dirty bastards," said Max smiling.

"I've been blocking anyone who asks for pictures," said Emily, wide-eyed.

"I don't send anything smutty, hon, just little flashes of flesh..." said Ashling. "I make sure they can't see my face, then take a little shot in my PJ's or bra and pants. They lap it up."

"But that's porn," said Emily.

"Hardly," said Ashling. "You see more flesh in the deodorant ads on the telly."

"It's what Sugar Babies do, darling," said Max. "There's nothing disgusting about it."

"Why do you think our donations have gone up?" said Ashling.

"I don't know. I just thought you had more Pigs than me," said Emily sheepishly.

"Look, hon, it's completely harmless. It can't be traced back to us. One dick pic is much like the next, isn't it, Max?" said Ashling.

"I'll have you know, mine is particularly photogenic!" he said.

"I don't know if I could do it, send pictures of myself..." said Emily.

"You won't know till you try, but it's up to you, hon. Do what you feel comfortable with," said Ashling.

Later on that evening, Emily was texting with a Pig who called himself Easy Rider. They'd been in touch for several weeks and though she'd refused to send him any pictures, their correspondence continued. There was something charming about him and she found herself texting him often. He'd sent a picture of himself working out – fully clothed in shorts and t-shirt, to her relief. He was very handsome, a bit older than her, maybe thirty. He'd sent regular 50-euro donations over the weeks, and their text chats had become more friendly. He loved dogs, and told her the picture of her and Moo was what had attracted him. With the money he'd sent Emily had bought new toys and a really cute coat for her dog. Easy Rider was happy to get pictures of Moo with the new stuff. Tonight, he asked if she liked his photo from the gym. Emily replied with a smiley face emoji.

I can send more if u like...

OK. I like...

Emily's phone pinged repeatedly as a series of photos came through. They were all of the same man in various places, some selfies, some obviously holiday pictures from trips abroad.

You're a bit of a poser...

Just a bit – aren't we all though... I just wanted to feel closer to u... and Moo, of course...

Of course...

Send me some pix... of u and Moo

Emily hesitated.

Maybe later...

OK... no pressure...

Emily lay back on her pillow and looked at Easy Rider's pictures. He was gorgeous, bearded, dark-haired and slim, with dark brown eyes. He looked fit but not overly muscle-bound, *not a gym bunny*. Just her type, and some of the photos showed him with a golden spaniel. He'd told her it was his parents' dog Hattie, and that he really missed the pet since he got his own place. Emily called Moo up from her basket at the foot of the bed. After several attempts, she managed to take a picture with her phone that showed Moo's head and just the top half of Emily's face leaning into the shot. It was a good picture. The dog was adorably sleepy and Emily could see the flash had made her own eyes smiley and sparkling. After much hesitation, she hit send. Easy Rider replied with heart emojis and a 100-euro payment.

A few days later when they checked the account, Ashling and Max were impressed.

"That's the biggest single donation we've had," said Ashling.

"You go, girl..." said Max. "Imagine what he'd pay for a nudie pic!"

Emily blushed and elbowed him sharply in the ribs.

"He's not like that. I think he likes Moo more than me, actually..."

"What's he like, this Super Spender?" asked Max.

"Cute, handsome..." said Emily.

"Minted, obviously," said Max.

"Obvs..." said Emily, smiling at all the attention.

She'd always been the quiet, studious one of the trio. This made a nice change. She didn't tell them about the other pictures. The ones she'd sent to Easy Rider. He was so sweet, he made her feel beautiful and confident.

THREE MONTHS LATER

WITH THEIR FIRST Year exams over, when term ended the three students went their separate ways, Ashling to rural Cork to help out on the family farm, and Max aboard the ferry to France in the hope of getting work picking grapes.

"Imagine, all the delicious French red you can drink, fromage and baguettes to beat the band, and lots of fit peasants all hot and sweaty after a day in the vines... it'll be heaven," he said, hugging each of the girls at the ferry port.

Emily was staying home, hoping to get a job in a coffee shop or bar. They'd decided to keep their respective Pay Pigs on tap during the break.

"We can't just drop them; they'll only find someone else to spend their money on," said Ashling. "Let's just keep them ticking over for the summer. We don't need to be together; we've all got the hang of it now. We'll let the dosh mount up, and we can split it up when we're back in college."

"Unless there's an emergency," said Emily. "What if one of us needs some cash urgently? What if Max gets the sack and he's stuck in the middle of France with no money?"

"He can take the credit card then. He *is* the one most likely to get in trouble," said Ashling.

"Your faith in me is touching," said Max pocketing the card. "I won't flog it, I promise, unless I'm stuck, or there's some handsome French waiter I want to woo... See what I did there? Alliteration! Just give me that First in English now!"

Laughing, they hugged again and the girls waved him off. Emily was a little tearful. The three had only met during Freshers Week, but they'd become really close and parting was a wrench. Ashling got the train to Cork that evening. Emily stayed put in Dublin, the old loneliness beginning to take hold as the days lengthened.

By the time they were back together that September something had changed. One of them was in too deep, and the other two didn't see the danger.

5

A WEEK LATER - JUNE 2010

Emily started a job in a coffee shop in Dun Laoghaire, a slightly faded but pretty seaside town just twenty minutes' walk from her home. It was pure drudgery. Most customers were nice, but some were downright rude. She'd done all of one day's training as a barista, so it was new to her, but the demands were ridiculous. There were a million different orders and it was hard to keep them in her head as she wrestled with the huge Italian coffee machine. Oat milk, almond milk, soya milk, milkmilk! Who knew there were so many milks? Espresso, macchiato, cappuccino, latte... with syrup, extra hot, not too hot, less foam, more foam... It was exhausting, and the pay was poor. Emily was cranky and missing her friends, even without the horrors of her job. The manager, a temperamental Croatian woman who was barely civil to the customers, was constantly picking fault with her 'milk art'.

"That is not a heart, it's a turnip, Emileee!"

So, the summer days dragged. Her brother Finn was creating havoc at home, so Emily had become invisible again. He had taken to sneaking out at night to meet gangs of other teenagers in local parks and get drunk. He'd already had to have his stomach pumped once, and her parents were mad with worry over him. Emily suspected he was smoking weed. *Her parents didn't know the half of it.*

There was only one bright spark on the horizon. The Pay Pig who called himself Easy Rider. He texted Emily every day, more often than Ashling and Max did. They both seemed to be having a better summer than hers. Ashling was dating a boy she knew from school who'd apparently 'turned into a ride' since she'd last seen him. Max rarely got in touch but when he did it was with fabulous photos of lavender or sunflower fields in the French sunshine, and boozy nights out with new friends.

Without her daily exchanges with Easy Rider, Emily felt the summer would have been a washout. Now he wanted to meet her, *in real life*. She couldn't tell the others. Ashling would freak out. *She could be very bossy.* For some reason keeping it secret made Emily feel brave. She'd have so much to tell them when September came, maybe even a new boyfriend.

For their first meeting Easy Rider said he'd pick her up from work. She brought a change of clothes and her make-up in a backpack and used the tiny staff toilet to change in. She wore a yellow strappy sundress she'd bought especially. It was flowy at the bottom and low cut at the top. It made her feel sexy. Between the barista work and the Pay Pig money, she'd been able to get expensive highlights in her light brown hair. Even her mum had noticed, amid all the Finn drama, and admired the new look. Emily told her a friend had done her hair, for free.

Easy Rider was just as handsome in person as the photos

he'd sent. He was wearing longish denim shorts and a white linen short-sleeved shirt, and he drove a BMW. He parked near the coffee shop and was sitting on the bonnet of the car when she got there. He leaned in and they exchanged cheek kisses, one on each side.

"You're even more pretty in person," he said.

Emily didn't reply. His scent and the touch of his hands on her arms had made her slightly breathless.

"Let's go somewhere and have a drink," he said, opening the passenger door for her.

"What will I call you?" he asked as they pulled away and headed out of the seaside town, going south towards Wicklow.

"My name is Emily. Some of my friends call me Ems. I don't mind either," she said. "What about you? I can't exactly call you Easy…"

"No, that would be weird. You can call me Dan, just as long as you call me often," he said.

Emily laughed.

"That's just pure cheese, you realise that?" she said.

The conversation flowed after that, light-hearted chat about their love of dogs, her tedious job and college. Much later she realised he'd revealed almost nothing personal, but on that first day, she was heady with his presence and didn't notice. She regaled him with funny stories of eccentric customers, her rude colleague and the madness of coffee choices. While he focused on the road she stole glances at him. He had nice arms, strong but not bulked up, and a good profile.

"You'd love me – I'm a simple Americano guy, none of that nonsense." He smiled.

"Thank God for that. If you were a soya macchiato with

syrup, extra hot and low foam, I might have to kill you," said Emily.

"I'll bear that in mind. Oh, and I always tip," he said.

"The perfect customer so," she said, then she told him how some kids had come in and stolen the tip jar while her back was turned working the coffee machine.

"Little shits! That's awful! Why do you stick it? Don't you make enough money from..." He paused and Emily's heart sank.

She'd been so stupid to think of this as a date. He saw it as a transaction.

"Not really. I don't have a lot of Pigs." The word was out of her mouth before she could stop it.

Emily could feel herself going bright red.

"That's a lousy name. I think of myself as a patron... of sorts." He laughed and she relaxed again.

That first day they had drinks in a quiet pub, miles from anywhere. He had two pints and Emily gulped down several vodkas with orange juice, to steady her nerves. She'd been out before with boys her own age, but Dan was different, confident and sophisticated, older. Most of the lads she'd dated could only talk about sport or video games, and down copious pints before moving in for a snog and a fumble. He didn't touch her apart from a guiding hand on her arm as they went into the pub. Dan seemed interested in everything she said, and she found herself telling him about her course, her family dramas, and eventually, the Sugar Babies.

"So there are just the three of you then?" he asked.

"Yes. We didn't want it to get out, what we were up to. Max said we didn't want to flood the market! As if! I just wanted to keep it quiet so my parents never know."

"So how many Pigs do you have?"

"They come and go, so the number goes up and down. But there are maybe four or five fairly regular ones," said Emily, now completely relaxed after the vodkas, "and you, of course."

"I hope I'm your favourite," he said, reaching out and stroking her bare shoulder with his fingertips.

"Oh, you are. You're the only one I've actually met!" she said with a smile, her heart beating a little faster at his touch.

"Good. Let's keep it that way, Ems," he said. "I want you all to myself."

There was something endearing about the way he used the abbreviated version of her name.

Soon he was picking her up from work every few days. They'd always drive somewhere out of the way. Emily was happy. In between their meetings, he texted her often, wanting to know what she was doing, asking for pictures, telling her how beautiful she was.

> I'm just going in the shower. Need to get the smell of coffee and milk off my hair!

> Send me a picture... from the shower.

Emily complied, feeling sexy, desirable and so grown up. Soon she was sending him more photos, ones she took when she was alone in her room, with the door locked. *What was the harm? Even twelve-year-olds were sexting these days.*

> Ur so gorgeous, Ems. I wish I was there with u.

> Me too...

THREE WEEKS LATER
MONDAY 21ST JUNE 2010

ON THEIR FIFTH meeting Dan took her to a half-built estate in the Dublin foothills. She knew he did something in property, but he'd always been vague about his work. This was a first, an insight into his life she relished. It was around seven in the evening and the site was quiet.

"You see these houses," he said. "They're going to cost two million each when they're finished."

"Wow, they must be pretty amazing."

Among the skeletons of homes in varying states of completion, one appeared finished, with a neatly landscaped front garden and a sign that said Show Home.

"Come on, I'll show you amazing!" he said.

They picked their way through the builders' equipment and debris. Dan held her hand and helped her step over any obstacles. At the Show Home he produced a key and opened the door.

"Voila," he said, "see how the other half live."

The large house was fully furnished. It was stunning, and Emily gasped as they went from room to room.

"Oh my God, it's so beautiful! It's worth two million!" she said.

"They might even go for more than that, and we've had a lot of interest," said Dan proudly.

"Will you make lots of money from this?" she asked peering into the un-filled hot tub on the vast deck at the back.

"Lots," he answered. "Come on, let's look upstairs."

There were five bedrooms, each more luxurious than the last. In the master bedroom they perched on the edge of the massive bed. Up until now they'd only kissed, but the atmosphere between them was electric. Emily knew this was it, the seduction, and she didn't mind one little bit. But she was wrong, so wrong.

EMILY CREPT into the darkened house, desperate not to disturb her family. Dan had dropped her at the end of the road, as she'd asked. He leaned over as she tried to open the car door. It was locked.

"Bye, sweetie. I'll see you soon," he said as he kissed her wet cheek. "Better tidy up before you go in; you look a bit rough."

He pressed the button to release the central locking, and she got out as quickly as she could. She was barely able to walk. Everything hurt.

Emily made it upstairs without waking the others. Painfully she took off her clothes in the bathroom, throwing her blood-stained underwear in the wastepaper bin. She climbed into the shower, turned on the water and slid down the tiles until she was hunched in the corner, knees pulled up to her chin and arms wrapped around herself. The warm water was soothing and stinging at the same time. After a while she was able to stand and pat herself dry with a towel, finding new hurts as she did so. In the bedroom her dog Moo waited. As if sensing something was wrong, he didn't jump up to greet her as usual, he just sat at her feet aiming an occasional lick at her toes. Emily crawled under the quilt and eventually fell into a deep tearful sleep with Moo snuggled beside her.

She called in sick to work the next day, telling her mum she had bad period pain. Susan was sympathetic and business-like, administering Solpadeine and a quick kiss on the forehead before heading off to her work as a nurse in the city centre.

The first text came at 9.30. The ping on Emily's phone woke her from a fitful sleep.

> How r u today?

She didn't reply. Ten minutes went by.

> I hope ur not sulking.

She thought about blocking Dan's number but she was afraid.

> See u when ur shift ends – wear something nice.

Panicking, she texted back.

> No.

> Y not?

> Sick.

> OK, get well soon. I miss u.

She didn't reply. Instead she went to the bathroom and

vomited until there was nothing left but acid and empty retching. The day passed slowly with bouts of crying and, whenever she closed her eyes, terrifying flashbacks. Mercifully, some of it was vague and blurry. She remembered screaming and struggling, but Dan had laughed and said, "Scream all you want, Ems. There's no one to hear you." She knew she'd passed out a couple of times when he'd choked her. Mostly she saw his face and felt him on her and inside every part of her, and saw the thrill in his eyes as he hurt her, again and again.

After two days Emily went back to work. Her parents didn't notice how pale and distraught she was. As usual, their attention was on her brother.

Finn had come home drunk again. He'd puked all over his bedding and Susan had spent the night sitting by his bed, in case he choked on his own vomit. That morning, picking up his dirty clothes for washing, she'd found weed in his jacket pocket. While he slept it off upstairs, Emily's parents were desperately trying to come up with a plan to 'fix' Finn. Apart from a quick goodbye as she made for the door, they paid no attention to her.

When her shift finished, Dan was waiting outside.

"Hi, sweetie. Feeling better?" he said.

Emily froze. There were people all around, tourists and families strolling in the sunshine. She wanted to scream at them all. *Help me.*

"Come for a drive. We'll get a nice drink somewhere," he said.

Then he walked over, took her arm and led her to the car. Inside he leaned over to fasten her seatbelt. Emily shrank back in her seat, sweating with fear.

"Here's the deal, Ems," he whispered, close to her face. "You look after me, and I won't send those naughty pictures and videos I have to your family, all your friends... and the college authorities."

Emily shuddered. Dan started the engine and they set off. He was smiling.

"There's plenty of porn sites that would pay good money for those shots I took when you were out of it. And the video... did I mention the video I filmed? It's steamy stuff, Ems. You look amazing. And once it's online... well, it's out there forever, for anyone to see."

He grinned and stepped on the accelerator. She was trapped, and they both knew it.

6

R ory was trying to locate the two students among the crowds milling around in the college canteen. Kate followed his lead, knowing he could probably identify Ashling Byrne and Max Egan from their online profiles. He stopped and pulled out his phone to double-check.

"I reckon that's them. Do you?" he asked, showing her an Instagram post of the two grinning into the camera and holding up cocktails in salute.

The pair he'd spotted were sitting in the farthest recess of the vast restaurant, as far away as possible from the mass of students.

"Less glammed up, but they look right to me," said Kate as they made their way around messy tables and chattering groups. The couple sat close together, hunched over paper coffee cups.

"Ashling Byrne?" enquired Rory.

The girl stood up. She had a mass of shiny red curls and

cornflower-blue eyes. She had been crying. Her companion, a boy with brown eyes and fair hair, answered.

"Yes, Officer, this is Ashling, and I'm Max."

Kate and Rory showed their IDs and the four sat down.

"Sorry to pull you away from your classes, but I expect you know what this is about," said Rory.

"It's about Emily," said the girl.

Her voice was barely above a whisper.

"So you've seen the video?" said Kate.

"Everyone's seen the video... It's the only thing anyone's talking about," said Max.

"And you're sure it's your friend, Emily Sweetman?"

Ashling sniffed, and once again it was Max who answered.

"Pretty sure."

"Why didn't you come forward?" asked Kate, her voice a little sharp.

She would play bad cop...

"We did..." Ashling blurted out.

"Yes, we both rang the Gardai, as soon as we saw it," said Max.

"We have no record of your names on the list of tip-offs."

Kate wasn't letting them off the hook.

"I didn't leave mine... I was too upset," said Ashling defensively.

"Me too. We were in bits," said Max.

Kate let it go for the moment.

"What do you make of the video?" asked Rory.

The two looked at each other, then Ashling spoke.

"I think Emily's really upset. I've never seen her so miserable."

"And do you think she would harm herself in such a way?"

The two went quiet.

"Maybe she didn't mean to... to do it, you know," said Ashling. "It could be a cry for help."

"Or a prank?" said Kate.

For a long moment the two students looked at one another, then Max answered.

"Emily's not the type to play a prank, not like this. And anyway, it's not even remotely funny."

There were dark circles under his eyes, and the two looked like they hadn't slept. Ashling's porcelain-white skin was tinged grey, making her freckles even more prominent. They were obviously extremely close, with Max reaching out to take the girl's hand whenever she sniffled or sobbed.

"So you think this was a genuine attempt?" said Rory.

"Yes," said Max.

"Maybe," said Ashling at the same time.

"Have you found her?" he asked.

"No, the search is still on-going," said Kate.

"Maybe she never went into the sea. She could be safe somewhere?" said the girl.

"That's what everyone is hoping. If that was the case, do you have any idea where Emily might go?" asked Rory.

"She'd definitely want to lie low after pulling a stunt like that," said the girl, a note of hope in her voice.

"But she'd have called us, Ash, wouldn't she? Even if she wanted to disappear, she'd have told us..." said Max.

Kate could see despair in his eyes. *He might not be crying, but he feared the worst.*

"But where would she go – to lie low, as you say," said Rory.

"That's the thing," said the girl. "If she didn't come to us, I've no clue where she'd go. We're her best friends."

"And she hasn't been in touch?" asked Kate.

"No, and we've been texting and leaving voice notes and DMs. We've basically been trying every way possible to get in touch with her since the video went up," said Max.

"We need to ask you some questions about Emily. Was she in any trouble that you know of? Was there any reason to think she was depressed?" asked Kate.

Something unspoken passed between the two. Max let go of Ashling's hand, took a sip of his coffee and crossed his arms over his chest.

"Ems has never been in trouble in her life, Detective. She's like the perfect student, straight As all the way," said the boy.

Not lately though, not according to her tutor.

"And were there any signs of depression, or anxiety?" said Rory.

"No. She was just the same as usual," said Ashling, too quickly.

Another lie.

The students explained how the three had met in First Year and become very close. Rory asked if Emily was in a relationship, or if there was an ex who might be in the picture. All the answers were a definite no. The conversation dried up soon, with nothing more forthcoming from the pair. Handing over their contact cards, the detectives left.

"They're lying about something..." said Rory.

"Through their perfect white teeth. And whatever it is, I think it's at the heart of this whole sorry affair," said Kate, as they made their way back to the car.

"Should we have another go at them?" he asked.

"Let's leave it for now, and see if anyone back at HQ has turned up something useful. They're just her friends, not witnesses. They don't have to speak to us while she's still a missing person, or even if she turns up dead."

"I know. This is not like other investigations," he said.

"Tell me about it. I can't help looking at everyone we talk to as a suspect, when the truth is – there hasn't even been a crime," said Kate.

Back at HQ most of the team were at their desks. Rory logged onto his computer. Kate went to find their boss, DI Jim Corcoran, in his office.

"We're pretty confident we've established the identity of the girl in the video."

"That didn't take long. Well, who is she?"

Kate filled him in.

"I'm not sure what else we can do until a body turns up, and if it doesn't, it's a missing person case, not one for us," she said.

"I know this is not your cup of tea, Hamilton, but I'm still getting pressure from the Commissioner. The news outlets have the story now, though the coverage won't be too big, hopefully. There's a code of conduct around the reporting of suicide that all of the mainstream media have to follow. The internet is another story, but nothing stays in the headlines for too long there," said Corcoran. "What's your gut feeling, Kate?"

"All day I've felt the video was genuine, and nothing we've found out has changed that. I think that poor girl took her own life last night," she said.

"And the family? They said she was a bit down lately?"

"They said she was different in the last few months, not necessarily depressed. Less bubbly – that's how they put it."

"But the friends saw none of that?"

"They say she was fine, no problems, grade-A student etc., etc."

"But?"

"But... Gardiner and I both felt they were lying, or at least not being entirely truthful. Something was going on with Emily Sweetman. Her grades were slipping, which the friends either didn't know or, more likely, lied about. Her family saw the change. So did her tutor. I can't believe her two best friends *didn't* see it. They're hiding something, but we can't exactly drag them in and get it out of them. This is not a murder enquiry," said Kate.

"Right. Until such time as there's a body, dead or alive, the uniform units and the coastguard can keep searching. I think we've done enough. I'm calling the Commissioner now and we'll bow out of this whole sorry mess. You can knock off now, Hamilton. Hopefully by tomorrow this one will be off our hands. Thanks."

7

T he Pay Pig was annoyed.

That stupid girl and her dramatics.

He'd been appalled when his wife showed him the video on her phone.

"Imagine, some poor girl recording and uploading her own suicide note. And right here, in Dublin," she said, over their morning coffees.

He'd watched the video through with mounting dread. *What the fuck? He knew the voice... Could that actually be Emily? Stupid bitch. He'd only been with her two days before. What if she'd left an actual note, naming him?*

He told himself there was nothing to worry about; she didn't even know his real name. He'd covered his tracks well... apart from the money trail. The payments had come from his personal account, the digital-only account that his wife knew nothing of. *Banking transactions were confidential, classified. They wouldn't find him that way. Anyway, teenagers killed themselves all the time, it was just a fact of life. It would be chalked up to 'mental health'.*

But he'd miss their assignations. He'd had her just where he wanted, available, compliant. *Why should he deny himself? He'd find another girl. They were two-a-penny online.*

8

Rory Gardiner knocked on Kate's door on the dot of 8 p.m.

"I brought dry white. Don't want a hangover in the morning and red is a killer," he said brightly.

"Good call," she answered, leading the way into the sitting room.

"What do you fancy? I'll get the takeaway since you brought the booze," she went on.

"We always have pizza, but we could be a bit more adventurous."

"I don't care. You choose."

"There's this new Greek place that delivers. They do lots of little dishes and I hear it's good," said Rory.

"Little dishes sound good. I'm not that hungry," said Kate.

"I'll order. You get the plates and glasses ready. Then you can tell me what this is all about," he said.

After a couple of years as partners and friends, Rory knew Kate's apartment well. He hung up his coat in the hall, phoned the restaurant and ordered their food, then went to sit on the sofa next to her. She had poured two glasses of wine already, and was swigging from hers. On the coffee table there was a large gift box covered in slightly faded blue and gold wrapping.

"Oh, you shouldn't have..." said Rory, smiling.

"Oh, I didn't..." answered Kate sarcastically.

"Right, the food is going to take at least half an hour. That gives you time to fill me in," he said, tapping the top of the box.

"Remember Bernie O'Toole?" she asked.

Rory's expression turned serious.

"I'm not likely to forget her, Kate. What's she got to do with this?"

Kate recounted how she had been contacted by Bernie's solicitor three months after the woman's death at the hands of the spree killer who'd also left Kate for dead.

"Her solicitor said Bernie had left this box of stuff for me. She'd made the bequest years ago, long before I even met her, years before she died," she said.

"Wow, that's strange. What's in the box?"

"I don't know. I haven't looked," said Kate.

"But you've had it for ages... Weren't you dying to know?"

"I wouldn't exactly put it that way..." she said with a hint of a smile.

"Shit, sorry, that didn't come out right," said Rory, "but how could you not look already?"

"I don't know... I wanted to put it all behind me. It wasn't just about the killings, it was about my past – my real past, that is. You know this."

Rory thought for a minute. They both sat looking at the box. Then he picked it up and shook it a little.

"Well, it's not gold bars, that's for sure. Might be diamonds though; they don't weigh much, do they?" he said.

Kate knew he was keeping things light for her sake, and she loved him for it. It was actually the reason she'd asked him to help her open the box which had been repulsing and attracting her in equal measure for so long. If anyone was going to get her through this, it was Rory. Greg was never here when she needed him. Whatever it revealed, her friend would help her process it in a way Greg couldn't, though she didn't doubt that he loved her.

"Will I get it open?" said Rory.

"Yes. I'm not sure I'm brave enough," said Kate.

"You're the bravest person I know, Kate Hamilton."

Rory slid a kitchen knife under the taped lid of the box. Both held their breath as he lifted off the top, and they leaned over to peer inside.

"Well, this isn't going to fund my early retirement," said Kate, surveying a pile of old letters and photos.

"You never know, there could be all sorts in here – wedges of cash, bearer bonds, *whatever they are*, stocks and shares... Bernie might have had shares in Apple going back decades. Imagine what they'd be worth now. People have made millions on those."

"Let's take a look at the photos first," she said.

The prints were mostly old black and white photos, the kind with a white border. Some were of a girl, clearly Bernie, as a teenager, fresh faced and pretty.

"God, you'd totally recognise her, wouldn't you," said Rory.

Kate didn't answer. She was staring at another photo, holding the edges with both hands. It showed two small babies, lying side by side in an old-fashioned pram, their heads close together. In the background was what looked like a park or garden. Gently, Rory prised the picture from Kate's hands and turned it over. On the back there was some handwriting, sloping and faded.

The twins, August 1968, St Mary's.

He read the words aloud, and put the photograph down on the coffee table. The front door buzzer broke the moment. Rory jumped to his feet.

"Dinner – just what we need," he said a bit too cheerfully.

Rory came back with several brown paper bags. Kate just sat, not saying anything. He moved the box and its contents onto the floor and laid out the food on the coffee table.

"Come on, Kate, let's eat... The box isn't going anywhere, and you look like you could do with something. You're very pale," he said.

Rory re-filled their glasses and Kate let him pick small tasters of everything from the spread. He handed her a fork and an over-filled plate.

"Are you going to chew it for me too?" she said.

"Not unless I have to."

They ate then, trying out the different dishes. Rory kept up a running commentary on his food. Kate only picked at hers. He opened the second bottle of wine and cleared away the remainder of their feast. Kate stayed where she was, drinking.

"Right, I've put all the leftovers in their trays in the fridge. There was plenty of room. That should feed you tomorrow night. Don't you ever do a big shop? You could starve to death in this house," he said.

"You'll make someone a lovely husband someday." She smiled.

"I will, if I ever find my Mr. Right," he said. "If not, you'll just have to put up with me."

Kate put the open box back on the table. Rory had a plan.

"You take the photos, and I'll go through the papers," he said, "and we won't stop 'till we've seen everything."

Twenty minutes later, they sat back. There were now several neat piles on the table and the box had been discarded, empty, on the floor. Kate had divided the photos by date, going from the earliest to the most recent. She'd then separated them into baby photos and non-baby photos. On the paper side were mostly handwritten letters. There was also a small pile Rory was calling miscellaneous, typed correspondence and an old tattered copybook.

"Right, fill me in," he said. "What have you got?"

"I've got a few pictures of Bernie as a girl, some with others, one with her parents I think," she said.

"And you're sure it's her?" he asked.

"You said it yourself; her face is the same as that of the woman we met in Churchtown, just younger," said Kate.

"And the rest?" He pointed to the other piles of pictures.

"Baby pictures, all of them. The twin one is the earliest of the dated ones. After that there are lots of one child, a boy going from toddler up to about six years old, I'd guess," she said.

"And do you recognise him?" Rory's voice was hesitant.

"It could be Larsson. I can't really say though," said Kate, holding a picture of a dark-haired little boy wearing a formal double breasted coat with a contrasting collar, possibly velvet. He was not smiling.

"Look at this," said Rory. "I think it's the same kid. I recognise the coat."

He handed over a fragile newspaper cutting with a photo. It was a scene that said a lot, even without the accompanying text. There was an old-fashioned commercial passenger plane. Kate didn't know what type. A set of steps was pushed up against the open cabin door and halfway down stood a smiling stewardess in uniform with a toddler in her arms. At the bottom of the steps a small welcoming party were gazing up. One was a middle-aged man in black wearing a religious collar, next to him a younger man in an Air Force uniform, and a woman in a smart fitted coat. The headline said:

WELCOME TO YOUR NEW HOME

The rest of the story was brief. Rory read it aloud, squinting at the tiny newsprint on the yellowing paper.

Monsignor Matthew O'Connor accompanies Captain and Mrs. Ronald Larsson as they welcome their new baby son all the way from Ireland. Captain and Mrs Larsson are adopting the adorable orphan, no doubt saving him from a life of poverty and deprivation. Air Stewardess Irene has accompanied the infant, together with several others, all the way across the Atlantic to a warm Stateside welcome and a prosperous new life with his adoptive family. Monsignor O'Connor told us he has been instrumental in many such adoptions, thanks to his close contacts in the Catholic clergy back home.

They both sat in silence for a minute. Then Rory took a

handwritten letter from his pile. It was dated 19th June 1969
and was on pale blue personal notepaper. Again, he read
aloud while Kate sipped on her wine.

Dear Sister Jacinta,

*I hope you are well and the Irish weather is kind this
summer. We're having our usual heatwave at the
moment, so it is very warm indeed. I wanted to let you
know how young Tim is doing, and I have enclosed a
lovely newspaper cutting from the day he got here, and
some pictures Ronald took. He is growing well and just
walking by himself, and he loves his food. Our nanny, a
nice Polish girl, takes good care of him, and Ron and
myself are growing very fond of the little angel.*

*Magda says he's a bit quiet for his age, and doesn't smile
enough, but he rarely cries. I think he's just a quiet little
soul. I'm enclosing another check for the order, just to
thank you and the other sisters for giving us our beloved
son, and to help with some of the other little ones in your
care. We will keep you always in our prayers.*

Yours sincerely,

Martha Larsson.

"Right, Hamilton, what do we know now that we didn't
before? It's the question you ask me about any evidence we
find, and this is clearly evidence."

"We already knew Tim Larsson was born in St Mary's

and adopted out to the States. Now we know a bit more about his adoptive family," said Kate.

"Exactly. We know the local Monsignor organised it, and who he was, though he's probably long dead. We know the parents' names, and that the dad was a captain in the Air Force. Also they were well off, because they had a Polish nanny to look after the child."

"And they sent money to St Mary's. The mother says, 'I'm enclosing another check'," she said.

"And we know how Larsson found his first victim, Irene – he must have started with this clipping... and then the Facebook group, and the TV programme," said Rory.

They paused for a while then, each remembering the case that had nearly killed Kate. It had also cemented their friendship.

Rory carried on sorting through the letters and papers.

"Forget about Larsson for the moment," he said.

"I wish I could forget about him forever," sighed Kate.

"There's a lot of stuff here about you too, Kate," said Rory.

"Really? What stuff?" She sat bolt upright and put down her near-empty glass.

Rory took a deep breath.

"You told me your birth mother's name was Rosie Jackson, right?" he said.

"That's what Bernie O'Toole said," she said.

"I've got a notebook here that's hers..."

Carefully, Rory handed Kate the old school copybook. For a long moment she looked at it, idly rubbing her fingertips across the faded and dog-eared green cover. In neat childish handwriting was Rosie's name, and underneath her address.

"Shit, this is the first time I've known her address..." said Kate in a whisper. "She was from Blackrock, County Dublin."

"Look inside," said Rory.

On the inside cover, in the same handwriting, it said:

In case of emergency: Contact Sean and Marina Jackson

It was followed by the same home address in Blackrock, and a landline number.

"Let's ring it," he said.

"God no! Let's not!" said Kate firmly.

"It might still be in use. People keep their numbers forever. Well, they do if they keep their landline," said Rory. "They might still live there – the Jacksons. They're your grandparents, Kate."

"Assuming that's true and they're still alive, they're also the people who abandoned me in the hospital, according to Bernie," said Kate, her voice tinged with anger. "What makes you think they'd want to hear from their long-lost grand-daughter now? They'd no interest in me back then, when I was barely alive and needed them."

Rory struggled to answer that.

"Read on. There's not much in it, just a few scribbled notes. It's not exactly a diary but Rosie talks about being in St Mary's," he said eventually.

Kate leafed through the pages of the copybook. Rosie had evidently started to keep a journal when she first got to St Mary's, but with little diligence or perseverance. At the start she wrote of hating everything – the nuns, the food, the endless prayers. She called it 'a holy prison'. In later notes she wrote fondly of her new friends, especially Bernie. The tone grew lighter as Kate turned the pages, many of which only had a line or two of writing and a date. Rosie talked of 'having a good laugh over our knitting' or 'making up silly nicknames for the nuns'. Once or twice she wrote about her physical state, complaining of dizzy spells, 'gross fat ankles' and her growing 'monstrous bump'. Rory and Kate were reading the entries together when she suddenly closed the copybook and threw it down on the table.

"What? What's wrong, what did I miss?" asked Rory.

"Read it for yourself."

Picking it up, Rory read the passage aloud.

"I hope Richard rots in hell. I hope he gets run over by a London bus, or gets cancer and dies in agony. He doesn't deserve his life to go on as normal, when mine is destroyed. Destroyed by him."

"Wow, that's angry!" said Rory. "Who's Richard?"

Kate had told her partner only sketchy details of the shocking truth she'd learned from Bernie O'Toole. Even now, he didn't know that Tim Larsson could be her brother. She knew that a simple DNA test would confirm it, but hadn't had the courage to get one. Rory also didn't know that Rosie Jackson had conceived as a result of rape, an act that Bernie said was perpetrated by her first cousin. Now, reading young Rosie's journal, it seemed likely that this 'Richard' was the rapist.

"No second name," said Rory. "She hasn't given him a second name. I wonder what he did to deserve such anger."

Kate sighed. At this stage she was ready to tell someone, and it might as well be Rory.

"My birth mother, according to Bernie O'Toole, was raped. She was only fourteen, and she told Bernie that her cousin did it…"

Rory tried to hide his shock.

"Fucking hell, Kate, are you sure?"

"I'm not sure. How can I be? This is all hearsay, third party hearsay from Bernie."

"Isn't there a way of confirming it? Can't you get a DNA test or something?"

"And compare it to what?"

"Don't you want to know? If what Bernie says is true, you could have a whole other family out there, brothers and sisters, your birth mother, even grandparents," said Rory.

"If Rosie Jackson was my mother, she's dead... and my father, my biological father, was a fucking rapist..." Kate paused, took a big swig of wine and continued, "Her own cousin – it's practically incest... And if all of that is true, Tim Larsson was my brother, my twin brother. Not exactly the kind of family you want to belong to."

As the silence lengthened Rory absently shuffled and neatened the piles of papers and photos on the table. Then he turned to Kate and drew her into a hug.

"Holy Christ Almighty, Kate, how are you not driven mental by all of this?"

"What makes you think I'm not..." she whispered into his shoulder.

9

ONE WEEK LATER - MONDAY JANUARY 31, 2011

Hugh Sweetman rang Kate every single day following his daughter's disappearance. Each conversation went the same way.

"This is Hugh Sweetman, Detective. Have you found Emily yet?"

She grew to dread the calls. The Serious Crimes Unit had stepped back. The search for The Girl in The Red Dress went on, though Kate knew there were few Garda resources being dedicated to it. She didn't tell Hugh that. Each day, she patiently explained that the search was on-going. No trace of Emily, dead or alive, had been found, since the infamous video was posted and the coat, identified as hers, had been retrieved from the beach. Kate finished the calls with as much reassurance as she could muster that 'no news is good news'. It was a hope she herself did not cling to, and she could hear the despair growing in Hugh's voice as each day went by.

A week after the video went up, just as the furore in the media was dying down, Kate was trawling through traffic camera surveillance as part of evidence gathering on an upcoming gangland murder trial. Jim Corcoran called her in to his office.

"A body has washed up in Anglesey, Wales. They think it might be Emily Sweetman," he said.

"Oh shit," said Kate. "Poor kid. When will we have confirmation?"

"The Welsh are going to do the post mortem and give us samples for DNA comparison. I think we lifted Emily's from her toothbrush; you'll have to check with Forensics," said Corcoran.

"How long before we know?"

"It'll be a few days. I want you to go and collect the samples, to speed things up. The Welsh labs are even more backed up than we are, so we'll extract and work up the DNA here. Otherwise we could be waiting weeks," he said, "and I want this over with, not least for the girl's parents."

"That would preserve the chain of evidence. Were there any signs of foul play?"

"The Welsh won't say. The body's been in the sea for a week. God knows what state it's in, or if they can even tell what killed her," he said. "You didn't dig up anything that might point to foul play, did you?"

"No, sir, but we didn't really find a reason for the suicide either," said Kate.

"That's the thing; sometimes it's just a tragic bloody mystery," said Corcoran.

"What will I do about the family, sir? You know the father rings me every day," she said.

"Tell them a set of remains has been found, and where. It's going to be in the media anyway. It's better coming from you. At least they know you," said Corcoran. "The Commissioner wants us to handle this since we were in it from the start."

"I take it there's still a lot of media interest? And the minister; is he involved?"

"Oh yes, he's still involved. More's the pity. The press office has been fielding calls from all over the world this last week. I told the Commissioner about the Anglesey body as soon as I heard. You can be sure she was straight onto the minister. Now it'll be on the front pages again, if it's her."

"That poor family. Maybe this'll give them some sort of peace, if they can bring her home..." said Kate.

"There's no peace after something like this," said Jim.

Kate decided to tell the Sweetman family in person. It wasn't the sort of thing you could relay over the phone. Rory went with her.

Susan Sweetman opened the door with dread written all over her face. She'd seen them walking up the short drive-way. She didn't bother with a greeting. Fear had robbed her of politeness.

"Have you found her?" she said.

"Mrs Sweetman," said Kate, "can we come in?"

The woman held back the door for them to enter, her shoulders slumping.

"I'll get Hugh," she said, heading towards the back of the house.

Rory and Kate made their own way into the sitting room and waited. The couple returned, their hands clasped tightly together. Susan looked like she might faint and Hugh led her to the couch and made her sit. He remained standing.

"I have some news for you but it's not what you want to hear," said Kate. "I'm sorry to tell you that some remains have been located in Anglesey, North Wales. There's reason to believe it might be Emily, but I must stress it's only a possibility."

Hugh sat down abruptly, as if his legs had failed to keep him up. No one said anything for a while. Susan turned her face away and rested her head on her husband's shoulder. He seemed frozen for a moment, just staring into space.

"The Welsh police are conducting their own investigation and will carry out a post mortem on the remains today, I believe. We'll then be provided with materials from which to create a DNA profile," said Kate, "for comparison."

Hugh finally spoke.

"Can I see her? If I go to Wales, now, today, will they let me see her?"

Kate hadn't expected this.

"I don't think so, Mr Sweetman. Until the remains are positively identified through DNA matching, they are officially in the possession of the Welsh police. It is simply a courtesy to An Garda Siochana that they are providing us with samples to run a DNA profile."

"How long?" asked Susan.

"It'll take several days. I'd estimate a week until we can do the comparison. We'll do our best to make it happen as quickly as possible."

"And if it's Emily..." said Hugh.

"You can make an application to re-patriate the remains to Ireland," answered Rory. "There would be some paperwork to complete, and the transport arrangements. There will have to be an inquest."

The couple went silent. Murmuring goodbye, Kate and Rory let themselves out, once again relieved to escape the despairing parents.

10

TUESDAY FEBRUARY 1, 2011

The following morning Kate took the fast ferry to Holyhead from Dublin Port. It took little more than 90 minutes, proving to be much quicker than a flight to Cardiff and the long drive up to Anglesey. The police HQ was less than half an hour away. There Kate found out that, despite extensive queries, the Welsh police were no closer to identifying the body. The sergeant said they were widening the search to the whole of the UK, but it could take months to establish an identity for the dead girl.

"The sad thing is just how many young women go missing, thousands every year in Britain," he said. "We might never know who the poor lass is."

Kate accepted his offer of tea and a sandwich in the police canteen, and she was able to complete the paperwork and take possession of the samples from the Duty Pathologist within a couple of hours. The return ferry was not until teatime, so she found herself hanging around the mortuary. The pathologist, a veteran police surgeon, found her sitting in the front desk area, scrolling news websites on her phone.

"Detective Hamilton, you're still here?" he said.

"I've got a few hours to kill before I hit the road," said Kate.

"This might seem like a strange offer, but would you like to see the remains? I know it's not every officer's favourite duty, but since you're here..."

Kate took a deep breath. The sandwich she'd had felt like a stone in her stomach.

"I should, while I'm here. Thank you," she said.

"Follow me. This is a small unit, and thankfully we don't have too many clients at the moment," said the doctor.

There were just four metal drawers in the cold room, testimony Kate recognised to the low-crime rural area. The pathologist checked the label on the door of one of the drawers with the paperwork in his hand and then slowly pulled it out.

Inside, as she expected, Kate saw the black rubber body bag, which, going by the shape, contained a slightly built individual.

"As you know, we believe these remains were in the water for some time, by our estimation about a week," said the doctor, "and in that time there has been some superficial damage, together with my cuts, of course. But the Irish Sea is damn cold this time of year, so decomp is only just beginning. Deep breath, Sergeant. It's not too bad, I assure you."

He must have noticed I'm squeamish, thought Kate, embarrassed. He unzipped the bag to about eighteen inches from the top and parted the rubber sides.

The face Kate saw had a grey-green hue and was bloated. There were small abrasions and grazes visible on the nose, chin and forehead, and the hair was matted. The top of the Y incision from the post mortem was visible, large black stitches stark against bruised skin. Kate could see the girl's features would have been delicate and pretty in life. She couldn't say for sure it was Emily Sweetman.

"Do you want to see any more?" asked the pathologist.

"No, thanks," said Kate.

"She's quite well preserved, actually, considering she's been in the water," he said, closing the body bag and sliding the drawer back into place.

Kate was relieved to leave the cold room and its occupants.

"And those cuts and bruises?" she said.

"They're to be expected when a body has been buffeted by the sea and thrown ashore by the waves. There's no sign of anything suspicious in my view, no blunt force trauma, just superficial damage. The condition of her lungs would suggest she died by drowning, and given the state of the body, probably no more than 7 to 10 days ago," he said, walking Kate back towards the reception area of the mortuary.

"Is there anything else of significance?"

"You'll have the full report by the time you get home, Sergeant, but for now I can say she was a healthy, well-nourished girl with no significant signs of injury or disease. Her blood alcohol level was very high at the time of death. No sign of drug abuse or long-term liver damage, so the alcohol was not a chronic issue. If it is ruled suicide or accidental, I would say it might have played a part," he said.

"Enough to cloud her judgement?" said Kate.

"I would say so, yes," he said.

"What happens now?" she asked.

"She'll stay here for the moment, unless we end up running out of room. If there's a positive identification and no suspicious circumstances, the body can be released to next of kin. If she's your girl, arrangements to send her home can be made in a matter of days," he replied.

Kate thanked the doctor and left, anxious to get away now from this place of death and decay.

Your girl... The pathologist's words echoed in her mind as she drove.

She's not my girl. I shouldn't even be here. This is no murder case.

She couldn't escape the fact that The Girl in The Red Dress had gotten under her skin – this story of a life and a death was one that wouldn't leave her. At Holyhead she found a quiet café, ordered coffee and got out her laptop. For the umpteenth time she watched Emily's video.

There must be a clue here.

What had Emily Sweetman done that had 'fucked up her life'? That was the big question. Kate made a list of the possibilities. Assuming the dead girl she'd just seen on the mortuary tray was Emily, she ruled out drugs. The same with pregnancy – the pathologist would have mentioned if the dead girl had been pregnant. Mental illness or depression? Kate put a question mark next to this one because her family had said she had been unusually quiet of late. Exam pressure was the next heading. Her grades had slipped, but even so, her tutor had said she wasn't failing. It was months away from the end of year exams. A brilliant student like Emily could have brought her grades back up easily enough. Money was next on the list and Kate underlined it, simply because she knew nothing of Emily's finances. The Sweetmans lived in a nice house in a fashionable suburb. Susan was a nursing sister and Hugh worked in finance. They looked prosperous, but that could be a façade. Lots of middle-class professionals in Ireland had been struggling since the financial crash of 2008.

Last on the list was Relationships. No one had mentioned a boy- or girl-friend. Emily Sweetman was pretty and bright. Was there an affair that had gone wrong? The café had emptied out of customers and the woman who'd served her coffee had already cleaned all the tables bar Kate's. It was time to join the queue of cars at the ferry terminal. Saving the list on her laptop under the title Emily, she decided the last two topics – Money and Relationships – were worthy of investigation. She couldn't shake the feeling that there was something more to this story, and for some reason she didn't really understand, Kate knew she had to find the answer.

ASHLING AND MAX were falling apart, and they couldn't help themselves. She cried at the slightest thing. He couldn't shed a tear. All they wanted to do was drink and smoke weed until oblivion took over. Nothing helped, and days passed slowly. They skipped lectures, and rejected all advances from their classmates to meet up.

"The bastards only want to ask us about Emily. They don't give a shit about her. They're vultures looking for gory details to post online," said Max.

The two stopped looking at their social media accounts, to avoid the careless comments and cruel speculation. Five days into their isolation the doorbell brought Max downstairs in the shabby student house they shared. He was expecting a pizza delivery. As soon as the door opened a man he didn't recognise barged into the hall, startling him.

"Max Egan, isn't it? I'm Emily's father," he said.

Max showed him into the living room littered with empty cans and takeaway boxes. He shouted upstairs for Ashling to come down. She came in her pyjamas and a dressing gown. When Max introduced the visitor, she barely spoke. Hugh Sweetman refused to sit on the scruffy sofa but paced up and down as he questioned them. By the time he left fifteen minutes later Ashling was shaking and Max was furious.

"Where does he get off attacking us like that?" he said.

"He's upset..."

"We're upset. Our best friend is missing presumed dead and he's blaming us... We should do something about that man. No wonder Emily never wanted to go home."

"You can't say that. He's in a state..." she said.

"I'm going to tell those detectives he's harassing us. He can't get away with it. I actually thought he was going to hit me," said Max. "We've done nothing wrong."

Ashling grabbed him by the shoulders and looked him in the eyes.

"We've done nothing wrong? That's what you're saying now, is it?" she said, her voice sharp. "We started the Sugar Babies, we got Emily involved, and you really think that's got nothing to do with her suicide?"

Max just stood and looked at her. Eventually he pushed away her hands.

"Why would you say that? We were all in it together. She took the money just like we did. What has any of that got to do with her disappearance?"

Even now, he found it hard to say the words death or suicide.

"I swear to God, Max Egan, you could dumb-ass for

Ireland! Have you not watched the video, like, a thousand times?"

"I can't bear to look at it anymore." He sat down and covered his eyes with his hands.

"It's all there in what she says – 'I've fucked up my life. I'm not that girl anymore. I'm all used up,' and the biggest clue of all..." Ashling said, almost shouting now.

"What?"

"You really didn't notice? Emily said, 'I'll keep this short and sweet. Sweet as sugar. LOL, that's me.' It was a message – just for us. She killed herself because of the Sugar Babies. It's all our fault," said Ashling, breaking down.

Eventually after a week of absence, Ashling and Max could no longer ignore the texts and emails from their tutors. They went back to college, but kept themselves apart from the other students, who wanted only to talk about Emily and the Red Dress video. In a way, it was a relief to get back to some semblance of normality, and they had course-work to catch up on and assignments to rush through. Ashling was feeling low.

"I'm broke, Max, and I'm not exactly in the mood to flirt with dirty old men, but I still need the cash. Maybe we should spend some time tonight, get back on the horse?"

"The Sugar Babies ride again," said Max. "There'll be less money coming in without Ems."

"For fuck's sake, Max!" Ashling was horrified.

"I'm just saying, Ash. You're the one who needs it most! Don't tell me you haven't thought it. Emily brought in good money, especially from that one Pig."

"She's our friend. We still don't know if she's dead or alive, and all you're worried about is the fucking Sugar Babies." She walked out then, leaving a red-faced Max.

After her classes Ashling made her way home. Emily's video was playing on a loop in her mind, her rent was overdue again, and she hated fighting with Max. In her room she opened up her private messages on the Sugar Babies site. There were several from her usual Pigs, asking for pictures and videos. Some were clearly getting impatient at her absence over the previous week. She would have to do some ego massaging to get them back on board. There was one message from a new source. Though she hated to admit it, *Max was right. They needed more Pigs, now that Emily was gone.* This one sounded sweet. He said he just wanted someone to talk to, that he was lonely, and had recently lost someone close to him. Ashling gave him the number of her burner phone.

11

THE NEXT DAY - WEDNESDAY FEBRUARY
2, 2011

I t was late when Kate got home. It had been a rough crossing. The high-speed ferry couldn't sail due to the stormy seas. The slower sailing took three and a half hours. Luckily she'd found a couch in one of the quieter lounges and stretched out to alleviate the nausea. As always, her apartment felt bleak and empty, and she was hungry. Happily there was some milk that was still in date, and her go-to late night meal – breakfast cereal, a childhood favourite that never failed her. By 1.45 she was asleep, dreaming she was in a boat endlessly crossing a choppy sea but never reaching land.

The next morning she made her way straight to the mortuary where State Pathologist Harriet Stilson worked. The quickest way to get the DNA results was to get Harriet to fast-track them. Kate believed the lab people were slightly scared of the pathologist, whereas they seemed to treat Garda requests as routine.

Harriet was just de-robing outside the cutting suite when they met.

"Kate, how nice to see you. Do you have a customer for me today? I hadn't heard you were coming in."

"I have a favour to ask, Doc. Can you get a rush on a DNA profile for me?"

"Come and have a coffee with me. I've only had the one this morning and I need a caffeine top-up. What's the case?" said Harriet.

"The Girl In The Red Dress," said Kate as they queued in the canteen where a chef was serving cooked breakfasts. *Nothing would induce her to eat in this place, but she hoped she could keep down a coffee.*

Harriet put a couple of slices of soda bread, butter and jam on her tray and insisted on buying the two black coffees.

"Tell me more..." said Harriet. "Of course, I know the headlines, but what's this profile you want? Have you found her? And why are Serious Crimes involved?"

Kate explained the background and handed over the samples she'd brought from Anglesey in a sealed evidence case.

"Did you get to see the remains?" asked Harriet.

"I did," said Kate, and gave the pathologist a quick description of the body she'd seen.

"That was brave of you. I know it's not your thing," said Harriet.

"Oh, is it that obvious?" Kate found herself blushing.

"Don't worry, you wouldn't be the first officer to go green around the gills every time I see you." The pathologist smiled.

"I wish I could get over it, this squeamishness, but I can't seem to," said Kate.

"Well, I might be able to help you with that, if you're up

for it," said Harriet. "I've found with my students that a short course of immersion does the trick."

Kate's heart sank. Not only was it common knowledge that she was a wimp, now she was being invited to delve more deeply into the world of blood and guts than she'd ever wanted to.

"What do you mean by a short course?" she asked.

"No need to look so worried. It's an hour or two for a couple of weeks and you'll see a difference very quickly, I'm sure of it," said Harriet. "I'll be here late on Wednesday. If you're free, pop in around six and we'll make a start. Oh, and make sure you have a good lunch, something carby."

Kate wasn't sure what to feel, dread or anticipation, but the word 'immersion' made her anxious. She agreed to come by if she could, and they parted company, with Harriet promising to fast-track the DNA test.

In the car, Kate's phone rang and she recognised Hugh Sweetman's number. She wanted to decline the call, but her conscience got the better of her. He didn't bother with hello.

"Is it Emily, the body in Anglesey? Is it her?"

"I'm afraid we won't know for several days, Mr. Sweetman," she said.

"But did you see her? Did you see the body they found?"

Kate wasn't sure how to answer. If she lied she'd feel bad, but if she said she'd seen the remains, the man would probably have a thousand questions.

"I only travelled over to collect the samples for the DNA profile," she said.

What was the point in telling him what she'd seen, when she had no answers for the poor man?

"I've been talking to her friends from college, Ashling

and Max," he said. "I'm sure they know something they're not saying."

Kate was taken aback. Understandably, the man was obsessed, but she hadn't expected him to be conducting an investigation that more or less dovetailed with her own. It was interesting that he suspected, like her, that the two students were hiding something.

"What exactly do you think they know?" she asked.

"The three of them have been joined at the hip since Emily started college. If they're so close to her, how come they had no clue about what she was going to do, or why? I'm sure they're hiding something."

"We have spoken to Emily's friends, Mr. Sweetman, and they were as shocked by that video as you are," said Kate. "Until we have proof otherwise, Emily is still a missing person."

"Have you even considered that she might have been abducted? That whole video could have been a ruse to cover her abduction by some maniac," he said. Kate could hear his mounting desperation.

"So far we've found nothing to suggest your daughter was taken by someone. Let's see what the DNA testing gives us, Mr. Sweetman. As soon as I know, you'll know," she said, and with some relief she said goodbye.

Back at Garda HQ, Kate went straight to see Jim Corcoran.

"How was Anglesey?"

"Green and quiet, mostly, very pretty. Though not so the morgue," she said.

"So you went there?"

"I did, and I saw the remains," she said. "The pathologist

offered so I thought I'd better take a look after going all that
way."

Kate knew what his next question would be.

"Sorry, boss, I can't say if it's her. The police surgeon said
even a week in the sea would have its effect, and it did. It
could be Emily. The height and weight match, and the age
too," she said.

"Do you think her family would recognise her?"

"Oh God, no. It would be traumatic for them to see the
remains; they're not a pretty sight," she said.

"Let's hope it's not her then," he said. "Once the profile is
done we'll know for sure and we can take it from there.
Thanks for doing the trip, Kate. The sooner that case is put
to bed the better. As far as I'm concerned it's not part of our
remit to investigate probable suicides, and I resent being
asked to put my people on it."

"It's fine, sir. If it's a choice between trawling through
hundreds of hours of CCTV for the Roche case and looking
into this one, I'd prefer this," she said. "There's something
about it that's niggling me... I can't get that girl out of my
mind. If it is her I saw in Anglesey, I want to know why."

"Just don't waste time on it. We might be in a bit of a lull
but the next murder we get in, you'll have to forget all about
The Girl In The Red Dress."

Back in the squad room Kate logged on to her computer
and started downloading new video files from the gangland
case. Two men were due on trial for shooting dead a rival drug
dealer named Roche as he waited for his kids to come out of
school. With the court date fast approaching, the team had to
build an airtight case for the prosecution. Her task was to trace
their movements in the days leading up to the killing, using

CCTV from all across the western suburbs of Dublin. So far she'd established the two men had been stalking their victim for weeks before the shooting. They'd been clever, using a variety of cars borrowed from relatives. Tracing those relationships and the cars involved was tedious and time consuming.

Rory was working on the same case. They had split the hundreds of hours of footage retrieved from traffic cameras, commercial premises and doorbell cameras. He came over to speak to her as soon as he saw her.

"How was Wales?" he asked, and she filled him in quickly.

"Are you around tonight?" he said. "I've got news."

"We could get a drink later..." she said. "We're going to need it after hours of this."

Quietly they agreed to meet in one of their favourite spots, a hotel bar in the city centre. By mid-afternoon Kate was both exhausted and wired after several strong coffees. She was struggling to keep focussed and had to keep pausing the video to take a breather. Rory had already left when she packed up her things, deciding to leave her car in the car park. Nights out with him tended to be boozy.

The Shelbourne Hotel was one of the oldest and most prestigious in the city. Even on a midweek night its Horse-shoe Bar was buzzing with politicos from the nearby parliament and a mixture of tourists and well-heeled Dubliners. Kate and Rory liked the atmosphere and the fact that they were unlikely to meet any of their colleagues, who frequented less expensive bars near HQ.

Rory had arrived first and secured a table. He'd ordered drinks, and Kate sighed with contentment as she sank onto a deep leather sofa and reached for her gin and tonic.

"This is a lifesaver," she said after a long sip from the

huge bowl-shaped glass adorned with cucumber, a straw and a crystal stirrer. Rory was nursing an espresso Martini, his usual.

"Considering the number of coffees you've guzzled today, I thought gin was the safest. Any more caffeine and you'll be climbing the walls," he said.

They chatted for a few minutes, commenting on the other customers, spotting a few well-known faces, reviewing their outfits. The clientele ranged in fashion from sober business suits on the men to designer dresses on the many single women 'on the pull', according to Rory.

By the second drink they'd relaxed and exhausted all the amusing possibilities of the crowded bar. Belatedly, Kate remembered the reason for meeting Rory.

"I almost forgot," she said. "You said you had news. What news?"

Rory took a sip of his cocktail.

"I'd better not have any more of these or I'll never sleep," he said.

Kate could see he was putting off telling her.

"Switch to gin; you'll sleep like a baby. Now, what have you done?" she said.

"After the other night, when we went through The Box..." He paused.

Kate's stomach clenched.

"Yes..."

"I did a bit of digging on your birth family."

"Oh," said Kate.

"I knew you were curious, but it's a big deal for you, starting the search, a big scary step. So I thought if I did it for you, then you could take or leave whatever I found. And you can... take it or leave it."

The waitress came to clear their glasses and Kate ordered another drink.

"So you found something?" she said.

"Are you sure you want to hear this now?" said Rory. "We could just park it for a while, or forget all about it. I don't want to upset you."

"Stop wittering, Rory. Tell me what you found. I won't shoot you. You've probably done me a favour," said Kate.

Rory sighed with relief. He adored Kate. She was his only close friend on the force, and he felt protective of her even if she was older and a rank above him.

"My mum is into genealogy – you know, family trees and all that stuff – so I picked her brains on how to get at official records of births, deaths and marriages, and census stuff," he said. "A lot of it is online now. You just have to know where to look."

"And…"

"I found Rosie Jackson's birth and death certificates, and her parents' marriage cert. Also her father's death certificate; he died only a year after her."

"And you're sure they're the right Jacksons?" Kate asked.

"The home address is the same as the one in Rosie's journal," he said.

"So what do we know now that we didn't know before?" said Kate.

"Jesus, Hamilton, we'll have to carve that on your gravestone!" said Rory, smiling. "This is what we know, and it's huge…" He paused, for too long.

"Did I say I wouldn't shoot you? I might have to change my mind," said Kate, gulping from her newly delivered glass.

"You have a grandmother, and she's still alive."

IT WAS LATE when Kate and Rory left The Shelbourne. Over several more drinks, which had helped to dull the shock, he had filled her in on the woman who might possibly be her grandmother, Marina Jackson. Under any other circumstances Kate would have found her fascinating. She had been widowed at only thirty-four, and as far as was known, had never re-married. Rory had tracked down Sean Jackson's will and it showed that, together with a majority shareholding in his construction firm, there were rental properties in Ireland and the UK, and a variety of shares and stocks that had made Marina a very wealthy woman.

"She still lives in the same house in Blackrock, a massive big place," said Rory.

"Have you seen it?" she asked.

"I used Google street view to take a look. It's a big old pile, but in good nick, and there's a massive garden and a big long drive," he said.

Kate wasn't sure what to think or say. She couldn't deny her curiosity about Rosie Jackson's family, but this felt like too much information, all at once.

"She's quite an elderly woman now, I reckon about seventy-six," he said, "but get this: she's still the main shareholder in her husband's company, and it's now one of the biggest in the state. She's mega-rich. And according to the Company Records she's been Executive Chairman, or chairperson, since the time her husband died in 1969."

"What does that mean?" asked Kate.

"It means he left her a fortune, but instead of living it up with all that dosh, Marina took over the running of the company and made it even more successful. Given this was when Ireland was still in the dark ages, a woman being CEO of a construction firm back then was unheard of. She must be a force of nature, this Marina."

"Jesus, Rory, you left no stone unturned," said Kate.

"Imagine if you're her granddaughter," he said. "You could be an heiress!"

They were both a bit drunk by now, Rory because he was a lightweight in the alcohol stakes, and Kate because his revelations had made her throw back the gins as fast as they were served. She wanted it to stop, to un-hear the facts he'd dug up about the Jacksons. As they shared a taxi to their respective homes, she realised the genie was out of the bottle now and nothing she could do would put it back in.

12

THURSDAY FEBRUARY 3, 2011

I n the morning, feeling more than a little unwell, Kate settled down to the gangland case, scanning through dodgy footage, fortified with coffee and painkillers and trying not to nod off. She could see Rory was suffering too, but felt little sympathy for her friend. Part of her wanted to throttle him. The revelations about the Jacksons had haunted her night, and even now her head was spinning with it all.

"Call for you, Sergeant Hamilton. Some Welsh bloke..." said one of the civilian clerks. "Line four."

Kate picked up the call.

"This is Sergeant Hamilton," she said.

"It's George Warner here, Sergeant, County Pathologist for Anglesey. We met a few days ago," said a warm voice.

"Hello, Doctor. How can I help you?" said Kate.

"Well, this is a little embarrassing, Sergeant, given I've already completed my PM report. But there's something I wanted to tell you. Some new findings. I'll have to issue an amended report."

Kate was intrigued.

"What have you found?"

"Well, we don't have a positive identification yet, but knowing your interest in this set of remains, I wanted to tell you something that may or may not be relevant, should your ID prove to be positive."

Kate wished he'd get to the point.

"Go on, Doctor," she said.

"As you saw for yourself, Sergeant, the body displayed a lot of haematomas – bruising, that is – almost all over the remains," he said.

"Yes, but that's to be expected, didn't you say?"

"Indeed, but I decided to have another look. I'm inclined to double-check my PMs, as I have no assistant and you never know what you might miss, working alone."

The pathologist sounded embarrassed. Kate's interest was piqued.

"And you found something..." she said.

"Yes, I did. Underneath the damage done by the sea and the body being deposited on a stony beach, underneath all of that, there was a considerable amount of old deep-tissue bruising, much of which only became obvious on a second viewing. This is ante-mortem bruising, going back a number of weeks."

Kate sat straight up in her chair, and almost dropped the phone.

"Could you say that again, Doctor..." she said.

"There's historic bruising, faded now but there beneath the skin. A specific type of bruising on the neck related to manual choking, plus some internal abrasions and soft-tissue damage. There were also shallow scars, mostly healed, that look like they were done with a blade of some sort. In summary, this girl had been hurt repeatedly before she died, weeks before she died," he said.

"And you're sure of this?" she said.

"Yes. I'm sorry I missed it at first. There's something else, Sergeant, that you should be aware of, if this is your girl," he said. "I've seen this kind of thing before, though rarely, thank goodness. The nature of the marks would suggest a sexual motive," said the pathologist. "I found old ligature marks that look like she might have been... hog-tied I think the expression is, and internal damage in various stages of healing. These abrasions were in the mouth, vaginal and rectal areas, which would suggest repeated incidents of violent assault. This poor young woman was the victim of some pretty serious sexual abuse, and over weeks if not months."

Kate's mind filled with imagined scenes that made her shudder.

"I take it you're still waiting on the DNA," he said, after her silence had gone on for some time.

"Yes, it'll be a couple of days. Thank you for the call, Doctor, and for taking another look. Please send me the amended PM report when it's ready, and I'll be in touch as soon as I've got the DNA results. To be honest, after what you've told me, I really hope it's not our girl. Thanks again," she said and put down the phone.

Kate sat back in her chair. What now? Without a positive ID there was nowhere to go with this new information. But she couldn't get Emily Sweetman out of her mind. Closing her eyes, she pictured again the cold and bloated grey face she'd looked at in the mortuary. For the first time she admitted to herself what she'd been so reluctant to confirm in Anglesey.

It was Emily. The Girl In The Red Dress was the poor

tortured young woman the pathologist spoke of. And now at last her death made sense. But who had hurt her so much it had driven her to suicide?

13

THE NEXT DAY - FRIDAY FEBRUARY 4, 2011

At six o'clock Kate arrived at the City Mortuary. Harriet Stilson was waiting. Fearing they were going straight to the cutting room, Kate looked for the paper coveralls and gloves she would need, but much to her relief, Harriet led her into her own office instead.

"For the moment you're only going into a virtual cutting room, Kate. Much less messy and completely odourless," said Harriet. "This is some new software using 3D animation based on digitally scanned bodies and autopsies. It's so life-like some of the med schools around the world are using it as a teaching aid. It's strictly licensed and only pathology departments can access it, so I can't give it to you to take away. Sit down and I'll log in, and I'll show you how to work through a full PM in a couple of hours," she said.

Kate was immediately sceptical. It was the sight, smell and sound of death that made her queasy. *How could a computer game help?* Harriet sensed her doubts.

"You'd be surprised how it takes the edge off, I promise. Look on the autopsy as a jigsaw puzzle, only in reverse.

You're starting with the picture complete and then taking it apart, into its pieces. That's where the answers lie." Harriet hit Start on the keyboard and left Kate to it.

She was right. The animation was so lifelike it was extraordinary. As the post-mortem unfolded bit by bit, with a pathologist figure in full garb, and scalpels and tools that glinted realistically, Kate found herself leaning in to the screen. With each stage of the PM the virtual view would zoom in to give a close-up of the cutting open, the removal of organs, the instruments, the examination under microscope. She was able to pause and rewind, to zoom in and change the angle of the shots on her screen, and all the time there was a voiceover giving step-by-step commentary. Despite herself, Kate was fascinated and the two hours passed quickly. Afterwards she met Harriet in the cutting room.

"Well? How did you find it?" said the pathologist.

"Amazing how lifelike it is for animation. It was fascinating," said Kate.

"I bet you're wondering how that's going to help you with the real thing."

Kate glanced towards the cutting table and was relieved to find it was empty.

"I am," she said.

"A few more sessions on that site and you'll be eager to see one of my PMs," said Harriet. "There are always going to be unpleasant sights and smells, and everyone has a physical reaction to that, even me. But you can overcome it. A drop of clove oil or Vicks under your nose and a mask and gloves do the trick. If you know almost exactly what's going to happen and what you're going to see, it takes away the fear of the unknown, and that's half the battle. By the time you've seen a few more virtual post mortems, you'll feel differently about coming in here."

"I do feel surprisingly OK," said Kate. "Are you finished now? Can I buy you a drink or a coffee to say thanks?"

"No need to thank me, Kate, but I'd kill for a quick glass of wine, and maybe something to eat? There's a nice little gastro pub up the road."

Over supper the two women chatted. Harriet revealed she was divorced, with two adult children, both students, still living at home. Kate told her about her long-distance boyfriend Greg, and how her mother had passed away a few months earlier.

"Sounds like you're flying solo, Kate. No brothers or sisters?"

"No," answered Kate.

"You had a close call last year, didn't you? That shootout in Churchtown. Are you OK now?"

Instantly Kate's hands went to her scar.

"I'm fine, fully recovered," she said. "Actually, there's something I need to ask you, and it's kind of related."

Kate found herself telling her about the St Mary's case. The pathologist had carried out the post mortems on the killer and Bernie O'Toole, but didn't know the background.

"I've got a favour to ask, and it needs to be kind of unofficial," she said eventually. "There's someone, an innocent party, who's afraid she might be related by birth to the killer. She doesn't want to go public or make an official request but she needs to know. If I can get a buccal swab from her, would you be able to get a DNA profile and comparison done? His will be on the database already," said Kate.

Harriet agreed to run the tests and Kate promised to drop in the swab the next day. They went on to discuss lighter subjects, including the enigmatic Jim Corcoran, Kate's boss.

"He's divorced too, you know," said Harriet, to Kate's surprise. "No kids though. I think it was a long time ago. In our line of work, it's hard to keep relationships going."

"Do you think he's got someone, though?" asked Kate.

"I don't know. He's an attractive guy. Those broad shoulders and smouldering eyes..." She smiled. "He can't be more than fifty. There are plenty of single women out there who'd leap at the chance."

"He's married to the job, Harriet. That's the problem."

On the way home Kate wondered if Harriet might have more than a passing interest in Jim Corcoran, but decided nothing would ever come of it. He seemed to live only to work. She couldn't ever remember him taking a holiday.

Before she fell asleep she texted Rory.

> I'm getting the DNA test done. Harriet's going to do it on the QT.

He answered immediately.

> Brave you – at least you'll know now.

THAT WEEKEND GREG was arriving from London and Kate felt both excited and anxious. It had been over a month since they were together. He'd been to various European cities chasing a big EU story, and this was their longest time apart since he moved over from Washington. Though they texted often and Face-Timed a couple of times a week, Kate knew she'd slipped back into singledom. It wasn't that she wanted to date other men; more that being on her own was comfortable and familiar. Like a well-washed old t-shirt, it just felt easy. Now she felt the need to smarten up, get her legs waxed and her hair done, put some food in the fridge and new linen on the bed. She bought fresh flowers in the supermarket and paid over ten euro a bottle for wine, almost a first for her. A few grey hairs had sprouted in the last year and needed urgent attention from a colour expert. It took half a dozen phone calls to salons and a patch test twenty-four hours in advance before she could get a (madly expensive) hair appointment at short notice. None of this came naturally to Kate – the preening – but she told herself she needed the boost in confidence.

Still, her heart beat faster when the buzzer sounded and it was Greg. The table was set for two, though she hadn't lit candles. *Too corny, and not her style.* Nor had she cooked. Marks and Spencer had taken care of the food. It just needed half an hour in the oven. *That was a step up from a takeaway, surely.*

Greg looked tired. They hugged at first, then he kissed her softly on the lips and ran his fingers through her hair. She began to relax.

"You look gorgeous, Kate. You've done something new with your hair."

Well, that was a whole other story involving harsh words with the colourist who'd ignored everything she'd asked for and put a chestnut tint on her dark brown. Maybe he was right, and it needed the lift... She should have left him a tip after all.

The evening went well, dinner was delicious, and after the second bottle of wine Kate vowed never to buy cheap plonk again. Greg filled her in on his assignments for the

Washington Post, which included writing occasional features.

"It's a sort of letter home from Europe, sometimes funny, sometimes serious, a bit like a travelogue. Eighty-five percent of Americans don't own a passport. So many have no clue about anything that's going on over here. Most of the time I'm door-stepping politicians, or chasing scandals and disasters, but I like doing these longer pieces."

Kate loved listening to Greg, though she was embarrassed that she hadn't read any of his recent work. So much of her time was spent with her head buried in a case, that most of what passed for world news escaped her notice. It was refreshing to forget, even for a few hours, the questions of life, death and the past that consumed her. He brought up The Girl In The Red Dress, which for a brief moment had been a global story, and she filled him in on her involvement. She told him that she'd finally opened the box bequeathed to her by Bernie O'Toole, and what Rory had discovered about the Jacksons. Soon they were too tired to talk or do anything other than cuddle up in bed and fall asleep.

14

SATURDAY FEBRUARY 5, 2011

Kate was off for the whole weekend, but on Saturday morning the phone woke her at 8.30. When the caller identified himself as a Garda Forensics Lab technician, her heart almost stopped.

"Detective Sergeant Hamilton, I hope you don't mind me ringing you on a weekend, but I thought you'd want to know. We've got a match on the DNA sample you submitted."

"Which sample is this?"

"Let me see."

There was a long pause, which did not help Kate's heart rate.

"It was submitted to query the identity of a set of remains that I believe were washed up somewhere in Wales."

"Yes, of course, thank you. You say you've got a match?"

"Yes indeed, Sergeant. There is a conclusive match between the two samples. Just to be clear, the DNA from the remains in Wales is a positive match for Emily Sweetman, based on the toothbrush sample. I'm emailing you the official comparison result now."

Kate thanked him for the call and hung up, the mood of her weekend shattered.

"You've got to go, don't you?" said Greg from under the quilt.

"Yes. I'm sorry, it's not something I can leave until Monday. Do you mind?"

"I mind because I'll miss you, but I understand, love."

"I'll be back as quickly as I can."

"Don't worry. I've got some work I can file, and if you're not back by the afternoon, I'll just hit up the bars and see if I can find another beautiful Irish woman to seduce!"

DRESSED AND READY TO GO, Kate rang Jim Corcoran. He picked up immediately.

Did he ever relax, even at the weekend?

"We've got a positive match for Emily Sweetman on the Welsh body," she said.

"Shit, that poor kid."

"I know. I thought it was her, but I couldn't be sure until now. There's something else I haven't told you, boss…"

Kate then recounted her conversation with the Welsh pathologist, and his belief that Emily had been repeatedly sexually assaulted in the weeks before her death.

"I didn't tell you because I really hoped it wasn't her in Anglesey."

"Jesus, Kate, what do we do with that?"

Corcoran sounded weary.

"I don't know, sir. It's not exactly something we can investigate easily, since the victim is dead."

"I know but it must have some bearing on her suicide, surely?"

"You'd think so."

"And the coroner is going to get the PM report, so it will all come out in the end anyway."

"That poor family..."

"We're going to have to tell them..."

"I know; that's why I rang you. Gardiner is away this weekend. I was hoping you'd come with me to tell the Sweetmans."

"I'll pick you up in fifteen minutes.. There's no point in taking two cars."

Corcoran was as good as his word and soon they were en route to the south Dublin suburbs.

"Do you want me to tell them?" he asked.

"I'll do it. They know me now. I've spoken to the dad every day for the last two weeks."

"Do you think they're ready?"

"Logically you'd think they'd have given up hope by now, but she's their daughter. I imagine they're still praying she'll turn up alive somewhere."

They drove in silence for a while but as they got closer to their destination, Kate grew more anxious.

"What about the PM results? Should I mention the findings, the old injuries?"

"Not today. Let's just tell them that she's been positively identified by DNA. We have to keep an open mind on the assault thing."

"I know, but those findings will come out at the inquest. That can't be the first time the parents find out what she went through."

"Who's to say the abuse happened outside the home?"

Kate knew Corcoran was only saying what she had wondered about herself, but still she was shocked.

"I know, it could be the father... but up until the last few months she was by all accounts a happy, bright young girl, loving life. Everyone says so. Wouldn't it be rare for the abuse to start at her age? She was nearly twenty and at college. If the dad was that way inclined wouldn't it have started sooner, when he could control her more easily, prevent her from disclosing?"

"It is unlikely. But she was victimised by some sick bastard, and it had to have had an effect on her state of mind. If we could prove who it was, there might be grounds to bring charges."

"We could talk to the friends again. They were definitely a bit cagey when we questioned them. Maybe they know who did this to her."

"That would mean opening an investigation, and I reckon there'll be no appetite for that at HQ. As far as the Commissioner and her political masters are concerned, they want this story to go away quietly."

They'd arrived at the Sweetman house by now. Taking a deep breath, Kate rang the doorbell, to be greeted by a flurry of excited barks. Hugh Sweetman opened the door. For a second no one spoke, but it was clear from his face that he knew why the officers were there. His head dropped and he put his hand over his eyes. The dog danced around his feet, then raced back inside.

"I'm so sorry, Mr. Sweetman," said Kate.

He stepped back and waved them inside, then he went towards the kitchen, stopping for a second to lean against the wall, as if he couldn't bear to carry on. Kate and Corcoran waited in the hall, watching. Hugh opened the kitchen door. Susan turned from her place at the breakfast bar.

"It's the Gardai, love. They want to speak to us."

As the four made their way into the sitting room, Susan began to shake convulsively. Her eyes were wide and brimming with tears, but no sound came from her.

"Mr and Mrs Sweetman, I'm very sorry to have to tell you that the remains in Wales have been identified as those of your daughter," said Jim Corcoran.

The room was silent then except for Susan's sobs. Finally Hugh spoke, his voice quiet and catching in his throat.

"Are you sure? Could it be a mistake? An error in the lab test or something?"

"We're sure, sir," said Corcoran. "It's been positively confirmed by DNA comparison."

The couple clung to one another as Kate and Corcoran stood awkwardly, looking on.

Then Susan spoke.

"Finn! We'll have to tell him..."

"I know, love. We will. We'll tell him together when we're a bit... stronger..."

Susan went on sobbing, her husband's arm around her.

"What happens now?" he asked.

Corcoran answered.

"We'll send the test results to Anglesey and liaise with our Welsh colleagues about repatriating the remains. You'll need to complete some paperwork but the Department of Foreign Affairs can help with that. I can contact them on your behalf, Mr. Sweetman."

"How long will it take? These arrangements. I'd like to go... to Wales, to bring her home... I don't want her all on her own... over there," said Hugh.

"We'll do our best to help, Mr. Sweetman. It won't take more than a few days. We'll make the necessary calls to the department and to the local police today," said Kate.

"Will I be able to see her?"

"The Welsh may need a positive identification from you before releasing the body," said Corcoran. "However, if they're OK with just the DNA results, I would advise against viewing the remains, sir."

Both Sweetmans looked aghast. Kate felt she had to speak, the vision of what she'd seen in the mortuary still fresh in her mind.

"When a body has been in the water for some time, I'm afraid it deteriorates... She'll likely be beyond recognition."

Susan broke into another bout of sobbing. Corcoran nodded to Kate, indicating it was time to leave. In the hall Kate asked Hugh if she could look at Emily's room. He nodded agreement. It was the first room on the right at the top of the stairs, and clearly the family had gone through it thoroughly after Emily's disappearance. Clothes were heaped on the bed, drawers emptied out. On the student desk in the corner was a laptop. Kate grabbed it and its charger. She was just about to leave when she went into the adjoining bathroom. Everything seemed normal. Lots of skin- and hair-care bottles lined the shelf and the shower tray. Underneath the tiny sink there was a stack of packets and boxes containing sanitary towels and tampons. Kate went through each one. In the bottom of a tampon box she found a small cell phone. Not a smart phone but a simple calls-and-texts-only device.

Now why would Emily have a second phone?

Downstairs Hugh and Corcoran were talking quietly. The DI was giving him details of how to go about repatriating Emily's body. Hugh barely seemed to notice the laptop and phone Kate had put into evidence bags.

"The coroner will want these examined prior to the inquest," she said.

"I'll be in touch, sir, and I'm very sorry for your loss."

They shook hands and made their way to the car.

"I'll see if the techies can find anything on these," said Kate.

"It'll be months before the inquest. No point wasting their time now. They've got enough going on," said Jim.

He dropped Kate back home.

"I'll take care of the calls, Kate," he said. "You've done enough on your day off. I need to let the Commissioner know first. Send me your contacts in Wales – the local sergeant and the pathologist. I'll start the ball rolling, and get the Department of Foreign Affairs on the case."

"I'll email those numbers. There are a couple of people I need to tell. The professor at UCD who first gave us her name – I promised I'd let him know. And I want to talk to the two friends again anyway, just for my own peace of mind. I'll get to them first thing Monday."

The weekend passed quickly. Greg did his best to lighten her mood but Kate struggled to shed the sadness she felt. In her absence he'd booked a table at one of their favourite Italian restaurants, and after an afternoon browsing the National Art Gallery and a couple of bookshops, they had dinner. Eventually the wine and the lively atmosphere helped, together with the warm welcome from the owner, who greeted them like old friends. The restaurant was just a few minutes from her apartment and they walked back hand in hand. Kate already dreaded Greg's departure.

"When do you think you'll be free to come to London?"

"I have another weekend off in two weeks. Unless there's a big case, I should be able to come over," she said.

"Good. I'll plan something fun to do. Now that's settled it won't feel so bad saying goodbye tomorrow."

Back home they watched a film. They were working their way through all of Alfred Hitchcock's movies. Tonight it was *Rear Window*, Kate's absolute favourite. Greg was adamant that *Vertigo* was the best. It was an old discussion, in which they both enjoyed arguing their points. As usual they had to agree to differ, but they did agree that James Stewart was superb in both. They spent the next morning with the Sunday newspapers followed by brunch in the city, then all too soon it was time for Greg to leave for the airport. He normally took a taxi, but this time Kate drove him, just to stretch out their time together. As usual, they kept their farewells brief.

"It won't be long 'till you're in London," he said, hugging her close.

"I know. The time will fly."

"Call me... OK?"

"Of course."

"And don't work too hard."

"I won't."

"We both know you will, Kate. Just try to leave all the murder and mayhem in the office, OK?"

15

MONDAY FEBRUARY 7, 2011

On Monday morning Kate was first in to the squad room. She'd done an hour of scanning CCTV footage for the Roche case by the time the others drifted in. When Rory arrived, she updated him on the DNA match.

"Oh shit, that poor family."

"And that's not all..."

Kate then told him about the findings of the post mortem.

"That's awful. She was just a kid... If someone was hurting her, it has to be the reason she did what she did."

He was upset, and Kate realised again what she'd known for a while. Rory had a good heart. He hadn't yet developed the hard shell that police officers needed just to survive the job. *But then, neither had she.*

"Come on – there are people to see, bad news to deliver," she said.

"The family?" he asked.

"No, I saw them on Saturday. I promised I'd let our

friendly professor know if we found her. I also want to track down her two buddies. The news will get out soon enough, but I want to be the one to tell them. If they know something about the violence she suffered before she died, this could be the time to find out."

Professor Grant took the news with stoicism, though he was clearly affected.

"There are a couple every year, you know, students who take their own lives. If you'd asked me a month ago who might be at risk, I'd never have picked Emily Sweetman, never. I suppose it's inevitable that one or two will falter, but it still causes the faculty distress and heart-searching. My colleagues and I will try to see if we could have picked up on her pain. I certainly didn't see it coming. The sad thing is, in my experience, these events are always tragic and almost always a mystery."

There wasn't anything else to say, and Kate and Rory left the office in a sombre mood. It was 11 o'clock, when most students had a fifteen-minute break between lectures or tutorials. They headed for the coffee bar first and quickly spotted Ashling Byrne and Max Egan, huddled over a laptop. The two officers were standing beside them before the students noticed. Max quickly shut the laptop. *Was it Kate's imagination or did they look guilty?*

"Do you have a few minutes? We need to talk to you," said Rory.

Ashling looked nervously at her phone.

"We're back in class soon," she said.

Kate and Rory sat down opposite the pair.

"I'm sorry to inform you that we have found your friend's remains. Emily's body washed up on the Welsh coast a few days ago and we've confirmed her identity with DNA."

The colour drained from their faces. Max gripped his friend's hand and she let her hair fall around her bowed head, hiding her face.

"Are you sure it's Emily?" asked Max.

"Yes, I'm afraid so."

"I can't believe she did this..." whispered Ashling.

"Please keep this to yourselves. Don't share it either in person or on social media. The last thing Emily's family need is another online storm," said Rory. They nodded agreement.

"There will be an inquest and you'll probably be asked to give evidence," said Kate.

The students' bowed heads shot up.

"But why us?" said Max. "We don't know why she did it!"

"You were her closest friends. While you may not think you know anything, you will be asked to tell the coroner and the court what you do know about Emily's last few months," Kate said.

The pair looked panic-stricken. Abruptly, Max stood up.

"Come on, Ash, we'll be late for class," he said. "Thanks for letting us know." With that, the two students almost ran out of the coffee bar.

"What the fuck do they know that they're so scared to tell us?" said Kate.

"Whatever it is, it's eating them up. Did you notice how thin and tired they look? They're hiding something; that's for sure."

"Yep, and I don't know if we'll ever get to the bottom of it."

"I could keep an eye on their social media, do some digging online..."

"Unofficially. Keep an eye on them, but as far as the Gardai are concerned this is a closed book."

Two days later Kate presented herself at the City Mortuary, nervously anticipating her second 'immersion' in the world of autopsies. Harriet Stilson was waiting for her.

"Come in, Kate. Sit down and I'll get you started on Lesson Two."

As before, the two hours passed quickly, the animated sequences of the surgery once again capturing her full attention. She had little time to notice the complete lack of nausea as she followed each step. When Harriet returned, she handed Kate an envelope.

"That DNA comparison you wanted," she said.

Kate felt her heart stop.

"Thanks, Doc," she said. "I'll pass that on."

"Right, so, shall we have a quick drink? I have half an hour before I have to head home. My youngest is cooking, so I have to show my face and eat whatever it is. I think he's doing something Mexican, God help us all!"

The two adjourned to the same pub as before. The envelope, squashed into Kate's bag, was burning a hole in her consciousness, and she found it hard to make small talk with the pathologist. Harriet wanted to know how she'd coped with the second autopsy, and Kate struggled to talk at all, much less give intelligent feedback on the video presentation.

"Are you alright, Kate? You seem a little distracted tonight. Was it the autopsy? Did it upset you?"

"Not at all. I found it fascinating. I can't believe I'm able to sit through these things."

"I told you it would work. A few more of those and you'll have to join me in the cutting room for the real thing."

"I hope you're right. Let's see how I get on with the next few videos, though. I'm not promising anything."

"You'll get there, I guarantee it. Now tell me about The Girl In The Red Dress. Did I hear rumours you've found her?"

Kate updated her friend on the case, including the disturbing findings of her Welsh counterpart.

"The PM report will come to me anyway, when the body is released. That poor kid, and her family! They're devastated enough without knowing what she went through before her death. Are you going to investigate?"

"I have to talk to Corcoran, to see if he'll authorise it. He was never happy taking on the case anyway, but this puts a different slant on it."

"Technically it might not be homicide, but someone brutalised that girl and they need to be stopped. Someone needs to find out who hurt her. From what you say it was prolonged and systematic. That means the abuser's got an appetite for it. There are bound to be other victims... She was a bright girl, her whole life in front of her. Why didn't she tell someone?" said Harriet with some emotion.

Kate wasn't surprised. Her friend was only saying what she'd been thinking. As they parted company, she vowed to tackle the DI about it the next morning. On the way to her car she texted Rory.

> I've got the DNA results.

And...

> I can't open them.

> Do you want me to come over?

> Yes but don't make me look at them.

> We'll put them in the box, OK?

> OK

THE FOLLOWING morning Kate tackled her boss about Emily Sweetman's abuse.

"It will probably come out in the coroner's inquest," said Jim Corcoran.

"But that might not be for months, and in the meantime the trail will go cold," said Kate.

"If the coroner finds that someone seriously assaulted Emily Sweetman and that's what may have driven her to suicide, we'll be asked to investigate – maybe not this team but the force. But even if we can identify the guy, it's going to be tricky to get evidence for a prosecution without the victim's testimony. No, it's not a good idea. You could find yourself down a rabbit hole on this one. Anyway, I can't spare you or Gardiner. I'm sorry, Kate, I know you have a personal interest, but I just can't sanction it."

"OK, we'll step back. Gardiner can keep an eye on her friends' social media. I know those two are hiding something. Eventually they'll let it out. They're all addicted to over-sharing. They won't be able to keep this secret for much longer. We'll do it in our down time, not on the job."

"Fine. Keep me in the loop."

16

A month to the day since her suicide, Emily's funeral was held in her local church. The death notices had said 'private service, close family and friends only' and the media stayed away. When the recovery and identification of the body had been announced, a couple of lines on the newsfeeds and scant paragraphs in the newspapers had marked the tragic death. Now news cycles had moved on, and The Girl In The Red Dress was yesterday's clickbait. In the church Ashling cried so much her face was blotchy and red. Max couldn't console her. The photo of Emily, young and smiling, that stood on top of the simple willow coffin broke their hearts.

Apart from the Sweetmans' extended family, there were students and staff from UCD, teachers and teenagers from Emily's old school, and dozens of neighbours and work colleagues of Hugh and Susan. When the solemn mass was over and the mourners lined up to pay their respects, the queue snaked all the way down the aisle of the church. Feeling like outsiders, Ashling and Max left and stood smoking in a corner of the churchyard. That's where the two officers found them.

"Nice service. Very sad," said Rory. "How are you two doing?"

Max mumbled, "OK." Ashling looked at her feet and didn't answer.

"I want to let you know that the inquest was opened and adjourned, to allow us to gather as much information as possible," said Kate. "You'll be summoned to attend by the Clerk of The Court in a few months probably."

"We'd like to talk to you both before then," said Rory, "just to paint a fuller picture of Emily's life."

Ashling looked nervously at Max.

"Are you talking about a police interview?" said Max, with a note of defiance.

"Nothing so formal. Just a more detailed chat. I know you guys are busy with college work, but we really would appreciate your help," said Rory.

"I'll have to speak to my father first," said Max. "He's a senior counsel, and he might not like me and Ashling getting involved in some sort of witch hunt."

Kate was struck by the term witch hunt.

Max believed someone was to blame for Emily's death. Or else why would he call it a witch hunt?

"You are involved, both of you," she said. "Something drove Emily, a young woman with no history of depression or mental illness... something drove her to take her own life, in a public and shocking way. Whether you like it or not, the coroner is going to find the truth, and you need to do all you can to help in that process."

Max grabbed Ashling's hand and the two walked away without another word.

"We'll be in touch," said Rory to their departing backs.

When weeks passed and they heard no more from the detectives, the two students almost felt that life was getting back to normal. Ashling was still broke and behind with the rent. Max hadn't told his father about the whole Emily business. As for the Sugar Babies, Max barely kept his Pigs ticking over. Ashling carried on but the funds were not so plentiful without Emily. There was one bright spot, though Max knew nothing about it. Aggrieved that he wasn't bothered with the Pay Pigs anymore, and desperate to keep the cash rather than share, Ashling had given one Pay Pig her personal account details. He was charming and generous, and she wanted to keep him all to herself.

17

MARCH 2011

The Roche case was taking up most of Kate and Rory's time. As the trial drew near there had been several more shootings in the gangland feud. One man was in hospital with spinal injuries, and another had taken a shot to the torso but was saved by his bullet-proof vest. While the rest of the squad pursued these new enquiries, Kate and Rory were busy cementing the case against the gunmen. It was tedious work, interviewing unco-operative associates and relatives of the victim and the shooters, watching endless hours of CCTV, tracking down witnesses. Few people were prepared to talk. In the tight-knit communities where the gangs operated, anyone believed to be talking to the Garda Siochana was a target. Houses were sprayed with gunfire in the night, beatings were meted out, threats issued. The gangs had enforcers, many of them young teenagers, high on crack cocaine and tripping on the sense of power a handgun gave them. When one teen was locked up, shot or overdosed, there was always another kid ready to step up. The drug kingpins directed operations from afar, in safe havens abroad, where they lived the high life on the profits of their trade and never dirtied their own hands with the blood of their rivals.

Liaising with senior counsel from the office of the Director of Public Prosecutions, weeks of slog had produced a substantial Book of Evidence, which the DPP was confident would make a compelling case. The trial date was a month away and soon there would be no more Kate and Rory could do to strengthen the prosecution case.

KATE SPENT a perfect weekend with Greg in London. Somehow, being away from Dublin meant she could leave her work and her personal worries behind. He was renting a riverside apartment in the revitalised Docklands, with a view over the Thames. At night, with lights twinkling from every block and tower, the city was breathtaking. He had booked tickets for an Agatha Christie play, *Witness for The Prosecution*, which was staged not in a theatre, but in the old council chamber in London's historic City Hall.

"I know it's a bit of a busman's holiday, but I didn't think you'd be into a musical, and to be honest everything else was booked out," he said as they took their seats in the elegant wood-panelled room full to the rafters with patrons.

They both loved the play and the walk back home, eagerly discussing the twist at the end and whether they'd seen it coming. On the Sunday they were up early and wandered among the boutiques and stalls in the trendy Spitalfields Market. Greg bought her tiny gold handmade earrings in the shape of starfish, and they had Pakistani street food on nearby Brick Lane. Her flight home was a late one, so they'd had time to really relax, which made their parting bittersweet. As the Heathrow Express train doors slid to a close, he promised to come to Dublin in a couple of weeks.

Being back in work on Monday morning was a bit of a comedown. Corcoran was in a bad mood. Two witnesses had withdrawn their statements in the Roche case and the Director of Public Prosecution wasn't happy. In gangland murder cases, jury trials had been suspended because of repeated jury tampering. The cases were now being heard before a panel of three judges in the Special Criminal Court. But witness intimidation was almost impossible to stop.

Kate and Rory visited both of the reluctant witnesses, but failed to persuade them to change their minds.

"You can't blame them, really. They have to live there, to send their kids to school and face their neighbours day-in, day-out," said Rory.

"And we can't protect them. Even if the shooters go down, these gangs have long memories. You'd have to think twice before going up against them."

"Look, we've got good forensics, and the CCTV evidence is strong. We don't absolutely need eye witnesses. A court would be mad to acquit the two shooters."

"Let's hope so. How bad would it be if they didn't go down after all the slog we've put in?"

Later, having filed their reports, they signed out of work and went to their favourite bar in The Shelbourne. Rory wanted to know all about the London trip and Kate was happy to re-live it. Two drinks in, he looked at her speculatively.

"Right, Ms Hamilton. Don't bite my head off... I have a question to ask you," he said.

"When did I ever bite your head off?" she said, laughing.

"You must be kidding. I was terrified of you when I first joined the team. You can be so fierce at times."

"Gotta be fierce in that bear-pit!"

"Well... speaking of fierceness... I think you need to open the envelope."

Kate was taken aback. She knew exactly what he was talking about. The DNA results were still unopened, shut away in the box she'd been left by the late Bernie O'Toole. She'd managed to keep the bequest and its contents at the back of her mind, and the back of her wardrobe, for weeks.

"That's not a question," said Kate.

"OK. When are you going to open the envelope?"

"I haven't really thought about it."

"Well, think about it now. You can't just let it rot in that box."

"I know. It's a big step. What if it's all true and that murdering bastard was my twin?"

"'You are not your brother's keeper' – never was a saying more apt. An accident of birth may connect you, but you're no more like him than I am. Even less, since I'm a man."

Kate sipped her third gin and tonic, and said nothing for a minute or two.

"The longer you wait the more it will eat away at you. It's like a ticking time bomb in the bottom of your wardrobe," he said.

"Now you're exaggerating. I haven't even thought about it for weeks."

"I don't believe that for one minute. The thing is, Kate, if Rosie was your mother you have a grandmother who's still alive. She's not going to live forever. She's already in her seventies. What if you leave it too late?"

"I don't know if I want a grandmother."

"But she might be adorable! Mine is. I don't know what I'd do without her."

"You're talking arse, Rory! Let's have another drink and some food and I'll think about it."

By the time they spilled out of the taxi at Kate's apartment block they were more than a little tipsy.

"Come on up. There's a bottle of nice wine in the fridge."

"That's a miracle, Kate. Did you actually go shopping?"

"Me? No! It's been sitting there since Greg was over. It's about the only thing in the fridge."

"Of course it is. I don't know how you don't just blow away in the breeze."

Rory opened the wine and got out the glasses. Kate fetched the box from her room and placed it on the coffee table. Then they sat, looking at it, in silence. Kate gulped her wine so quickly she had a coughing fit and Rory had to thump her on the back. It didn't help. Finally she put down her glass and raised the lid of the box.

The envelope was on the top. It looked very new and bright among the faded photos and letters.

"Here goes…"

Kate ripped open the envelope and unfolded the sheet of paper. It wasn't easy to make sense of the technical language. Rory leaned over her shoulder to read it.

"What does it say?" she said, handing him the sheet.

"Do you really want me to tell you?" he asked, scanning it carefully.

"Yes, I do. I can't make head nor tail of it. Too much gin. But don't fuck it up."

Rory re-read the paper and put it down. Suddenly it felt like it might burn his skin.

"I think it says that the probability, the mathematically overwhelming probability is... that the two samples are from siblings who share the same parents."

Kate was quiet. They both stared at the paper on the coffee table.

"Are you sure?" she whispered.

"I've read it three times. I'm sure."

Again they went silent.

"Do they deliver alcohol on Deliveroo?" asked Kate.

THE NEXT MORNING at work Kate was finding it hard to concentrate. She was hung over, and the DNA results were like grenades going off in her already aching head. She could think of nothing else. Rory, also visibly suffering, kept them going with coffee and pastries all morning. At lunchtime he made her come to the canteen, though she refused any more food. He ordered steak pie and chips.

"Soakage," he said as he tucked in. "It's practically medicinal. Go on, have a chip."

Kate ate some chips from his plate and had to admit it helped. She was quiet, and as he finished his plate Rory knew he had to say something.

"Look, you ripped the sticking plaster off and it hurt. I know that, but knowing the truth must be better than wondering."

"I'm not sure it is..."

"It's been hanging over your head since the shootout. That's more than a year. It's a wonder you're not demented."

"OK. Maybe you're right. But now that I know, what am I supposed to do with it? Everything Bernie told me must be true. My birth mother, St Mary's, my mam and dad, the two people I loved and trusted most in this world. It turns out they were little short of criminals. I don't even know if my passport is valid, since it's based on a fake birth certificate. Everything I believed about myself is a lie."

"You're catastrophising, Kate. Firstly, your parents weren't criminals. At worst it was a civil offence. Secondly, they adored you and gave you a brilliant childhood. They made you the person you are. Everything else is just biology. None of this changes who you are. None of it."

"Stop being so bloody sensible. Allow me some wallowing," said Kate.

"No, you've done enough. Now's the time for action. You've taken the first step, even if it took a massive drinks bill at the Shelbourne to get you there! You've got to contact Rosie's mum, your grandmother."

"I don't want to meet her. Why would she want to meet me? If it wasn't for my birth she'd still have her daughter."

"Now you're being melodramatic. It's not your fault you were born. None of this is your fault. And if she doesn't want to meet you, fine! You move on with your life."

"It's that simple, is it?"

"It's not simple. I know it's not," Rory said gently, fearing he might have gone too far, "but somehow or other, you have to put the past behind you, and unless you take the next step you won't be able to."

"God, I hate you, Rory Gardiner," said Kate ruefully. "You're like my very own Jiminy Cricket – nag, nag, nag."

"So... when are you going to contact Marina Jackson?" He said it like he was planning a treat. "She's a busy woman. She still sits on the board of her company, but she's not going to live forever."

"Alright already," said Kate. "Send me her contact details."

With two weeks to go until their next weekend together, Kate couldn't wait that long to tell Greg. That night she Face-Timed him and told him about the DNA results. To her annoyance, he said the same thing as Rory, though he was a bit more tactful.

"It's your choice, Kate, what you do now. Try to look at the positives – there could be a whole other family out there who'd love to know you. Rosie's mum sounds like quite a character, strong and resilient. Just like you. Don't you want to get to know her, before it's too late?"

"It's not that easy, reaching out to a stranger."

"You don't do 'easy', Kate. I reckon 'easy' would bore you to death. Take a chance; what's the worst thing that could happen?"

"Have you been talking to Rory? He's on exactly the same page as you."

"Sensible guy, Rory, and he cares about you, like me."

After the call, Kate took out the contact details Rory had handed her on a sticky note. There was a landline, and, before second thoughts could derail her, she keyed the number into her phone and hit the call button.

18

The voice that answered was strong and warm. The woman had picked up the call so quickly Kate nearly dropped her phone in shock.

"Hello?'

What to say?

"Hello. Who's calling?"

Kate went into automatic pilot.

"My name is Kate Hamilton, I'm a detective sergeant with the Garda Siochana. Is that Mrs Jackson?"

"Yes. How can I help you?" The woman sounded curious but friendly.

Kate panicked.

"We're conducting Home Security briefings in your area and I wondered if I might visit to have a chat. I can check out the residence and advise on any improvements. May I ask if you live alone?"

How easily the lies came! She even surprised herself.

"Yes, I do. I had an alarm installed a while ago, but I

suppose a check wouldn't do any harm. When would you be in the Blackrock area?"

"I can call in on Monday, if that would be convenient."

"I'm around in the morning until about one o'clock, but I'll have to check your credentials, Sergeant."

"Of course, Mrs. Jackson. You can never be too careful. I'll call in at about ten a.m. if that suits?"

"I'll see you then so. Bye-bye."

Kate almost collapsed with relief when Marina Jackson hung up. Her heart was pounding. She replayed the conversation over and over in her head. The woman had sounded mature but not frail. *How much can you tell from a voice?* There was a faint accent... maybe English? For hours she wavered between horror at what she'd done and apprehension at meeting Marina. *What could she say? She'd already lied on their very first encounter.* Maybe she could just do a quick check on the house and leave, and never contact her again? She rang Rory. He came straight over.

"Before you say anything, I've no alcohol in the house and I'm not drinking," said Kate, switching on the coffee machine.

"Agreed," said Rory. "I'll make the coffee. You sit down and tell me everything."

Kate recounted the brief conversation.

"Well, if she lives alone in that big house she probably needs some security advice."

"I panicked. I couldn't just say 'Hi, I'm your long-lost granddaughter', could I?"

"No, you'd give the poor woman a heart attack. You have to tell her the truth on Monday, though. You can't start off your relationship with a pack of lies."

"Relationship? She'll probably show me the door. I've blown it already."

"Don't be silly, you haven't blown it. She sounded nice, didn't she? Not too doddery?"

"As much as you can tell from a voice over the phone, she sounded nice. Not like a little old lady, anyway; more like a strong mature woman."

"There you go. The apple doesn't fall far from the tree; you're strong."

"I don't feel strong, I feel shit-scared. What am I going to say?"

"We'll work it out. We have all night and the weekend to think of a way to tell her who you are. It'll be fine."

19

FRIDAY APRIL 1, 2011

For the first time since Emily's death Ashling had a date. Max knew she was going out when she disappeared off to the bathrooms straight after their last lecture. When she returned fifteen minutes later she'd changed from her habitual jeans and t-shirt into a dress and was wearing makeup.

"Another date with Beamer man?" said Max.

"How did you know..." said Ashling.

"I saw you come home the other night. And you're all dressed up, and it's not for my benefit."

"He's picking me up in half an hour. I've time for a coffee."

Max could tell she was dying to tell him about her new man.

"So who's the rich guy?"

They were sitting in their favourite corner of the café, steaming cappuccinos in hand.

"His name is Dan and he's gorgeous."

"Where did you meet him? Rich and gorgeous isn't easy to find!"

Ashling blushed. Max sensed she was playing for time.

"Come on, who is he? And does he have a gay identical twin for me?"

"I don't think so. At least he hasn't mentioned one so far. He's... or at least he was... one of my Pigs."

For once Max was speechless. Ashling had never met up with a Pig before. She'd always said it was too risky.

"He's not a Pig anymore," she lied, not wanting to disclose that Dan had been sending her money privately. Max didn't need to know she'd cut him out of the Sugar Babies' profits.

"We're going out, kind of..."

"But Ash, you always said you wouldn't go near the Pigs."

"I know, but we were texting for ages, and he's nice. I just thought, why not?"

"So, how many times have you been out with him? Tell me everything."

Ashling filled him in on her three dates with Dan.

"He's such a good listener. I told him all about Emily and home and everything, and he totally gets me."

"So what does he do for a living, and how old is he?"

"He works for a property company. They build fancy houses. He's promised to show me some of the sites one day, and he's around thirty, I think."

"You don't know?"

"I haven't asked him; it seems a bit rude."

"That's like ten years older than you, Ash. It's a lot."

"Age doesn't matter. He's still young, free and single."

"Are you sure?"

"Of course I'm sure. He's a nice guy, Max. I've been chatted up by married men before. I can see them coming a mile off."

"Do I get to meet this paragon then?"

"Not yet. This is only the fourth date, and we don't go to studenty places! He's taken me out to some really cute little country pubs for drinks and food. It makes a change from burgers at McDonald's with other boys."

"He's not a boy, though, is he? He's a grown-up. Are you sure you're ready for that?"

"You're just jealous, Max Egan, that I've found a man and you're still single!" Ashling laughed and stood up. "I'm off. Don't want to keep him waiting. See you later."

"Be good, Ash, and if you can't be good..."

"I know, be careful!"

THE NEXT DAY
SATURDAY APRIL 2ND 2011

WHEN ASHLING CAME to she had no idea where she was. It was pitch dark and she could feel hard cold walls around her. She couldn't move her arms and legs. Closing her eyes, she shook her head violently. It hurt. A lot. *This must be a dream. She just had to wake herself up and it would be fine.* But when she opened her eyes again it wasn't over. She wasn't at home in her bed. She was in a small dank space, and the reason she couldn't move was that her hands and feet were bound. *Was she in her grave? Was this what death was?* As her head cleared she started to remember. Dan... their date...

that perfect house... but then she remembered the bedroom and what happened there. That was worse, far worse than now. She longed for oblivion. *And water... Nothing more, just some cold, blessed water, or she would actually die.*

DAN WASN'T a man to panic. He'd been in tight spots before and gotten out unscathed. There was a girl in college who'd threatened to go to the Gardai. He'd taken care of her. In the end she couldn't face a court case and the judgement of her parents and friends. He'd convinced her no one would believe her. The others knew better than to go public; he had sex tapes that could destroy them.

He just needed time to come up with a plan. He'd underestimated this girl. Nothing he said or did would subdue her, until he shut her up with his fists. She could expose him and ruin everything. He had to get her out of the picture, and he knew just who could help; his friends on the Dark Web. They'd know what to do with the stupid bitch.

There were plenty of suggestions. Some of the others offered to take the girl off his hands, but they were scattered all over the world, from San Francisco to Melbourne. The idea of shipping her out was too outrageous, even for him. Others opted for a worse fate for Ashling, and they wanted to see video proof. He had watched so-called 'snuff' movies. *Even if they were genuine, it was a step too far. Though it could make him a lot of money, and he'd be a legend. But he didn't need the money, and after all, he wasn't a killer. He just liked things a bit rough.* He rubbished the snuff movie suggestion mentally, while giving the impression online that he was giving it some thought.

As he pondered his options he told himself he should have tried harder to find a willing partner, but he didn't like the city's BDSM community. He'd been to a couple of specialist clubs. It was all safe words, sweaty men in vinyl, and ugly domineering women, not the younger girls he preferred. Anyway, Dublin was small. He was scared he'd be seen and outed by some busybody. His life would be in the toilet overnight.

Now, damn it, he'd have to do something with her, and soon. She'd been stashed away for more than twenty-four hours. He'd bring her some food and water, then he could talk sense into her. He'd get her to agree to keep quiet, somehow. He had to.

ASHLING WAS FALLING in and out of sleep, dozing off, leaning against the wall on her right side, then waking with a jerk, aching and stiff. She wasn't sure how long she'd been in this dark hole of a place, but each waking moment was more torturous than the last. She was so thirsty her lips were cracking and her tongue was sticking to the roof of her mouth. Her throat felt like it would close and then she was afraid she wouldn't be able to get any air into her lungs. Forcing herself to take in slow, deep breaths, she tried to calm her anxiety. In for four, hold for four, out for four. It was something Emily had taught her before their exams. And it worked. She'd been shouting on and off for hours, but all she could hear was the hum of traffic on a distant road, and birdsong. Then, without warning, there was a loud clanging noise close by. Light flooded the space, almost blinding her. She realised she was inside some form of shipping container, with huge stacks of builders' blocks forming a wall on her left. There was a narrow opening a metre or so from her bound feet. Someone had opened the door and was walking towards her.

"Help! Help me, please..." Her voice was croaky and weak.

No one answered.

Then he appeared.

"There's no point shouting. No one can hear you but me," he said.

"Water... Please, I need water..." Ashling was crying now, partly from relief that someone had come, partly from dread that it was Dan, the person who'd put her here. He bent down and used a Stanley knife to cut the duct tape on her hands, then he handed her a bottle of water. Her hands were so numb she dropped it, and she had to shake them repeatedly to get the feeling back. He took back the bottle, opened the lid and held it to her mouth. She gulped almost half the bottle without stopping, finally taking it from him when she could feel her fingers again.

"Please, Dan, let me go. I won't tell anyone," she said.

"I'd like to believe that, Ashling. But how do I know you'll keep your mouth shut?"

She gulped some more water, playing for time. Her mind was spinning. Could she get her feet free from the bindings and make a run for it? Then she realised how weak she was, after sitting in the same position for so long. Even if she could run, he would catch her easily.

"Look, I know I overreacted. It's just... I'm not very experienced with men, and I wasn't expecting it to be like that..."

She tried to make her words conciliatory, though the sight of him filled her with fear and disgust.

"It was a big misunderstanding. I just lashed out in that moment."

"You nearly broke my nose," he said.

"Sorry, Dan..."

"If I let you go, what will you tell your friends... about the marks?" He gestured towards her bruised and swollen face. One eye was half-closed.

"I'll say I fell over, drunk. I'm really clumsy. I'm always tripping up and hurting myself."

For a moment she thought she'd won. He seemed to consider removing the bindings on her knees and ankles. Then he grabbed the roll of tape and her hands in one quick move, and began to wrap them tightly together again.

Ashling lost it.

"You bastard, you sick perverted bastard!" She was screaming and struggling now. "You can't do this to me. You have to let me go or I'll die here."

"Shut up, you stupid bitch. Did you think that I'd fall for your little act?"

"It's not an act. Let me go and I promise I won't tell."

"You're such a liar, just like your Sugar Baby friend."

He crouched beside her in the tight space, put his face close to hers and pressed his hand to her swollen cheek.

"You sell yourselves like you're up for anything, but when it comes to the crunch you can't hack it."

He almost spat the words. Ashling closed her eyes and shrank into the corner.

"I'm sorry. Please let me go... I'll do anything you want..."

"Oh you will, sweetheart, you will. I have big plans for you. You're going to be an internet sensation."

Standing up, he threw a second bottle of water and a

packet of crisps at her, then he left, locking the heavy doors and securing them with a chain. In the silence, the awful truth dawned on Ashling. Dan had mentioned 'her Sugar Baby friend'. Could he be talking about Emily? Was he the reason she'd committed suicide?

20

MONDAY APRIL 4, 2011

"**D**o you want me to come with you?" asked Rory.

Kate was due to visit Marina Jackson at ten o'clock. She'd met her partner at eight in a coffee shop near HQ.

"I do and I don't," she said.

"Well, you've time still to make up your mind. You know what you're going to say; we went through it last night. You'll be fine. It should be private between you and her."

"I know. It's just very scary."

"Not scary – exciting. Think of it that way."

"Who are you, my therapist?" said Kate.

"Near as damned," he said.

After an hour in work, she clocked out on the duty roster, claiming a dental appointment. Rory gave her a thumbs-up as she left. Blasting out music on the car radio to stop her swirling thoughts, she arrived at the Jackson home fifteen minutes early and parked outside the imposing gates. The house lay at the end of a winding driveway with lush gardens on either side. It was a solid two-storey mansion, painted cream, neo-Georgian in style. A rich red ivy creeper trailed over some of the walls. At exactly three minutes to ten Kate pulled her car in next to the gates, and as she was about to get out and press the buzzer, they opened. She spotted a camera perched on the high perimeter wall.

She parked the car to the left of the front door on the gravel driveway and made herself climb the two broad granite steps to ring the bell. It echoed in the large house, but the door opened in a matter of seconds. An elegant woman in a business suit smiled at Kate. She looked to be in her mid-thirties.

"Detective Sergeant Hamilton?"

"Yes."

Kate had her Garda ID ready and handed it over. The young woman looked at it quickly before returning it.

"I'm Karen, Mrs. Jackson's PA. She's just having her morning coffee in the conservatory. Would you like to follow me?"

Kate's heart was thumping painfully. She wanted to turn and run, but it was too late now. Returning her badge to her waistband, she followed the young woman.

"This is a lovely house," she said.

"It is, isn't it? I'm lucky I get to work in such a nice place," said Karen.

"Do you live here too?"

"I stay over occasionally if we work late or have an early start, but I have my own place in town. Mind you, it's just a little apartment, not a patch on this house."

"You could fit my entire apartment into the hall," said Kate, aware she was making nervous small talk.

"Mine too," said Karen with a grin. Then she opened the door to a vast sitting room with pale leather button-back couches and chairs. The ceiling was high and decorated with ornate plaster carvings round the edge. A huge plaster ceiling rose framed a delicate chandelier. There was a piano in the corner, and an attractive mix of traditional and modern artworks on the light walls. Wide French doors led to a conservatory filled with greenery. Kate could see a figure seated at a table among the plants, bathed in sunshine. For a second she couldn't get her breath. This was Marina Jackson, her grandmother, *maybe*. *What in God's name would she say?*

The PA led Kate across the deep-carpeted room and opened the doors.

"Detective Sergeant Hamilton is here, Marina," she said.

"Why don't you come and have some coffee with me, Detective," said the woman, getting to her feet.

Kate walked out into the conservatory and shook hands. Her knees were trembling so she was glad to sit when Marina did. The table was laid with coffee and biscuits.

"I'll leave you to it. I've got some calls to make," said Karen.

"It's exciting to have a visit from the Gardai," said Marina.

Not sure she could speak, Kate smiled and sipped the coffee she had been handed. She could not take her eyes off Marina Jackson. She was tall and slim, with no hint of a stoop. Her hair was a perfect silvery white, cut short and slightly wavy. She was dressed impeccably in a navy pencil skirt and a cream silk blouse. Every inch the successful corporate CEO, she didn't look her age.

"You have a lovely home, Mrs. Jackson," Kate said.

"Thank you. I'm very lucky; the house was in my late husband's family for several generations, so it's quite the responsibility. I just try to keep it nice and make sure it doesn't feel like a museum!"

Marina had a rich, warm voice.

"Now, tell me about this security check you're doing. I hadn't heard of such a thing before."

Kate's voice froze in her throat. *Now was the time to come clean, but could she do it?* She gulped the hot coffee.

"Anyone can ask the Gardai to check their home over for safety and security. We're happy to provide advice."

"But I didn't ask—"

"I know, Mrs Jackson... but it's a good idea to get these things done. You have a lot of very beautiful things here; I can see that. It could make the house a target for thieves."

"You're right, of course. Let me show you the security measures we've already taken, then you can advise on what else we should be doing."

Marina produced a folder of papers which included details of a state of the art house alarm, the CCTV system in the house and grounds, window and door locks and a 24-hour monitoring contract with the alarm company, plus a connection to the local station.

"This looks very impressive, Mrs Jackson, and this was all installed recently?" said Kate.

"Yes. We'd had an alarm system for years but I decided to upgrade the whole lot just last year."

"And do you live here alone?"

"Most of the time. Karen stays over sometimes. I have a housekeeper who comes in every day, and a gardener who keeps the grounds nice. So there are people around during the day but not at night. Would you like to see the rest of the house?"

Kate accepted the invitation with relief, as she was

running out of things to say about home security. Marina led the way back into the main body of the house. In an attempt to keep up her cover story, Kate made a point of inspecting the window and door locks, and the alarm sensors.

Upstairs there were four bedrooms with bathrooms, and a spacious office suite where they could see Karen working. She waved as they passed the glass-fronted office. Then Marina led the way downstairs to the back of the house and the kitchen. Once there, she showed Kate to a seat at the table.

"Well... what's the verdict, Detective?" said Marina.

"All very good, I think. I would advise that you activate the alarm when you're home alone. There's a setting that only activates when the perimeter is breached, say one of the windows or doors. That way you won't be setting it off yourself as you move about the house."

"Good. I'll take that on board. I should really have been doing that all along. It's just... well... this house has been my home for more than forty years. I feel safe here."

"And so you should. I think you've taken all the right precautions. This is a low-crime area. Just keep the local station number on your mobile. You could also consider getting a panic alarm to wear on your person, just in case. They're really simple. If you had a fall or you couldn't get to a phone, you just press a button and the Guards are alerted, plus an emergency contact, like Karen."

"That's a good idea. I hadn't thought of it, but then we never like to think of ourselves as vulnerable, do we? Now I have a question for you..."

Kate had almost begun to relax. *She would leave now and never come back to bother this nice woman.*

"Yes?"

"What's the real reason you're here?"

***

RORY WAS ANXIOUS. Kate had promised to ring him but, with no word from her, he was finding it hard to concentrate. When his mobile vibrated in his pocket it made him jump. Quickly, he made his way to the tiny kitchen down the hall from the squad room. He was disappointed to see that it was from an unknown number.

"Rory Gardiner speaking."

"Is that Detective Gardiner?"

"Yes. Who's calling?"

"It's Max Egan... Emily Sweetman's friend. We spoke once or twice."

"Hi, Max. How are you?"

"Not so good right now... I need to speak to you, and it's kind of urgent."

Rory was intrigued. *Was he finally going to get the truth out of the student?*

"Do you want to meet, Max? I can come out to Belfield."

"I'm not in college today. Can you come to the house?"

Max called out his address, which was close to the UCD campus. Rory grabbed his jacket, signed out on the Ops Board and booked out a car from the transport unit in the basement. He tried calling Kate, but it went unanswered. *What was going on in that big house in Blackrock?*

Max opened the door to him. He looked rough; hollow-cheeked and pasty.

"Come in to the kitchen. I need coffee," he said.

Max washed two mugs from a pile of dirty ones in the sink. Rory sat at the breakfast bar, watching. The place was untidy but no more so than he'd expect for a student house. Max himself was more interesting. He'd always seemed fairly together, even in the midst of his distress at Emily's disappearance and death. Today he looked like he was falling apart. His hands trembled when he spooned the instant coffee into the mugs, several times he ran his fingers through his lank hair, and he was still in a t-shirt and boxer shorts though it was almost one o'clock. He was even thinner than before. His shoulder blades were sticking out through the cotton top. Rory let the silence sit between them. Finally, having slopped the coffee onto the breakfast bar when he passed over the cup, and without the offer of milk or sugar, Max sat down opposite Rory.

"It's Ashling. I think something's happened to her," he said.

"Go on..."

"I haven't seen her in two days, and she hasn't been in class either."

"Two days! Why did you wait until now to raise the alarm?"

"I just kept thinking she'd be back any minute. She's stayed out before, a couple of times, but only for one night, never this long. I didn't want to piss her off if she was just having fun. I called her family but they haven't heard from her. I told them not to worry, that she's probably off having a great time. I think they believed me..."

The boy's voice tailed off.

"And what makes you think she's not?"

"She won't answer my texts or calls. They're going straight to voicemail. That's not like her. Ash is never off her phone."

"Right. When did you last see her?"

"Friday after class. She was going out, on a date."

"Who with?"

"That's just it, I don't know. Some guy called Dan she's been seeing for a couple of weeks. I think he's older... He drives a dark BMW and he has a beard. I got a quick look at him when he dropped her home one night."

"Anything else you know about him, like a surname?"

"No. I'm not sure Ashling even knows his surname. She said he worked in property, but that's all she told me."

"Would she normally tell you about her dates?"

"She's an open book, and I'm her best friend; she tells me everything. None of this is like her... Ash never skips class. She has an assignment due today. She'd normally be cramming all weekend."

"Did she say where they were going?"

"No, just that they didn't go to student hangouts, like he was taking her somewhere special maybe... She said they went to country pubs."

"Are you sure she's not off on some romantic getaway?"

"Ash would tell me if she was going to be gone for a few days. It's not like her to disappear like this and not send me a text or anything. And there's something else, something I haven't told you..."

Finally, the truth, thought Rory.

"He's one of her Pay Pigs."

Max then told him about the Sugar Babies, how it all started, and about Emily's involvement. Rory wrote frantically in his notebook. He let the boy talk, conscious that this might be the breakthrough they needed to make sense of Emily's suicide.

He'd heard of Sugar Daddies and Sugar Babies but not Pay Pigs.

This was a new twist.

"Right, I'm going to need a formal statement from you. I'll also need yours and Ashling's computers and passwords. Get dressed and come back to HQ with me. Bring a recent photo of Ashling. We'll file a Missing Persons report."

With Max's permission, Rory took a close look at Ashling's room. It was, as he'd expected, a chaotic mix of books and academic paperwork, piles of clothes, makeup and toiletries. He scanned the notebooks and checked drawers and wardrobes to no avail. It didn't look like she'd packed spare clothes, her backpack was still there, and there was an empty weekend case in the bottom of the wardrobe. Her phone charger was plugged into the wall. This might explain why she hadn't texted or called Max. Still, Rory had an uneasy feeling. Knowing what these students had been up to, he couldn't help but feel something bad could have happened to Ashling, just like Emily. He took her laptop, a toothbrush and a hairbrush for DNA, and put them in evidence bags.

Max was waiting on the landing when Rory finished his search. He went in, rummaged under the mattress at the foot of Ashling's bed and pulled out a cell phone.

"This is her other phone, the one she used for the Pay Pigs."

Rory opened another evidence bag. Max dropped in the phone. Now dressed in jeans and a creased shirt, he still looked terrible. For the first time since he'd known him, Rory felt sorry for the boy who'd seemed so feisty when they'd first met. Now, written on his face was pure fear. He'd lost one close friend, and he was scared he'd lose another.

21

K ate was floored by Marina's question. Her elaborate ploy had failed and now she'd have to come clean.

"Well, Detective?" she said, still smiling warmly.

"You're right, Mrs. Jackson, I did come here under somewhat false pretences... but everything I've done and said is genuine. An Garda Siochana is tasked with protecting and serving the public, and in particular anyone who might be vulnerable."

"I know you're genuine, my dear. I checked you out. You've got quite a high profile as a murder detective, don't you? But what has that got to do with me?"

Kate felt her breath coming in short gasps. Where to start? All the rehearsed words fled her mind.

"You probably know about the shooting in Churchtown a little over a year ago?"

"Yes, I do. That was a terrible business. I read that you were wounded quite badly that day."

Kate's hand flew to her neck, but she couldn't make

fingertip contact with her scar. She had dressed carefully for this day, and put on a silk scarf to cover it.

"I was shot, yes... and the woman I was there to protect... well... she died."

As usual, Kate felt a lump in her throat when she talked about that awful day.

"Yes, I remember, and so too did the killer, didn't he?"

Oh God, this was all going wrong... There was nothing to do but keep talking.

"Yes, he was shot by one of the Armed Support Unit. We were investigating him for a series of killings. You might remember, the murders happened in just a matter of days. It was all over the media. Even though it was impossible to prove, we believe he was responsible for all four, plus a fifth victim, the woman I was with that day, Bernie O'Toole."

"My God, what a terrible business. I take it you're fully recovered, Detective?"

"I am, thank you. Does that name, Bernie O'Toole, mean anything to you?"

"I don't think so..."

"Her maiden name was Bernadette Murphy... and she was in St Mary's in Donnybrook... at the same time as your daughter."

Marina's hand went to her mouth and her eyes widened. The colour drained from her face. She didn't speak, just sat staring at Kate.

"I'm sorry to have to bring you back to that time, Mrs. Jackson. I know it must have been devastating for you."

"You can't possibly know..." the woman whispered.

Kate let some moments go by.

"Bernie told me she was close to your daughter Rose..."

"Rosie... We called her Rosie... I remember she did make a friend, a girl she really liked."

"That was Bernie. She spoke very warmly of your daughter."

"And she's the woman who died?"

"Yes, I'm afraid so."

"But what... what has this got to do with me? Now, all these years later?"

Marina's strength seemed to be returning. Kate thought she could discern a hint of the core of steel she must have needed to survive the tragedy in her life.

"Bernie told me about Rosie, and how she died... I'm so sorry for your loss, Mrs Jackson."

"Loss isn't a big enough word... not for what happened to us. I lost them both, Rosie and her father."

Kate felt like she was turning the knife in a wound that was clearly still raw. *What else did she expect?*

"I can show you a picture if you like, of Rosie," said Marina softly.

She stood up and led the way back to the lounge at the front of the house. From a drawer at the bottom of a ceiling-high bookshelf she pulled out a photo album. Then she crossed to the sofa and beckoned for Kate to sit beside her.

"I used to have photos everywhere of Rosie, and her dad, all over the house. But it was too painful. I couldn't bear to look at them. Now I only take them out on certain days – her birthday or around Christmas, when I miss her most."

She started leafing through the album. Kate felt her heart thump and her breath quicken. *This was it... she was going to see her mother's face.*

22

R ory took Max Egan into HQ, and helped him to make a Missing Persons report. Max was nervous and monosyllabic. Rory put that down to anxiety. Once the desk sergeant had taken Ashling's details and opened a file, Rory took the boy to an interview room.

"Firstly, Max, I want to let you know that you are not under caution. This is just somewhere we can talk and I can make a recording so my notes are complete and accurate. I'll ask you to sign a witness statement at the end to confirm we've got the details right. Do you understand?"

"Yes."

"Let's go over what you've said already, OK? Ashling went out on a date on Friday?"

"Yes."

"What time did you last see her and did you see the person she was meeting?"

"It was about five o'clock and I didn't see him, but she did tell me she was meeting the same guy she'd been out with before."

"This man is the one you believe you saw drop her home after a previous meeting?"

"Yes. It was dark so I didn't see very much. Just the BMW and a man with dark hair and a beard."

"And you believe he's called Dan, and that he works in property."

"Yes, but that's pretty much all she told me."

"You know a little more than that though, Max, don't you? You know how she met him..."

Max looked uncomfortable.

"She met him through the Sugar Babies group we set up, Ash, me and Emily... He was one of her Pay Pigs."

Once again, the boy explained what the three students had begun the previous year.

"Do I have your permission to go through your laptop and phones, Max?"

"If it's going to help find Ashling, you can go through anything I have."

"We'll also examine her laptop. I'll need you to provide our technical examiners with your logins and passwords, and Ashling's as well, if you know them."

"OK."

Rory took Max to meet the Technical Intelligence team and checked in the two laptops, Ashling's spare phone and the boy's two phones. Max wrote down the logins and passwords he knew and handed them over. Quickly briefing one of the officers on the missing student, Rory also asked him to retrieve Emily Sweetman's laptop and phone from the Evidence Room. They'd been shelved as 'non-urgent', pending a date for the inquest. When the examiner raised an objection, Rory explained the two cases were linked.

"The two girls were best friends. One's dead and the

other is missing. There has to be a connection."

Rory brought the boy to the canteen, got him soup and a sandwich and left him there, with strict instructions not to leave the building.

Rory went to find Corcoran and bring him up to speed. The DI was surprised but Rory could see he was also intrigued.

"I didn't know you were still looking into the Sweetman case," he said.

"We weren't, not actively. This boy rang me this morning in a bit of a state."

"Tell me more about this Sugar Baby thing..." he said.

Referring to his notes, Rory explained exactly what the students, including Emily, had been involved in.

"And now this girl has gone off with one of her... let's call them 'clients'?"

"Yes. According to Max Egan, she went out with one of the Pay Pigs on Friday and hasn't come back."

"She could just be having a good time with a rich sugar daddy... God, what are these kids thinking of? It's barely a step up from street-walking."

"According to the boy, it never involves meeting or having sex with the Pay Pigs; it's all conducted online."

"She went off somewhere with a Pay Pig. That's more than online! Even if these men are harmless fools with more money than sense, it leaves those kids open to actual predators. They're putting themselves at risk whatever way you look at it."

"I agree. That's why I'm concerned for Ashling's welfare. Max says it's completely out of character for her to go missing. She's skipped classes today, and she had an assignment due. He's worried sick."

"Jealous boyfriend, is he?"

"He's not her boyfriend. They're best mates. He's not into girls."

"You don't think we're looking at another suicide, do you?"

"There's nothing to indicate she was thinking that way, sir."

"Fuck it, Rory, these things come in clusters, you know that. There's hardly a small town in the country that hasn't had a bunch of suicides one after another."

"I know, but I'm more concerned about this man she's with. What if he's harmed her?"

"Tell Missing Persons this one's a priority. See if they can triangulate her whereabouts from her cell phone. I don't like the sound of this one little bit."

Rory checked in with the technical officer. He was done with Max Egan's two phones, having downloaded the contents. Rory went to find Max and give him back his phones. The boy was curled up on one of the battered and faintly smelly old sofas that had once constituted the smoking area of the canteen. He looked asleep but stirred as Rory reached him.

"Any news?" he asked, rubbing his red-rimmed eyes.

"Nothing yet. You can go home now, but get in touch if you hear anything or she contacts you, OK?"

He walked him out of the building.

"Try not to worry."

"Something's wrong. I know it," said Max. "You've got to find her."

Rory said nothing. This wasn't the time to be making promises.

23

Marina's photo album was full to bursting point and Kate couldn't take her eyes off it. The older woman flicked through the first few pages, but Kate managed to get a glimpse of some early photos; Marina and Sean Jackson on their wedding day, and one of Sean in a hard hat. Within a couple of pages all the photos were of Rosie, as a tiny baby, a toddler and then through the early years of school. Every stage, first steps, first tricycle, every birthday and Christmas, they were all here. Marina kept turning pages until she got to the last few.

"This is Rosie as I remember her. She was growing up so quickly, my little girl."

Kate stared, holding her breath. It was like looking at her own face back in her teenage years. Same hair and eyes, same smile. The shock of it nearly made her cry. *Would Marina see it too?* The older woman handed Kate the album, stood up and walked to the window. Kate could see she was mopping her eyes. After a moment she turned back towards the sofa.

"It's been a while since I looked at those photos; you'll have to excuse my tears. It always happens, even after all these years."

What to say?

"There has been an investigation going on, ever since the shootings, into how St Mary's operated back then."

"Is that why you've come to see me?"

"Yes. We have found records of the girls and women who were there, and their babies."

"I'm not sure there's anything I can tell you. Rosie went in there on the day after Christmas 1967 and she never came home."

"It's our understanding that the nuns were involved in an illegal adoption operation. Were you aware of that, Mrs Jackson?"

Marina Jackson sat down, her face pale and still wet with tears.

"We weren't aware it was illegal, no, but we knew the babies were adopted out. It was part of the service they offered... To this day I don't know why we didn't just keep Rosie with us and let her have the child. We could have sorted something out... We could have taken care of her. But back then if a girl got pregnant out of wedlock her life was destroyed. I wish I'd had the courage to say no. The Church had such a grip on us all, we were like sheep, stupid ignorant sheep."

Marina hung her head. The two sat in silence for what seemed like forever. Finally, she spoke again.

"These are things I've never spoken of in more than forty years. It's not easy."

If ever there was a moment to speak, this was it.

"Do you know what became of your daughter's child?"

Marina sighed.

"Rosie was carrying twins. Nobody picked it up until she went into labour two months early. Her body couldn't cope. If they'd found out sooner they could have saved her... My husband wanted to sue the doctor, and the nuns, for negligence. He was mad with grief and rage. But then he died too, a little over a year after Rosie. I dropped the case. What was the point? It wouldn't bring either of them back."

"And the babies? Did you know what happened to them?"

"They didn't survive. They were too premature."

Jesus, what to say now? Kate took a deep breath.

"According to the records we've recovered from the nuns, Rosie's babies survived, Mrs. Jackson."

RORY WAITED IMPATIENTLY for a report on the phones and laptops from the technical examiner. He wanted to talk to Kate, but she still hadn't returned. Finally, the technical examiner called him up to the lab.

"There's not much on Ashling Byrne's phone or laptop. I can see she's been in communication with one particular person, a Pay Pig who calls himself Dan. It's the usual flirty stuff. She sent him a few selfies, nothing very raunchy. They've had a few dates already and they made an arrangement to meet last Friday. I can't trace him yet. He uses multiple VPNs, to hide his identity. Could be he's married... or just cautious; I can't say. The other phone is much more interesting – the Sweetman girl's device. She was in touch with a person using the name Easy Rider, also one of her Pay Pigs. From what I've seen he groomed her for a while, and she agreed to meet him. Then, within a few weeks, it became a coercive relationship. She was pleading to be left alone. He was insisting they meet. She was afraid of him. He was threatening to release a compromising video online, a sex tape."

Rory asked for a transcript of the communications between Emily and the Pay Pig and went to Corcoran with the news.

"That might explain Emily Sweetman's suicide. What was it she said on that video... 'I've fucked up my life.' Apparently she was being blackmailed," said Rory.

"Then we have to assume that he was the one who abused her. Going by her PM results, he's a violent sadist," said the DI. "What does Kate make of all this?"

"She hasn't seen it yet. She had to go out... dentist appointment."

"Bring her up to speed as soon as she's back. Any response to the Twitter appeal for Ashling?"

"Not much. A few vague sightings, none confirmed. Her family in Cork have been in touch. Her mother is on her way to Dublin now. The dad can't leave the farm."

Rory's mobile purred in his jeans pocket. Corcoran frowned as he took out the phone but Rory ignored him. *It might be Kate...*

"Sorry, sir, it's the tech examiner – he's got something he wants me to see."

"Keep me in the loop."

Rory took the stairs two at a time to the Technical Bureau lab. The examiner was looking pleased with himself.

"I think we're talking about the same guy – both girls were involved with the same Pay Pig. Easy Rider and Dan are one person. I ran the texts through a Forensic Linguistics programme. It came back as an extremely likely match. He used different emails but the same VPNs to cover his tracks, but the words and language in both cases are pretty much identical. He groomed each girl in the same way."

"So who is this guy? Can we identify him from the texts?"

"He calls himself Easy Rider, and sometimes she calls him Dan, but that's all we've got so far."

"And his mobile?"

"It's an unregistered pay as you go."

Rory reported back to Corcoran.

"A burner phone... of course it is. He was covering his tracks. See if you can trace the purchase. There must be a way to find him. What about emails?"

"He's been careful to remain anonymous there too, using multiple VPNs to hide behind."

"Well, let's hope the techies can get an ID for him."

"Do you think he's abducted Ashling?" asked Rory.

"Possibly, or he went too far, hurt her too much..."

"We know he's a sexual sadist... but killing her would be a big escalation..."

"Focus on finding out who this guy is... then maybe we'll locate the girl. Now go and find Kate and bring her up to speed."

24

I n Blackrock, Kate feared Marina was going to pass out. Her perfectly made-up face had gone white and she was leaning back in the sofa with her eyes closed and one hand held over her mouth.

"Are you OK, Mrs Jackson?" Kate asked.

The older woman nodded but didn't reply.

"Shall I get your assistant?"

"No. I'll be alright in a moment." Her voice was so faint Kate could barely hear it.

Minutes passed. Kate couldn't take her eyes off the photo album. It was open on a double page of holiday photos – Rosie with her parents in some sunny destination, swimming, sunbathing, cycling and boating. It reminded Kate of her own teenage years and holidays in Spain with her parents. *Adoptive parents.* She too had been an only child, so obviously adored, so like Rosie.

"That was the summer of 1966, our first package holiday."

Kate could see Marina was trying to regain her composure. *But was she strong enough?*

"You've come to tell me about the babies, haven't you?"

What to say?

Kate couldn't keep up the pretence anymore. She wanted to rip the photos from the album and hold them close, to study the face and the body language of the girl she now believed was her birth mother. Her blood.

"Yes." Her voice came out as a whisper. Marina looked at her closely.

"What is it, dear? You look like you've seen a ghost."

"There was a boy and a girl... He was sent to the States. I'm afraid he died."

"And the girl?"

Kate took a deep breath.

"She was adopted here in Ireland... by a Garda and his wife."

"Is she alive?"

"Yes... she's alive."

Kate couldn't say another word. There was a massive lump in her throat. Marina watched her in a puzzled silence. Finally she looked again at the album on the table. Carefully, she removed the adhesive corners from a close-up shot of Rosie. She held the photo in her hand. Moments passed as Kate struggled to hold back tears. Finally Marina spoke, her voice barely above a whisper.

"I need some time... to... to process all of this. If you'll excuse me, I'll call Karen to show you out."

Kate felt her stomach sink. *This was not how she'd hoped the meeting would go.* Marina went to a phone.

"Karen, can you please come down and see the detective sergeant out?"

"I'll leave my card in case you want to get in touch," said Kate.

Marina stood by the piano, her face turned away towards the French doors. Karen came and showed Kate out of the sitting room. Marina didn't reply when Kate said a quiet goodbye.

It was only eleven fifteen, but it felt like a lifetime since she'd driven up the drive to the Jackson home. She hadn't known what to expect, but she was completely unprepared for the tidal wave of emotion she'd felt on meeting Marina, and seeing those pictures of Rosie.

For so long everything she'd been told by Bernie O'Toole had seemed like someone else's story. St Mary's, the girls and their babies – they were part of another world, another country. Now, for the first time, the faded figures in the photos were real. Rosie Jackson's face was one Kate knew so well, a mirror image of her own.

WHEN RORY GOT BACK to his desk Kate had returned from Blackrock.

"How was it?" he asked.

"You don't want to know," she said.

"That sounds ominous."

"I'll tell you later."

"OK, grand, but in the meantime a lot has happened."

Rory told her about the call from Max Egan, Ashling's disappearance and the findings of the technical examiner.

"Jesus, this was one morning I should have been here," said Kate.

Rory handed her Max's statement. On her screen, he pulled up the transcripts of the texts found on both girl's phones. Kate scanned them.

"This goes a long way towards explaining Emily's suicide," she said.

"It does, and it looks like the same guy has been grooming Ashling, if that's the right term."

"Whatever you want to call it, it looks like she's with him and we know he's a violent man. How can these kids be so stupid? They need a bit of pocket money so they offer themselves up to creeps and predators," said Kate.

"According to Max, it was always meant to stay online, no in-person meetings. And it's more than pocket money for Ashling; she needed it for rent."

"I get that, but the whole thing shows how bloody naïve they are. Don't they know there's no such thing as free money? Did the techies have any joy in identifying this Easy Rider?"

"Not yet. He uses multiple VPNs and two different pay-as-you-go cell phones. They're working on it, but it's a long, slow trail to follow."

"Right. Let's go out to Belfield and see if we can get CCTV of the car. That's where he picked her up, right?"

"Shit, I should have thought of that. I'll ring ahead and arrange to meet campus security."

"And I'll tell Corcoran where we're going."

Kate hurried to the DI's office.

"How are the teeth?" he asked.

For a moment she was baffled.

"Oh, grand, nothing too major to get done," she lied.

"Good. Now, what do you make of this missing girl?"

"It's very worrying when you look at the person that she probably went missing with," said Kate.

"Agreed. Make her your priority today. We don't want another dead student on our hands."

She left to meet Rory in the basement, where he'd secured an unmarked car for their use. It took just twenty minutes to get to the Belfield campus. On the way Kate told him what had happened with Marina Jackson.

"So that's it, game over," she finished up.

"That's not it, Kate. Not game over! You just took her by surprise, that's all. What else would you expect? She lost her only child over forty years ago and now you've brought back all that grief and pain. She's in shock. That's why she reacted like she did."

"One minute she was showing me pictures of Rosie and the next she was asking me to leave..."

"And...? It's not an unreasonable reaction. It's not personal. She doesn't know yet that you're her granddaughter... As far as she's concerned, you're just a stranger who's delivering shocking news."

"I don't know... She looked at me very closely. She had a photo of Rosie in her hand, like she almost knew..."

"So why didn't you speak up?"

"I couldn't. Seeing those pictures blew my mind. It was like looking at photos of myself as a teenager."

"If ever there was a moment to fess up..."

"That was it, and I bottled it."

"Look, it's not over yet. The ball's in her court. When she gets over the shock she'll be in touch. She won't be able to just forget it, not now that she knows she has a granddaughter. You're her only link to the truth."

"D'you really think she'll contact me?"

"I do, and soon."

"I don't know if I want her to."

Rory turned the car into a parking space by the admin

block at Belfield. As he switched off the engine he turned to look at Kate.

"You know you do want to hear from her, or else why did you go out there?"

"You made me... and Greg..."

"You're a detective – you investigate things. This was a story you had to get to the bottom of, because you're at the heart of it. Admit it."

"Oh, shut up."

They made their way in silence to the office of the Chief of Campus Security on the ground floor. He took them into the hub of the operation, a room with dozens of screens showing video from cameras all over the campus. A security guard was on observation.

"How long do you keep the footage?" asked Rory.

"We have a thirty-day turnaround," he said.

Rory gave him the day and the location where Ashling was picked up. It took a while, and was interrupted when a stray dog appeared on one of the screens, frantically chasing a student on a bike.

"Bloody dogs, we get them all the time. People bring them here to walk them in the grounds, then they let them off the lead. The next thing is someone's been bitten or knocked off their bike, or the dog goes missing and the owners expect us to find it."

While he got on the radio to locate a mobile security unit, Kate and Rory waited impatiently, passing the time by watching the multiple screens.

"This would do my head in," he said.

"Me too. You just don't know where to look at any given time. It's a head wreck."

"You get used to it," said the guard, having finished his radio conversation. "Now let's find your footage."

Searching through archived files, the security man located four cameras which showed the exit from the coffee shop on the previous Friday. They had narrowed the time frame down to about half an hour, between four forty-five and five fifteen, based on Max's recollection. It was a busy time, since most lectures and tutorials finished at half past four. Hundreds of students wandered in and out of shot but eventually they located a girl they believed to be Ashling. At about seven minutes past five she could be seen leaving the café and walking towards a nearby set-down parking area. As they followed her progress through different camera angles, you could see she was in a good mood. While those around her walked mostly with their heads down, staring at their phones, Ashling almost bounced along.

"Is it me or is there a spring in her step?" said Rory.

"Looks that way. She looks happy to be going out, anyway," said Kate.

"Is this the girl who's gone missing? I saw something on Twitter," asked the security guard.

"Yes, this may be the last sighting we have of her," said Kate.

"I hope she's alright," he said.

"There's the car, waiting for her!" said Rory.

"Fuck! I can't see the registration. Can you pause it there?" she said.

The guard did as she asked, but while the make and colour of the car were clear, all the camera angles were from high up, and the registration plate was not readable. There was no clear shot of the driver.

"Any chance you could make the image sharper?" said Kate.

"We don't have that kind of kit. It's not often we have to go back and look at something. The occasional car theft or a stray dog, like I said. We're not equipped to do anything with the picture quality. I can download the files and send them to you. Your lads must have better software than us."

Accepting the offer, Rory gave the man his email address for the files, and they thanked him and left.

"Where to?" he asked.

"Back to HQ. We know the car make and colour, and the time it left here. We need to start tracing the route it took. We might get lucky," said Kate.

It was almost seventy-two hours since Ashling had walked jauntily across the concrete pathways and climbed into that car. Kate couldn't help but feel a deep unease that the pretty student's date had not turned out as she'd expected.

The two worked late into the evening, eating near-stale canteen sandwiches as they tried to access the footage and find the dark blue sedan car. There had been heavy Friday evening congestion on the busy roads around UCD. Dozens of similar cars could be seen but nothing that was useful or definitive. Finally, at almost 9 p.m., they gave up, signed out and left the squad room.

"Do you want to go for a drink?" asked Rory.

"No, not tonight. I'm worn out," said Kate.

"You've had a day of it."

"Bath and bed for me. I'll see you in the morning."

"Back here, bright-eyed and bushy-tailed at nine."

"I've never in my life been bright-eyed or bushy-tailed!"

25

Gardai are concerned for the wellbeing of nineteen-year-old student Ashling Byrne, last seen on Friday in the vicinity of UCD Belfield. Anyone with information on her whereabouts should contact Garda HQ in Harcourt Street or their local station.

The post went up on the Garda Twitter account on Monday afternoon. It came up as an alert on his news feed at work.

Fuck, no... This was serious. What would he do with her now?

He had meetings all day, but found it hard to concentrate. Then he had an idea. Money... He would pay her off. Students were always broke. He'd make it worth her while to keep quiet. Another night locked up and she'd be happy to take a couple of thousand to keep her mouth shut.

Let the little bitch make up some story to explain her disappearance. The whole thing was her own fault.

The text came in at ten past five, when the boss had finally left and he was about to finish up.

WE KNOW WHAT YOU'VE DONE

His blood ran cold.

Who is this?

YOUR WORST NIGHTMARE

Fuck off

CAR PARK, NEWTOWNSMITH DUN LAOGHAIRE 5 a.m. TOMORROW – OR YOUR WIFE FINDS OUT EVERYTHING

He couldn't breathe. He just made it to the bathrooms in time and threw up.

Was this a scam or did someone really know? He wouldn't go; it would be madness. He'd call their bluff.

But what if he didn't go... and whoever it was made good on their threat?

He stopped for a coffee to clear his head, but it only gave him acid. He drove the twenty or so miles to the site. As always, it was deserted – one of the ghost estates his company had ditched after the financial crash of 2008 and sold on to a vulture fund. Real profits lay in the high-end houses they were now building. The rich stayed rich no matter what happened further down the ladder.

This site consisted of a dozen half-finished three-bed homes in a remote corner of Wicklow, some built to roof height but still open to the sky, others little more than foundations. It was miles from anywhere and slowly returning to nature, with weeds taking over the downstairs rooms of the windowless houses and young saplings pushing through the block walls. Driving along the rutted mud roadway that traversed the field surrounded by woodland and the Wicklow hills, he grew more and more anxious. He'd put the girl in a cargo container where materials had been kept during construction. He didn't want to see her. He wanted to forget she ever existed. *He didn't even fancy her anymore. She was no use to him.* He felt like turning the car around and driving away.

THE CLANGING of the chain on the container door woke Ashling with a jolt. All the water was gone and her stomach was cramping with hunger. She'd wet herself and was freezing cold. In the hours since Dan had left her screaming in despair she'd come up with a plan and rehearsed it over and over in her head. She would not get angry. She would not cry or plead. She'd reason with Dan.

He didn't speak, and she could see in the dim light that he looked bad – not angry-bad, but jittery, not his usual confident self. Once again, he slit the duct tape with the Stanley knife. He gave her a bottle of water and a sandwich. It was the uninspiring kind you get in a petrol station, and she crammed it into her mouth in great handfuls. Dan stood back watching her, his face disgusted. She knew she smelt; there was no mistaking it.

"Thank you," she said when the food was all gone.

"You stink."

Ashling forced herself to stay calm.

"I know, but the facilities aren't great here, are they? Zero stars on Trip Advisor."

He didn't smile.

"When can I go home?"

"As soon as I know you won't blab."

"I've told you I won't say a word."

"Liar."

"Look, Dan, I've been thinking a lot. I know now this is all my fault. I got myself into something I didn't really understand. You were right – the whole Sugar Babies thing was a stupid scam. We were dumb to do it."

"Too right."

"If you let me go I won't ever tell anyone. If I did, I'd have to admit that I offered myself to strangers for money. My family would disown me. I'd probably get thrown out of college."

"You're a tart, basically."

Ashling swallowed back her rage.

Keep calm. He's coming round to the idea.

"OK, I deserve that," she said.

After a moment Dan started wrapping her wrists in duct tape again. Ashling felt tears coming.

He was never letting her go.

"Please, Dan, I promise…"

"Shut up. I need to think. I'll be back tomorrow and we'll come up with a plan. You need to work out what you're going to say to your family and friends. The fucking Gardai are looking for you now."

"OK, I'll have a good story ready. Can't you let me go now, please?"

"No. I've got things to do. I'll bring you some clean clothes and washing stuff tomorrow, OK?"

"OK, Dan. You won't be sorry, I promise. Thank you, thank you."

He threw her another bottle of water and a bag of mini

Mars bars, then he was gone. Ripping open the pack with her teeth, Ashling sobbed with relief. Then she started chewing her way through the chocolate as if her life depended on it.

Just one more night in this shithole and Dan would let her go. He'd promised, hadn't he? More or less...

He must have been distracted before he left, because he'd taped her hands carelessly. She was able to free herself with a lot of painful wriggling and by using her teeth on the duct tape. Her knees and ankles were another thing altogether. Even with her hands free, it took a long time to get the tape off. She had to find the end point and slowly unstick and un-wind each piece, on first her knees and then her ankles, and all this in almost total darkness. As she stood up for the first time in three days, her head was spinning and her limbs ached. Slowly, she made herself stretch and pace on the spot to get back her strength. She'd become used to the smell of her clothes, though she was grateful that fear or lack of food meant they were only wet. She made her way towards the entrance of the container and tried rattling the doors. Putting her face next to the millimetre-wide gap at floor height, she shouted for help. No one came. Apart from the usual birdsong and distant cars, there was no sound of activity outside.

She used her new-found freedom and space to keep moving, even trying some yoga she remembered from school, until eventually she was tired enough to sleep. Wrapping herself in a tarpaulin she'd found by feeling her way around every inch of her prison, she sipped the water Dan had left, saving some for the morning. She closed her eyes and felt almost giddy with hope.

26

TUESDAY APRIL 5, 2011

Kate was in work by nine, still overwrought after a bad night's sleep. Determinedly, she pushed her personal life to the back of her mind, telling herself that the sorry saga of her birth was over. She just had to get back to normal life, and that meant work.

There had been no confirmed sightings of Ashling Byrne overnight, and little response to the Garda appeal. As she pored over traffic camera footage from the previous Friday night in the hope of finding the car again, Corcoran strode into the squad room and immediately commanded the attention of all present.

"We've got a suspicious death in Dun Laoghaire, a young male, late twenties or thirties, found in his car."

"Was it a crash?"

"No. He's parked up, no damage to the car. The dead man was found sitting in the driver's seat."

Someone murmured 'heart attack' at the back of the room.

"Maybe, or some sort of seizure or an overdose. We won't know until the pathologist gets him on the table."

Corcoran approached Kate's desk and gestured for Rory to come over.

"This might be nothing more than a sudden natural death, so I'm not putting the whole team on it yet. But I want you to take a look. The local Guards are on site. They've preserved the scene, though I believe it's a bit chaotic. Dr Stilson is on her way. Here's the address. Call me when you've had a first look."

Two Garda cars and an ambulance surrounded the car on the Dun Laoghaire seafront. One officer was directing people away from the scene, ushering families and dog walkers into their cars and out of the car park. Still, the scene was hectic. Onlookers gathered only feet from the car and more kept coming despite being repeatedly asked to leave. Many had their mobile phones out, taking pictures. Paramedics had pronounced the man dead. Still he sat, eyes staring out to sea. Two Gardai stood on either side of the car, attempting to shield from sight the dead man. They'd thrown a hi-vis Garda jacket across the windscreen to prevent the body being seen from the front.

When Kate and Rory arrived they had to push their way through the crowd.

"Right, you're the Log Man. That makes you in charge of the scene," she said to one of the officers. "You need to get these people away from here. Some of them have children with them for God's sake! Make a log of every adult's name and contact number. No one comes in. Clear the car park and close the entrance. I want a perimeter of at least twenty metres around the car. And get the Technical Bureau here. Tell them we'll need a large crime scene tent."

Rory helped with clearing away the crowd, while Kate donned gloves and white crime scene overalls and approached the car. She used her camera phone to record video, including her own initial observations.

"Dark blue, late model BMW. One occupant in driver seat, male 25-35 years, dark hair, bearded, pale complexion, eyes open. There may be some petechial spots in the eyes, to be confirmed. No visible signs of violence. Deceased is wearing a striped shirt, red tie and jeans. The interior of the car is tidy, keys are in the ignition, there's a jacket on the back seat. Paramedics pronounced death at nine twenty. The exterior of the car is clean and undamaged. We're waiting for CSI to check for prints before opening the doors. The driver's door has been opened by attending paramedics wearing gloves. They report the body was almost cold to the touch."

She stepped back to check out her surroundings. The car park was located in a public park bordering the rocky stretch of coast between Dun Laoghaire and Sandycove, just a few kilometres from the city centre. It was a scenic spot, popular with locals and visitors. There was a broad concrete promenade with steps down to the water's edge. Cormorants, gulls and other seabirds swooped and dived into the water, and it wasn't unusual to see grey seals pop up their heads or bask on the rocks only a few metres from the shore. Dogs and children played and people strolled or jogged by the sea. The car park had room for fifty or sixty cars. The Gardai closed off the entrance, and as walkers returned to their cars they were directed out onto the road, so the spaces were gradually emptying out. On the opposite side of the narrow road were a number of imposing three-storey period houses, a couple of restaurants and an ice cream shop. Kate scanned the facades for cameras, but found none. Rory jogged over to her.

"The local Garda can handle the exit without me. There's not many left," he said.

"I don't suppose he's been taking registration numbers, has he?" asked Kate.

"He's used his personal mobile phone to photograph every license plate. I was impressed."

"Good job. If this is a homicide, the killer could have been in one of those cars, watching all the action; you never know. I want to speak to whoever found him."

"That man over there with the two kids and the dog."

Kate and Rory approached the anxious-looking dad.

After a brief conversation they had little new information, apart from confirming that the occupant of the BMW was probably dead at around eight o'clock when the witness had arrived. He couldn't recall any other cars or people in the vicinity. They took his details and let him go.

"Do we have an ID on the dead guy?" asked Rory.

"According to the DLV in Shannon, the car is registered to a David Hunter, with an address somewhere in Rathmichael, which I think is a few miles inland from here."

"So what do we do next?"

"We'll wait for the Technical Bureau and the pathologist. I've had a quick look but we're not going any closer until they've examined the car, inside and out."

"What do you reckon? Heart attack, Sudden Adult Death?"

"He's a bit young for natural causes, and I think there are suspicious signs in the eyes, petechial haemorrhages," said Kate.

"Wow, so, strangulation..."

"Maybe. We'll have to see."

Within an hour Harriet Stilson and the Technical Bureau had arrived, and a white tent had been erected around the car. While they waited for the pathologist's initial examination, Rory searched for the name David Hunter online and Kate rang Jim Corcoran.

"D'you think it's suspicious?" he asked.

"I can't say until Harriet's had a look. She's examining the body now."

"Do you have an ID?"

"We know who the car belongs to. My next stop will be the address on record for the registered owner."

Rory interrupted her call, showing her an image on his phone, a wedding photo of a man, with a pretty blonde bride.

"This is David Hunter. Looks like our body," said Rory.

"Gardiner has found the dead man online. It seems to be the owner of the car," said Kate.

"Better get straight over to the home address and break the news before someone on social media spills the beans."

Kate went to speak to Harriet.

"Interesting one, this," said the pathologist. "Looks like asphyxiation. No ligature marks or manual bruising on the neck, but definite petechial bleeding in the eyes. Could be our old friend, the plastic bag over the head."

"Any signs of a struggle?"

"Not that I can see, and no plastic bag, so it wasn't self-inflicted. You'd imagine he'd have to be restrained, for a couple of minutes at least, while the bag did its work."

"Are you pronouncing homicide?"

"Too soon. Let's call it a suspicious death until I've done the post mortem," said Harriet. "I'll be finished here soon and get the body removed to the mortuary. If Corcoran asks, tell him I'll get cutting after lunch, say two o'clock."

As Kate turned to leave, Harriet called to her.

"You could sit in... I think you're ready."

Kate gulped. *Was she ready*? She'd had four sessions with the virtual autopsies, but the real thing?

"If I can make it, I'll be there," she said. "I'm off to inform next of kin."

"Good. I'll hope to see you around two then. Here, you might want to take this..."

The pathologist handed her an evidence bag with a wallet inside.

"That belongs to someone called David Hunter," she said. "It was in the jacket pocket."

27

The drive to Hunter's home address took less than twenty minutes. It was a smart townhouse in a newish development. The area was hilly and wooded. For a Dublin suburb, it was very pretty and rural, though it was just a short drive to the city centre.

"These houses cost a small fortune," said Rory.

"How do you know?"

"I've been looking to buy for months now. I'm fed up paying rent; it's dead money."

"And have you looked at this development?"

"God no. This is way out of my league. I just comb the property websites all the time, so I've got a good idea of house prices. Property is a bit of an obsession."

"For you and the rest of the country. So our dead guy is rich?"

"You don't get one of these on the average industrial wage, that's for sure, plus late-model BMWs don't come cheap. He has to be fairly well off."

"Not anymore, poor bastard."

It was nearing eleven as they approached the detached house. There was a brand new white Mini Cooper in the drive.

"So we know he's married, from Facebook. I wonder if there are kids," said Rory.

"The second car is too small. I'd expect a people carrier in a place like this if they had children," said Kate. "God, I hate this part of the job."

The door was answered by a young woman dressed in designer leisure wear. Kate and Rory showed their warrant cards.

"Mrs Hunter?"

"Yes, I'm Mrs Hunter, but I go by my maiden name, Sherwin, Chloe Sherwin. What's this about?"

Kate introduced herself and Rory. The woman invited them in and led them to a huge kitchen at the back of the house. It was a beautiful room, filled with light, with a sleek range of cabinets, luxury appliances and a massive kitchen island.

"I've just brewed some coffee. Would you like some?" said Chloe.

Rory and Kate both accepted eagerly. It had been a long, cold morning on the seafront.

As she poured their drinks, Chloe said, "What can I do for you, Officers? Is it about the robberies?"

"Robberies?" said Rory.

"Yes. The Smyths next door were done, and the Brophys over the road. We're all on tenterhooks to see who'll be next."

"We're not here about the robberies," said Rory.

"I need to ask you about your husband," said Kate. "Is he at home?"

"No, David went out hours ago. He's probably in work, or he might be out on a site. He works for the family firm Sherwin Developments," said Chloe.

"We've found your husband's car in Dun Laoghaire," said Kate.

"No way! Has something happened to his car? It's only new. He'll be furious if it's been damaged."

"The car seems to be fine, Chloe, but a body has been found in the driver's seat... and we have reason to suspect that it might be your husband."

Chloe's right hand went to her mouth and her face turned ashen. She grasped the edge of the counter, and she swayed slightly. Rory went to stand beside her.

"Sorry, could you say that again? I'm not sure I heard you..." she whispered.

Rory put his hand on her arm.

"I think you should sit down," he said gently.

He pulled out one of the stools.

"I'm sorry to say we've found a body in your husband's car, and it's possible it's David," said Kate.

Chloe Sherwin's hands scrabbled in her tracksuit pocket and she pulled out a mobile phone. With shaking fingers, she pressed buttons then held it to her ear.

"David, it's me. Ring me when you get this. The police are here and I need to talk to you. Ring me now," she said. Then, as soon as she pressed End, she dialled again.

"Answer your phone, David. Please answer your phone." Her voice was shrill. They could all hear David Hunter's voicemail message for the second time.

"Ms Sherwin... Chloe, please put the phone down for a moment. I need to ask you some questions," said Kate.

"There must be some mistake. Some little scumbag stole

David's car and then overdosed or something. They're all on drugs, aren't they, these thieves?" said Chloe.

"When did you see your husband last?"

"Last night. He was gone before I woke up this morning. He's always up early," she said shakily.

"And what were your movements yesterday and in the evening?"

"Erm, let me think... I got home around six thirty. David got back a bit later. We had dinner. He had work to do so he spent an hour or two in his home office. I watched TV and went to bed around eleven. He came up later."

"And this morning?"

"He was gone when I woke up at about ten o'clock. I'm working from home today. He might come back..." Her voice faltered.

"Do you have a recent photo of David?"

Chloe again reached for her phone, scrolled for a few seconds, then handed it to Kate.

"We were in Andorra in February, skiing. That's just a few weeks ago."

Kate examined the picture closely. There was no mistaking it – David Hunter was the man in the car.

"I'm going to have to ask you to come with us, Chloe..."

"Where? What if David comes home and I'm not here? He'll be worried."

Kate and Rory both looked at the woman silently. Her eyes moved from one to the other in panic.

"Can I ring my dad? Please. He'll know what to do."

Kate nodded, then she motioned to Rory to stay put and let herself out into the hallway. She rang Harriet at the mortuary.

"Yes, Kate, what can I do for you?"

"I'm bringing Chloe, David Hunter's wife, to the mortuary. Can you hold off on the post mortem until she's given us a positive identification?"

"Right so. I'll wait for you and have the poor chap ready for her," said the pathologist.

Tom Sherwin arrived at his daughter's house within fifteen minutes. A tall, well-built man, he was wearing golfing gear; dark shiny trousers, colourful shoes and a lemon Argyle-pattern sweater. He took the news calmly.

"Chloe told me on the phone. Where is she?"

Kate explained that she was getting changed and her father went straight upstairs. A few minutes later they returned. Chloe had changed into smart trousers and a black jumper. Her hair was tied back in a pony-tail. She was white faced and shaky. Her father held her hand as they made their way out of the house. Before locking the door, she activated the house alarm.

"I'll drive. Just give me the address and I'll programme the SatNav. We'll meet you there," said the father.

The two climbed into his Land Rover and the cavalcade set off, leaving behind the quiet suburbs and heading for north Dublin and a drab industrial estate, where the grey, windowless mortuary sat between a car showroom and a tile shop.

"Well, what do you make of the wife?" said Kate as Rory drove.

"Good-looking girl. You can nearly smell the privilege off her," said Rory.

"And her reaction?"

"She seemed genuinely shocked," he said. "What did you think of her?"

"I'm still not convinced she believes us. The ID will be awful for her."

"A nightmare. She woke up this morning thinking her hubby was gone to the gym. Now she's about to see him stretched out on a slab."

"The father was very calm," said Kate.

"I expect being a captain of industry gives you nerves of steel. He's quite the tycoon – Sherwin's build some of the most expensive houses in the country. As far as I know he's the major shareholder too."

"You really do know your property info!"

"Like I said, I'm a bit obsessed, especially with houses I'll never be able to buy."

"Mmm, we'll see how he holds up at the mortuary," she said. "If this is a homicide it'll be big news. It's not every day a guy like David Hunter is murdered."

28

Tom Sherwin's Land Rover was already parked up when they got to the mortuary. Harriet met the four of them at the door, shook hands and led the way to what was known as the Chapel of Rest. It wasn't actually a chapel, despite the crucifix on the wall; it was a viewing room. Chloe gripped her father's arm tightly as they stood in the corridor outside.

"You don't have to go in, Ms Sherwin," said Kate. "There's a room next door with a viewing window."

Chloe seemed frozen to the spot. Her father nodded to Kate and they made their way to the next door. Inside the small room was a curtained internal window.

"Are you ready?" said Harriet. "There's no rush. Please take your time."

Tom Sherwin answered.

"Best to get it over with," he said quietly. "Chloe can do this, can't you, love?"

His daughter nodded, and the two walked to the viewing window. Harriet gestured to her assistant, who flicked a switch on the wall. The curtains parted and a dimmer light slowly went on in the chapel. The body was in view side on, with a white sheet pulled up to the neck.

Chloe gasped and turned away immediately, burying her head in her father's shoulder.

"Ms Sherwin? Can I confirm the identification, please?" said Kate.

"That's my son-in-law, David Hunter," said Tom Sherwin.

"I'm sorry, sir, as the closest next of kin, I need to hear it from Chloe..."

Chloe raised a face raked with tears.

"That's my husband, David," she said.

"I'm very sorry for your loss," said Kate, "and thank you for making the identification. I know it must be a terrible ordeal."

"What happened to him? How did he die?" asked Chloe.

Harriet Stilson answered.

"We won't know until I've completed the post mortem, I'm afraid."

Tom Sherwin led his daughter from the room as the motorised curtains slowly closed over the window. In the corridor he turned to speak, keeping his arm around a sobbing Chloe.

"I'm taking her home now," he said. "She's pregnant, and it's early days. A shock like this is risky. I'll take her back to my house. Her mother and I will look after her. If you need to speak to her again, please contact me first. Any more stress could put the baby in danger."

He produced a business card.

"You can get me on that number."

Kate and Rory walked them out to their car, handing

over their own cards with contact numbers, then watched as they drove off.

"Well, that's that. We have an ID. Now we just need a cause of death. What do you make of those two?" said Kate.

"They're not the kind of people you expect to meet in a place like this. I'd say it hasn't even sunk in yet. He's holding up well. She's in bits. Plus, she's expecting; can't be easy."

"Poor woman. Now I suppose she's afraid she'll lose the baby too."

"At least she'll have her parents. They seem very close, she and her dad," said Rory.

"Come on, let's grab something quick to eat. There's a gastro pub down the road. I'm going to need something substantial if I'm sitting in on the autopsy."

Rory laughed.

"Kate Hamilton willingly sitting in on a PM! Don't talk rubbish, you!"

Over a lunch of fish and chips in the pub, she explained how the pathologist had put her through her paces on the virtual software. Rory was impressed.

"Fair play, Kate, that takes guts! Oh, sorry, didn't mean to mention guts over lunch! Not when you'll be staring at them in half an hour."

As they walked back to the mortuary, Kate prayed her stomach wouldn't let her down, despite her confident assertion to Rory.

"There's no point in both of us spending two or three hours here. Go back to HQ and do some digging on the dead man," she said. "Contact his office, find his friends, sniff out what you can about him. It's probably going to be our only line of enquiry, unless the CSIs find something on the car. If this is a homicide – and Harriet seems to think it is – it's a strange one. If it was a robbery, surely they'd have taken the car. There are gangs in this city that would have it shipped to the Middle East in a matter of hours."

"If the motive wasn't theft, then what?" said Rory. "Maybe he's done something to piss someone off... a drugs debt, an affair... He could have had his hand in the till?"

"Let's see what the PM turns up, and whatever you can find in his background. We'll brief the team around six."

Rory wished her luck and drove off. Kate took a deep breath and entered the nondescript concrete building. She put on green surgical robes in the small anteroom, and pushed the door into the Cutting Room. The pathologist and her assistant were waiting by the steel table. Kate smeared some Vicks VapoRub just under her nose, slipped on her mask and went to stand beside them.

"Right, let's get started," said Harriet, and drew back the sheet.

The post mortem took over two hours. Kate was pleased to get to the end without feeling too nauseous.

"You're holding up well," said Harriet.

"I know! I'm quite proud of myself."

"I knew those sessions would sort you out."

"You were right; it's definitely made a difference."

"OK, down to business then – shall I tell you what I think happened to our subject?"

DI Jim Corcoran arrived just in time to hear her.

"Fire away, Harriet," he said. "What killed him?"

"Well, firstly we can rule out natural causes. He was as healthy as any man in his thirties, and fit. No sign of heart disease, cancer, excessive drinking or substance abuse. Nothing underlying that I can see."

"So what was the cause of death?"

"He was asphyxiated, no doubt about it."

"Go on..."

"There are faint marks on the wrists and abdomen. They suggest something was tied around his hands and waist. A belt or rope, some kind of ligature, probably thrown over him from behind and secured somehow. This would have restrained him, restricted his movements. He had no chance to defend himself. Then a plastic bag or something similar was placed over his head and held there until he stopped breathing. It wasn't a gag as far as I can tell. There are no abrasions or fibres around or in the mouth. But there are faint marks on the neck consistent with something being tied or taped around him. The petechial haemorrhaging in the eyes confirms asphyxiation. He was killed where he sat, sometime between 2 a.m. and 6 a.m."

"There's no chance it was suicide?"

"No bag at the scene, and those restraint marks would indicate another person was involved."

"It's not one of those auto-erotic jobs, is it?" asked Corcoran.

"You mean some sort of sex game gone wrong?" asked Harriet.

"Exactly."

"I suppose it's possible, but if he was alone, trying out something, we'd have found the ligature or the bag, wouldn't we?"

"Any sign of sexual activity?" asked Kate.

"No recent activity."

"So, we're looking at a homicide," said Corcoran.

"That would be my conclusion."

Kate and Corcoran thanked the pathologist and left. On the way back to HQ Corcoran was all fired up. They'd had a year of gangland shootings and horrific domestic-abuse killings. This was clearly a very different case; on first impressions a complete mystery.

"Right, let's see what Gardiner has turned up about our man," he said. "Take whatever info he's got and dig into it. At the moment all we have is the victim. I'll get on to the CSI supervisor, see if they've found anything in the car. The crime scene must give us something."

In the squad room Corcoran briefed the team, and a Murder Board was set up. Several officers had been sent to the area where the body was discovered in search of CCTV from traffic cameras, local businesses, ATMs – any source available. They were also to liaise with the local Guards in Dun Laoghaire and help with door-to-door enquiries.

"The pathologist has put the time of death as somewhere between 2 a.m. and 6 a.m., and the body was first observed at 8," said Corcoran. "Get hold of any CCTV in the surrounding streets from midnight onwards. There can't be that much traffic in the area in the middle of the night. I want registrations for every car you spot, and pictures and descriptions of anyone on foot."

Rory printed off photos from the dead man's social media pages and some of Kate's pictures from the crime scene. These were pinned up on the murder wall.

"Not much to go on, is there?" she said, as they studied the board while Corcoran handed out assignments.

"It's a bit of a whodunit. I can't find anything in David Hunter's life that would make you think he'd end up like this," said Rory.

He shared all the notes he'd made with Kate. He'd succeeded in tracking down a number of David's close friends via social media. By direct messaging them from his

Garda email, he'd been able to get mobile numbers and speak to some of them. None had heard the news of their friend's death, so it had been a series of difficult conversations. However, even through their evident shock and distress, Rory found that they were forthcoming. All his friends described Hunter as a great guy, sporty, sociable and successful. He was mainly involved in sales of the up-market houses and apartments built by Sherwin Developments.

"One man admitted that they used cocaine, but he was emphatic that it wasn't a habit," said Rory. "The others denied there was any drug use. Reading between the lines, I'd say he was a bit of a ladies' man. They called him a charmer. One even used the term 'babe magnet'. Who talks like that these days? On the other hand, they said he was happily married and they didn't think he was having affairs. But that could be the usual circling of the wagons. Someone dies and instantly becomes a saint."

"Harriet found no signs of serious drug use or addiction, so they're probably telling the truth. I reckon there's hardly a dinner party in South County Dublin that doesn't feature a few lines of coke. Dip your toe in that world and it can get you into serious shit. We're going to have to question the wife again," said Kate. "In the meantime we need to get his computers, at home and at work, and any other devices, tablets, phones, etc. And we need to do it before anyone has time to tamper with them."

"I'll call Tom Sherwin and get him to meet us at the house."

"And see if you can get access to the dead man's office as well."

"They'll be closed by now. But he's the boss; he should be able to get us in."

"They'll probably close the office tomorrow as a mark of respect. If we can gain access we'll check it out in the morning. We need to talk to his co-workers. Get contact details from Sherwin. What about other family?"

"Both his parents are dead. There's a younger sister in Australia. The local police are tracking her down."

"Any Garda record?"

"A couple of fines for speeding. Nothing else."

"So, no criminal history... an unlikely victim. Talk to that friend who mentioned the coke again. We'll interview him and get a formal statement. If David was in deeper than his mates, he could have been meeting someone to score and the deal went south. We need to find out what he was doing there in the early hours of the morning..."

"And who benefits from his death?"

"That too. Tell me what you've found on the wife."

"Well, she's the one with the money. She's an only child, has a good job and no shortage of cash. That fancy house was a wedding present from her dad. When he's gone she'll inherit the company and his fortune. That's the gossip among the dead man's mates."

"Any signs of domestic abuse? Were there call-outs to the house? Unexplained injuries?"

"Her or him?"

"Either... Contact the local station. they'll know. Get Mr Sherwin to meet us at the house tonight. Whoever did this has a head start on us. We need to move quickly."

29

"You can't speak to Chloe at the moment. We've had the doctor out to see her and he's worried the shock and stress might bring on a miscarriage. She can't have a sedative or something to calm her down because of the pregnancy."

Kate and Rory were standing outside the Hunter house in Rathmichael. Tom Sherwin had arrived soon after the appointed time of six o'clock. He looked grey in the face in the dusk light, Kate thought.

"The post mortem results mean we're treating this as a suspicious death. We will have to speak to Chloe soon," she said.

Sherwin nodded, took a set of keys from his jacket pocket, opened the front door and disarmed the beeping alarm. As they followed him into the house, he switched on the lights and headed for the kitchen.

He didn't flinch when suspicious death was mentioned.

"I'm happy to answer any questions you have, Detective. We're a very close family, and David worked for me too. I can tell you all you need to know. Chloe needs time to recover from the shock."

Kate decided that pushing to see Chloe immediately would be pointless. Tom Sherwin wasn't asking for their patience, he was insisting on it.

"In that case I'd like you to come to HQ tomorrow to make a formal statement. Under the circumstances, we'll need to take away any relevant devices or materials."

"Work away. I'll wait here. The master bedroom is on the right at the top of the stairs, and David's home office is down here at the back, off the dining room."

Kate sent Rory upstairs and took the home office herself. It was a big room, with a computer desk and chair, and some shelves holding a printer and a few box files. One half of the room accommodated an expensive exercise bike and a set of training weights.

David Hunter took his fitness seriously.

It was extremely neat and empty of clutter. Even the waste-basket was bare. There wasn't a speck of dust anywhere.

Who kept their office this tidy? Had someone cleaned up in the hours since they'd first been at the house?

Kate put on latex gloves and bagged the laptop, then she filled a cardboard crate from the car with the box files. There were no drawers to search, but on instinct she crouched down to look under the computer desk. Taped to the underside was a slim padded envelope. Using her phone she took photos of the concealment. Then, although desperate to see inside, she decided to leave it in situ for the Technical Bureau to examine and remove. Everything, including the adhesive tape and the envelope, would have to be forensically examined before the contents were looked at. She could hear Rory moving about upstairs, and the opening and closing of drawers. Kate dialled HQ and got through to the Technical Bureau. It was six thirty, almost the end of the day shift, but she managed to get hold of one of the officers she knew.

"It's the suspicious death we picked up this morning, Ben. I'm at the victim's house and I've found something I need an evidence technician to recover."

"Can it not wait until the morning, Kate? I'm off in half an hour."

"Sorry, Ben, this is important. I have a feeling the house has been scrubbed clean already. I can't afford to leave this in case it gets the same treatment. And I've no authority at this stage to seal the premises."

"Right so. I'll be with you as quick as I can. I could do with the overtime anyway. Send me the address."

"You're a star, Ben. Thanks."

Satisfied that she'd completed a thorough search in the office, Kate went back to the kitchen. Tom Sherwin was nowhere to be seen. She found him in the sitting room. A sleek black heater was on, producing authentic amber flames in the huge, modern fireplace. Sherwin was on the sofa, apparently watching the local news bulletin. He got to his feet when she came into the room.

"I take it you're done now?" he said.

"I'm afraid not, Mr Sherwin. My colleague is still at work, and one of our evidence technicians is on his way out from HQ to help."

Kate thought she saw a glimmer of annoyance in the man's face.

"I see. I hadn't expected this to take so long."

"We have to be thorough. I'm sure you'll understand that."

He sat down again and muted the TV sound with the remote control.

"It seems like we'll be here a while then," he said. "I have some questions for you if that's the case."

I'll be asking the questions... not you...

"I will need a formal statement from you, Mr Sherwin, but I'll tell you what I can..."

Kate tried to keep her own annoyance under wraps. She hadn't warmed to Tom Sherwin. It seemed like he was used to everyone doing exactly what he wanted.

"What do you mean by suspicious death?" he asked.

Finally, he asks the one thing anyone else would have asked half an hour ago...

"We have reason to believe that David did not die of natural causes," she said.

"Well, of course he didn't. He was thirty-two years old and still had the fitness of an athlete."

"That certainly chimes with the findings of the post mortem."

"So what killed him, then? Was there some kind of car accident?"

"We don't believe so, but I'm not in a position now to give you any further information. I can say that a full investigation has begun and as soon as we have news we'll be in touch with you and your daughter."

"So you think it's murder, do you? Or suicide..."

He doesn't beat around the bush, does he?

"We're treating it as a suspicious death. Now, I have some questions. I'll be making notes and recording this on my phone. It will serve as a preliminary to the formal interview."

Priming her phone to record, Kate got out her notebook and pen. She was taking her time, totally aware that this might irritate her interviewee. She wanted to unsettle him, to get him off guard. He seemed to her to be way too calm for a man who'd lost a member of his 'close family'. Over the next half hour she was disappointed to find out little that she didn't already know about the victim. Sherwin told her how Chloe had met David at university, where he was something of a high flier on the sports field, if not academically. They were married soon after graduating. Tom had offered David a position in his company, at his daughter's request.

"Graduate jobs were scarce or non-existent back then. There was talk of David emigrating, and Chloe would have gone with him. We didn't want to lose her. She's our only child, and very close to her mother and me," he said. "We started him off in the office, to learn the ropes. After a couple of years he became part of the Marketing and Sales team. He was good at that."

"So he got on well at work, but how was their relationship, in your opinion?"

"There was nothing wrong with their relationship. Chloe is a wonderful girl and David adored her."

"So you're not aware of any marital difficulties?" said Kate.

"No, none at all. They were happily married…"

"And expecting a child…"

"Yes, after years of trying, Chloe found out she was pregnant just a little while ago. We were overjoyed."

"And David?"

"He was delighted, of course he was."

You don't sound so convinced…

The doorbell sounded then and Kate switched off the voice-recording app on her phone.

"That'll be my evidence technician. I'll go," she said.

Sherwin made as if to get up, but Kate stalled him.

"I'll show him in, Mr Sherwin. No need for you to get up."

Ben Tyler was one of the most senior CSIs in the Gardai, and Kate was genuinely pleased to see him. There would be no forensic cock-ups with him on board. She showed him to the home office and the concealment.

"Not very original as a hiding place..." he said.

"Nope, not at all, but that's our good luck," she replied. "I'm off to see how Rory's doing in the other rooms, and if we need you to collect anything other than this little gem."

"Grand. I'll photograph it, retrieve it, and dust for prints while I'm here."

"Thanks, I really appreciate it," said Kate, shutting the office door behind her. She didn't want Tom Sherwin wandering in while Ben was at work.

Upstairs Kate headed for the master bedroom. It was beyond luxurious, and not a thing was out of place. A king-size bed was immaculately made up with pure white linens and an abundance of colourful cushions. A big dressing table groaned with neatly lined-up perfumes, makeup and skincare items. The brands were ones she recognised but could never have afforded. Off the bedroom there was a walk-in wardrobe, clearly divided about sixty percent to forty between Chloe and David. A separate en-suite was bigger than Kate's full bathroom at home, with his and hers sinks, a free-standing bath and a shower. The medicine cabinet held nothing more than the usual; flu remedies, over the counter painkillers, muscle pain heat pads. No prescription meds at all. Rory had been careful to put every-thing back as he'd found it, and Kate knew he was thorough. If he'd found something of significance, he would have called her. She left the master bedroom and went to find him.

"Well, any joy?" she said.

Rory was lying on the rug half under a double bed in the second bedroom. He bumped his head as he slid out to speak to her.

"Thanks for making me jump!" he said, rubbing his forehead.

"Sorry. I thought you'd hear me coming."

"In answer to your question, no smoking gun…"

"What *have* you found?"

"This is the cleanest, tidiest house I've ever been in. It's like a show-house, not somewhere where people actually live. The other bedrooms are squeaky clean," he said.

"I know what you mean."

"No one is this tidy. I think someone's been in today and scrubbed the place from top to bottom."

"I thought that too. When Chloe changed her clothes this morning, after we told her about David, I can't believe she left her room like that. She was in an absolute state. And yet there wasn't a thing out of place, not even in the walk-in wardrobe."

"I'd say Daddy got the cleaners in, but why? What are we missing?'

"I don't know. It's definitely fishy. Your son-in-law dies suddenly in mysterious circumstances. Your first thought can't be 'must get the house cleaned'."

"Unless you're trying to hide something…"

"Or find something…"

"We might have got lucky on that... *I* found something the clean-up crew obviously missed."

Kate told Rory about the envelope hidden in the office.

"I can't wait to see what's inside that little package," he said. "I haven't had that kind of luck. The only thing that's a bit odd, apart from the whole clean-freak thing, is some very high-end camera equipment."

"Hardly odd; this pair are minted. I expect they've got high-end gadgets all over the place," said Kate.

"Sure they do. I've bagged up her laptop and an iPad as well, but I found this tucked away on David's side of the walk-in wardrobe. And by tucked away, I mean hidden in a secret compartment of his gym bag. Unless you knew it was there, you'd be unlikely to find it. It's small but powerful. It'll shoot stills and HD video – really high quality. There's a fold-up tripod too. Quite the home movie kit."

"Right, let's take it into evidence. What kind of stuff was he filming?"

"That's the thing; there was no SD card in it, and no spares in the bag."

"Might be nothing. They travel a fair bit; it's probably for holiday videos."

"Yes, but where are these movies? Why no SD cards? And why keep it in his gym bag?"

"Men are weird. Maybe he films himself working out. He wouldn't be the first gym bunny to post his six-pack on Instagram."

"True. I'll have another look at his Insta."

There was a noise from below that startled them both.

"What the fuck..." said Rory as they headed for the stairs.

Tom Sherwin was standing toe to toe with Ben the CSI, shouting.

"I must insist that you leave this house immediately."

"I just need to check with the detectives first, sir," the latter was saying, in the kind of voice you'd use when talking to a small child having a supermarket tantrum.

"I should not have let any of you in here, not without a warrant. This intrusion into a... a... grieving household is outrageous."

Kate put a gentle hand on the older man's arm.

"Calm down, Mr Sherwin. We're almost done here. My colleague is only doing his job."

"He's removing things from the office, and Chloe hasn't given permission," said Sherwin, his tone no less belligerent.

"If you wish to get your daughter here now..." said Kate, hoping she was playing an ace card.

"No, no, that won't be necessary. She couldn't possibly..." he said.

He stepped back, allowing the CSI to get by.

"There's just the kitchen and living room to look through now. We'll be out of your way very soon," she said in a voice that did not invite resistance. "With three of us, it'll be even quicker."

"I should have asked you for a warrant, Detective. That was my mistake."

"In a case like this Gardai have the right to conduct a search of the residence, in particular as this was the last known whereabouts of the deceased. There is no requirement for a warrant in exigent circumstances."

Tom Sherwin gave her a steely glare.

"I'll be consulting my solicitor about this."

Ben had returned from his Garda van, having secured the envelope into a locked evidence box. While the older man waited in the kitchen, the three officers worked their way through the sitting-room.

"What brought that on?" asked Kate quietly.

"He came into the office just as I was removing the envelope from under the desk," said Ben.

Kate felt a surge of optimism. *Whatever was in that envelope was dynamite, or else why was Tom Sherwin so angry?* She couldn't wait to get back to HQ and examine the contents. It was nearly eight o'clock. The sitting room had yielded nothing of interest, no home movies or holiday films. There was only the kitchen left.

"Mr Sherwin, would you like to return to the sitting room now? We're all done there," she said from the hall.

Passing her by on his way, he still looked angry.

"What time would suit you to come in to Garda HQ tomorrow?"

She was being very polite. He was not.

"I'm a busy man. I can't just drop everything and sail into town to suit you."

"We could come to your home if you'd prefer…"

"That won't be necessary. My assistant will phone you in the morning to arrange a time," he snapped and strode off into the sitting room.

He doesn't want me anywhere near Chloe, thought Kate, *But why? Could she have killed her husband and Daddy is protecting her?*

It took only fifteen minutes to go through the numerous cupboards and drawers in the kitchen. The fridge had a few beers and wines, and some basic foods like milk, yoghurt and butter, and an array of expensive ready meals.

"That's funny," said Rory.

Ben and Kate were by his side in a moment.

"What?"

"There's a full container of baking powder."

"So..." said Kate.

"My mam is mad for baking. She'd always have this stuff, but not on its own... There's no flour, or baking tins for that matter. These two don't seem like the baking kind."

"I would be surprised if they cook at all. The fridge is full of booze and ready meals," said Kate.

Ben took the small cardboard tub from Rory and sniffed the contents gently.

"Yep, baking powder," he said.

Then he replaced the lid and turned the tub upside down. He prised the plastic underside of the container off. Inside there was a second chamber. It held a cluster of tiny wraps filled with white powder.

"Jesus, these people are amateurs. Envelopes stuck under the desk and coke in the baking powder," said Ben.

"Are you sure?"

"I can do a presumptive test here that'll give a fairly accurate result, and we can confirm it in the lab."

He went out to his van to get the test kit.

"How much do you reckon is in there?" asked Rory.

Kate took the container and counted what she could see.

"A gram each wrap, probably a thousand euros' worth at street prices. A defence solicitor could argue that counts as personal use, just about, but it's still Class A."

The presumptive test was a tiny plastic bag containing a reactive chemical. Ben carefully opened one of the wraps, dropped a few grains of the contents into the bag, sealed it and shook it gently. Within seconds the chemical went from colourless to light and then dark blue.

"Cocaine, and quite a pure sample too," he said.

"I wonder if Daddy knows his little girl likes nose candy," said Rory.

"You've been watching too many American cop shows," said Kate.

The doorbell rang, startling the trio of officers. Tom Sherwin got there first, and returned to the kitchen with another man, of a similar age, but dressed more formally, in a suit and tie.

"This is the family solicitor, Edward Simms," said Mr Sherwin.

The two men took in the scene before them and Simms was the first to react.

"As my client, Chloe Sherwin has not given express permission for this search. I suggest you leave immediately. "

Kate was not going to take this lying down.

"Mrs Hunter's husband has died in suspicious circumstances, and Mr Sherwin, acting on her behalf, gave us full access to the house."

"Be that as it may, it is my client's wish that any such permission be withdrawn at this point."

Reminding herself that she was dealing with the family of a victim, not a suspect, Kate conceded defeat.

"There are certain items that may be of evidential value which we'll be removing from the house. For the moment I will suspend the search, but we will return if our investigation requires it. My colleague will provide you with a receipt for the items, Mr Sherwin."

Kate nodded to Ben, who dropped the baking powder tub and all of its contents into an evidence bag, which he then numbered and labelled. Rory drew up a short list, which included: two laptop computers; one tablet; one envelope, contents unknown; one small container labelled

Baking Powder; four box files, contents unknown; one digital camera; bag and tripod. Kate signed the list and handed it to Tom Sherwin. He snatched it with little grace, turned on his heel and returned to the sitting room, closing the door with something of a slam. Without another word, the solicitor showed the three of them to the door.

"What do you make of that?" asked Ben.

The trio had stopped by their cars to chat.

"The father knew there was coke in the house, hence the clean-up this afternoon. They didn't find it, or not all of it, anyway. That's what's making him mad. I suppose he doesn't want a scandal," said Rory.

"If he didn't know where it was hidden, then either Chloe didn't tell him, or she didn't know it was there," said Kate speculatively.

"Surely she'd know if her husband was using..." said Rory.

"You'd think so..." said Kate.

Ben laughed.

"Clearly neither of you have ever been married," he said, then got into his Garda Technical Bureau van and rolled down the window.

"I'll get the wraps into the lab for definitive testing, and give the devices to the cybercops. I'll do the envelope first thing in the morning, and call you when I have something. The box files will be in the evidence store when you're ready to go through them."

Kate waved him off. As they made to leave, she glanced back at the house in the rear-view mirror. Tom Sherwin was standing at the picture window, a dark silhouette against the lights within.

K ate called Corcoran and brought him up to date. He was still in his office when they reached the squad room, although it was almost ten p.m.

"So our murder victim isn't the squeaky-clean pillar of the community we were led to believe... What did you get at his home besides coke?"

Kate told him about the concealed envelope they had recovered at Hunter's house.

"What had Hunter got to hide? Maybe he had his hand in the till, or was cheating on his wife. Either could get him killed," said Jim.

Kate called the Technical Bureau, where only a single staff member was usually on duty overnight.

"Good news," she told the other two. "Ben came straight back here from Hunter's house. He's examining the envelope now. We should be quick getting results," she said.

Kate found Ben Tyler in his lab. Suited and masked, he was looking through a microscope.

"I thought you'd gone home," she said.

"Curiosity got the better of me. I came in to drop off the stuff and couldn't resist taking a look."

Kate put on latex gloves and a mask.

"Mind if I join you? What have you got so far?"

"One good set of prints on the tape. I'll get our print person to check them against the victim's. We'll need to get prints from the wife too."

"And the envelope?"

"I'm just about to look inside."

Ben cut across the envelope below the sticky seam that sealed the package to preserve it, and tipped the contents out onto a sterile metal tray.

There were three SDI cards, and two USB thumb drives.

"No smoking gun, then..." said Ben.

"Those are camera cards, aren't they?" said Kate.

"Yes, they store stills or video footage."

"Do you need to check them for prints or DNA?"

"I do. Give me about half an hour."

Kate left the lab and made her way to the office of the information technology examiners – the cybercops, as they were dubbed. The room was in semi-darkness, but the blue flickering light from a screen betrayed the presence of one of the team. Kate was delighted to see who it was.

"Keeva, are you still on duty?"

The young woman had long, pink-hued fair hair and wore Goth clothes and Doc Martens. She cut an unusual figure among the male-dominated and conservative staff at Garda HQ. She and Kate had often shared coffee and a chat.

"Strictly speaking I'm on standby at home, but I got stuck into a game and kind of lost track of time..." she said.

"Consider yourself off standby, then. I'm glad I don't have to drag you in from home. I've got an urgent job from a murder we caught this morning. Ben's examining three SD camera cards and two USB sticks we seized earlier for prints and DNA. When he's done I need to see what's on them. Can you do that?"

"Of course. That could be a lot of material, depending on the memory size. Do you want to sit in?"

"Definitely. Give me a shout when you've got something to show me."

KATE TOLD Corcoran and Rory what Ben had found in the envelope.

"I wonder what's on them that someone felt the need to hide them," said Rory.

"We'll know soon. Ben will give them to Keeva when he's done lifting prints and DNA."

Kate made her way to the vending machine in the tiny kitchen. Fishing for change in her pockets and emptying out her purse, she bought crisps and chocolate bars for herself, Rory and Corcoran, and brewed three strong teas. Back in the squad room, the two men wolfed down the snacks gratefully.

"What if Ashling wasn't abducted at all?" said Corcoran between mouthfuls.

"Why did she disappear, then?" said Rory.

Kate's phone vibrated. It was a text from the Technical Bureau.

"Right, Keeva's got the camera cards and USB sticks. I'm going up to see what's on them."

"Me too," said Rory, and Corcoran followed.

In the Technical Bureau Keeva wheeled over three chairs

from the other desks and they all sat expectantly around her screen.

"I've downloaded all the files from the first card," she said. "They were encrypted but I've used some of our specialised software to open them. It wasn't that sophisticated an encryption program. Fairly bog-standard... Anyway, here goes..." She pressed play on the video file.

ALL DAY ASHLING had kept her hopes up. She'd eked out the litre bottle of water, only taking sips when she was desperate. She practised her yoga, and did stretches and star jumps to keep her limbs from stiffening again. She sang songs when she could remember the words, and planned the first meal she would have on her release; her mother's roast chicken dinner.

But as night fell and the birds went quiet, the water was all gone, and so was her optimism. Rain began to fall on the roof and she spent ages trying to find a tiny leak she could hear dripping into the dark space. When she eventually found the gap in the top right hand corner of the back doors, it proved to be useless. She couldn't get the bottle into a position to collect the drops, and ended up standing with her tongue against the door, catching only an occasional single drop of rusty water. It passed the time, but now she was weak from the effort. She cursed herself for eating all the chocolate bars. *How could she have been so stupid, so greedy?* Now her stomach cramped with hunger and she tried vainly to ignore her growing thirst.

Wrapping herself in the smelly tarpaulin against the

damp and cold, she lay down. Despite her tiredness she couldn't sleep. She thought about her family.

Her mother was such a softie, she'd be climbing the walls with worry. And her dad... how would he cope with all the farm work when his little girl was missing? And Max and all her other friends... would they be thinking of her, looking for her? Dan had said the Gardai were searching, so why hadn't they found her?

Where was Dan? He'd promised to come back with clean clothes... and set her free...

He wouldn't leave her here to die... would he?

31

WEDNESDAY APRIL 6, 2011

It was almost two in the morning when Kate, Rory and Corcoran left the Technical Bureau. They were subdued as they trooped downstairs to the squad room.

"That's not the kind of stuff they prepare you for in training..." said Rory sombrely.

"I don't think you can be prepared for that," said Jim. "Hunter was one sick bastard."

The SDI cards had revealed a catalogue of sexual violence. David Hunter had filmed himself with women as he violated and abused them. His particular appetite was for choking his victims to the point of unconsciousness, then raping them every way he could, even using objects to penetrate their bodies. As well as biting and slapping his victims, he used a knife to draw shallow trails of blood on their skin. The victims often woke screaming in pain, which only seemed to encourage him. The Technical Examiner had been able to access the metadata from the files and could date each recording.

Most shocking of all was that Kate was convinced that Emily Sweetman, a.k.a. Red Dress Girl, was his most recent victim. Both she and Rory had identified her in the footage, based on the photos they'd obtained from her family. There were a number of videos of her. There were three other women he had filmed himself abusing, and these went back a couple of years. His techniques had become more practiced and ever more cruel over time.

"I don't think I'll ever sleep again," said Rory.

"We need to get access to Hunter's work laptop. He was performing for the camera. This wasn't just for his own sick perversion. I bet he's either sold or shared that footage online," said Kate.

She was trying very hard to stay unemotional when all she felt was an overwhelming disgust. *The bastard deserved all he got.*

"There are no videos of his wife," said Rory.

"She's the one with the money. His job, his home, his fancy car, they're all down to her; he wouldn't dare jeopardise that," said Corcoran.

"We need to identify those other women. They've all got a strong motive to kill David Hunter," said Kate.

"That's not going to be easy. If we had facial recognition software, it might help," said Rory.

"Dream on, sonny," said Corcoran.

"Let's see what his laptop turns up. He must have met them somewhere, probably online. There'll be a digital trail," said Kate.

"It's late. You two need to get some sleep. Go home and be back here at eight," said Corcoran.

"What about Ashling? If David Hunter is the man she was dating, the one who brutalised Emily, she's either one of his victims or a prime suspect. She's key to this whole thing," said Kate.

"Keeva might find something once she cracks his laptop, and I'll hit his office first thing and seize his work computer. There has to be some way to find out what he's done to her," said Rory as they parted ways in the car park.

Only hours later at eight in the morning, Corcoran briefed the full murder team on the findings from Hunter's house. Lawless and Sutton were tasked with interviewing the dead man's friends and finding David Hunter's cocaine dealer, and they left immediately. After a couple of hours of fitful sleep, Kate had gone straight to the Technical Bureau. A tired-looking Keeva had finally gained access to Hunter's laptop. It contained dozens of locked and encrypted files. Soon afterwards, Rory arrived with the dead man's work laptop. A second technician took the device.

"This one's been sanitised," he said, almost immediately, "and professionally so."

"What does that mean?" said Kate.

"Everything on the memory has been deleted – wiped. A program was run to erase the memory, and recently too."

"How recent?" asked Rory.

"Two days ago... at about seven p.m."

"Can you get it back?"

"I can try, but no guarantees."

Rory and Kate left the two officers to their work, and reported back to Corcoran. He looked about as exhausted as they felt. Kate wondered if he'd been home at all overnight.

"Did you recognise the location in those videos? Is it his house?"

"It doesn't look like any of the rooms in the family home," said Rory.

"So does he have another property? A holiday home, his parents' place?"

"One of the lads spoke to his sister in Australia. She confirms their parents are both dead and the family home was sold years ago."

"Hang on," said Kate. "He worked for Sherwin's. They must have dozens of properties on their books."

"Right. Go and check out the videos again, get some stills of the bedroom and take it to the Sherwin office. Someone might recognise the décor. It could be a vacant property Hunter had access to," said Corcoran.

"A show house would be convenient, wouldn't it?" said Kate as she and Rory went back upstairs to the Technical Bureau.

Quickly, they got the technician to take a screenshot of the bedroom from one of the videos downloaded from the SDI cards. He managed to find a frame where neither Hunter nor his victim were in the picture, and sent it to both their phones.

"Sherwin Developments is closed, as a mark of respect..." said Rory.

"You've got phone numbers for his co-workers, don't you?" said Kate. "Ring them all and text them that image from the video, see if anyone recognises the room. We need to find the location, and fast."

"Do you think Ashling might be there?"

"It's a long shot. It's been five days. How would he keep her out of sight? Surely someone would find her, even if he has her locked in or chained to a radiator. I'm going down to the inspection pit to see if they've turned up anything in the BMW," she said.

In the basement of Garda HQ David Hunter's BMW was

being meticulously processed for evidence. Kate found Ben Tyler and another CSI combing through every inch of the interior.

"Any joy?" she asked.

"We found some tiny bloodstains in the boot, on the carpet," said Ben.

"How tiny?"

"Little more than a few drops. Could be nothing... I've sent them to the lab for a profile."

Kate felt a chill of foreboding. *Had David Hunter killed Ashling?* Her phone vibrated. It was a text from the digital investigator who was examining Hunter's work laptop.

Can you come up to me? ASAP. I've something to show you.

Kate took the stairs two at a time.

"I've managed to retrieve some of the deleted data, including browser history," he said.

"And... what have you found?"

"I can see why someone wiped this clean, and it was done expertly. It's taken our most sophisticated programs to recover the data. And I've only got bits and pieces so far. However, I can tell you that this guy has a serious appetite for hardcore, violent porn."

"We kind of know that already..." said Kate, disappointed.

"He's an active member of a group on the Dark Web..."

"What do you mean 'active'?"

"He downloads dozens of video files, everything from violent BDSM to so-called 'snuff movies'. Nasty stuff. And he's uploaded some of his own. Those videos Keeva found on the SDI cards. He's quite the hit in the chat rooms."

"Sick bastard."

"This is what I wanted to show you."

The technician opened a file showing an online conversation. None of the participants used real names.

"Hunter used Easy Rider..." said the technician.

"We knew that too."

"He posted this still, and look at the chat that follows..."

Kate pulled her chair in closer to the screen. For a moment she held her breath, as she took in the exchanges between the chat room members.

"Can you enlarge that still?" she asked.

The technician did so.

"Send it to my email, and a screenshot of the chat. Thanks for this. I can't tell you how important it is."

Kate's phone pinged as she ran back downstairs. It was a text from Rory.

> I think I've found the place.

He was in Corcoran's office, and her phone pinged again just as she got there. It was the still from Hunter's laptop and screenshots from the chatroom.

"You were right," said Rory excitedly. "We've found the place where Hunter filmed himself and Emily. It's a show house in Wicklow, just outside Blessington."

"He posted a picture of Ashling online. Look," said Kate grimly as she showed the other two her phone. "Hunter was in touch with other sickos on the Dark Web. He posted this for his mates."

"Shit... Is she alive?" said Rory.

The photo showed Ashling lying in a foetal position, bound with duct tape. She was in a small dark space, her eyes were closed and there were cuts and bruises visible on her face.

"Hard to tell. Let's hope so," said Corcoran. "Where did he post this?"

Kate showed them the online conversation.

"It's a chat room where they share and discuss violent sexual content. He's basically asking the other guys what to do with her," she said.

"And they're full of helpful suggestions," said Rory, taking the phone from her.

"Such as?" asked Corcoran.

"Well, the consensus is he should either ship her out to one of these other guys, or kill her and film it for their enjoyment..." said Kate.

The three went quiet.

"When did he put this up?" asked Rory.

"Monday afternoon."

"He left work on Monday around five, and his wife said he wasn't home until seven thirty. His camera was still in his wardrobe on Tuesday so he probably didn't have time to do what he'd planned..." said Rory.

"And the cybercops haven't found any video of Ashling..." said Corcoran, a hint of hope in his voice.

"So she's probably still alive? Is that what we're saying?" asked Kate.

"We have to assume she is."

"Someone tried to erase everything on his laptop a couple of hours after that last post... but who? It can't have been him. He wasn't in the office then," said Kate.

"He couldn't have had time to kill her and make his snuff movie..."

"It's not on any of the SDI cards, or either of his laptops. Let's hope he didn't."

"Right, follow me."

Corcoran led them to the squad room and called the team together to brief the others.

"For the moment, David Hunter's murder enquiry takes second place. Our priority for now is to find Ashling Byrne. We've uncovered strong evidence, actual video footage, that Hunter was a sexual predator, into rape and violent abuse of young women. Now we believe Hunter abducted Ashling last Friday. Kate will show you the image he posted of the girl. I want everyone to study it to see if we can identify her location. This is time sensitive. If she's still alive she's probably in a bad way."

The team gathered round Kate's screen.

"Could be a basement, or a cellar somewhere..." said one detective.

"There's a bottle of water on the floor..." said another.

"And some sweet wrappers..."

"Hunter uploaded this on Monday afternoon, before he left work," said Kate.

The room fell silent.

"That's not two days' worth of water..." said a sombre voice.

"He might have been to see her after work on Monday. There's a gap of two hours between him leaving work and his arrival home to Rathmichael, some five miles away," said Kate.

Corcoran pulled a huge paper map of the greater Dublin area down from the wall and spread it on a desk.

"Let's work out how far he could have travelled in that time..."

A detective stuck a pin in the map at the location of the café. Using red string, he started to draw a search area.

"It's no good – that's too big. Where would we start?" said Kate.

Rory put sticky notes in locations around the south side of Dublin city and the surrounding counties.

"These are Sherwin developments still in the building stage. He would have had access to them all. Maybe he used a show house again..." he said.

Everyone clustered round the map. There were five developments roughly within the search area.

"According to the website, they've all been *closed as a mark of respect following the sudden death of David Hunter*," said an officer, reading from his screen.

"There's bound to be security on those sites, surely?" said Kate.

Corcoran checked his watch. Only a couple of hours' worth of daylight left. "I'll get on to Tom Sherwin. We don't have time to wait for warrants. He has to let us search them now!" said Corcoran, hurrying from the squad room.

"Right, everyone pick a location. Go and conduct a thorough search. If that girl is still alive, we need to find her in the next couple of hours," said Kate. "Unless you hear otherwise, let's assume we have full permission to search, with or without warrants."

Kate and Rory took the Sherwin site in west Wicklow, the one Hunter's co-workers had identified from the still of the bedroom. Before leaving, Kate checked in with Ben Tyler in the basement garage. He was still examining the BMW.

"We've found hairs and fibres as well as the blood. What colour hair has the missing girl?" he asked.

"She's a redhead."

"We've got a couple of long reddish hairs from the boot," he said.

"Hunter must have moved her in the boot. We think he stashed her away somewhere. He posted a photo of her online, bound and unconscious. She was showing signs of minor injuries," said Kate. "That would explain the blood."

"I'll get one of the cybercops down here to decode and access the BMW's SatNav and its history, then we'll know where the car went," said Ben.

Kate felt like hugging him.

"Forget the trace evidence. Get the info off his SatNav as soon as you can – we need to know exactly where he's been since Friday evening. Text me when you've got it. There's still a chance the girl's alive."

Rory had secured a squad car and was waiting with the engine running.

"Hop out, Rory. I'll drive. I'm expecting SatNav data from Ben and you'll need to be hands-free to go through it. Where are we headed again?"

"Blessington area. It's about an hour away," said Rory.

"Have any of the other search teams reached their sites?"

"No word yet."

Jim Corcoran took a while to get on to Tom Sherwin. The murder victim's father-in-law had his assistant fielding calls, and she took some persuading to put him through. By the time they spoke, the detective inspector's patience was wearing thin. "My officers need to get access to all of your sites in the greater Dublin area," he said.

"What on earth for? Those sites are closed for the rest of the week, as a mark of respect."

"I understand that, Mr. Sherwin, but we have an urgent need to search them. Surely you must have security patrols on duty?"

"That's as may be, but you still haven't told me why you need to search my sites."

"We are now sure that your son-in-law was killed unlawfully. This is a murder investigation. Consequently there are good operational reasons, which I'm not at liberty to reveal, why we need to retrace his steps over the last few days," said Corcoran.

The line went quiet.

"Mr Sherwin, time is of the essence. I can get search warrants but that could take hours. In the meantime I have officers en route to five different sites in the Dublin area. I need your co-operation, please."

"Very well, Detective Inspector. I'll contact the security teams and tell them to grant access to your people. But I expect your officers to treat my properties with respect. I don't want to find my valuable assets damaged or ransacked; is that clear?"

"Thank you for your assistance, Mr. Sherwin."

Corcoran radioed to the detective units.

"Report to on-site security; they'll be expecting you. And leave no stone unturned. You all know what's at stake," he said.

32

Kate and Rory arrived at the site outside Blessington within fifty minutes, just as the sky was beginning to darken. It was a gated development of twenty or so large detached houses, some minutes outside the town in a pretty valley overlooking a lake. All of the houses were fully built to roof level, with most having windows and doors fitted. Only one, the show house, looked fully ready for sale. Kate made the security guard take them there first. Inside, it was beautifully furnished and decorated, and eerily quiet.

On the first floor Kate and Rory recognised the master bedroom from David Hunter's video.

"This is it, isn't it?" she said.

"For sure, but he's done a good job covering his tracks."

The room looked immaculate, down to crisp fresh linen on the bed and soft wool throws and cushions.

"Do we need to seal this off?" asked Rory, opening wardrobe doors and sliding out drawers with gloved hands.

"Yes. Get some tape from the car, and we'll lock it from

the outside. Tell your man downstairs this house is off limits until the CSIs have cleared it."

They moved on to the other houses one by one. These were a different story. As they made their way through each building, guided by the security man, they found bare unplastered walls, wiring ducts sticking out and gaps in the floors for the utilities. Here and there hard hats and bits of equipment had been left in the empty rooms, as if the workers had simply dropped their tools where they stood the day before, when news of David Hunter's death had broken. Within half an hour they'd completed the search of the site, but found no trace of Ashling.

"Is that it? No more outbuildings or sheds?" Kate asked the security man.

"We use containers for the valuable stuff, the portable generators and the bigger power tools. The diggers aren't left here at night – too easy to steal. There's gangs out there that travel all over robbing building sites."

"What kind of containers?" asked Kate.

"Big steel shipping containers. There's usually one or two on every site. They're locked and alarmed – to keep the robbers out. There's only one left here. This way..."

The man led the way through trees along a well-trodden path. Concealed behind some shrubs they found a large rust-coloured container. It was padlocked and the lock had an electronic keypad attached with a tiny blinking red light. The guard keyed in a number and the padlock clicked open. He shone a flashlight as they stepped into the void. The interior was dry and pitch dark. There were pieces of machinery neatly organised in rows and a portable ramp inside the door so that they could be wheeled out. Pallets of blocks and sacks of cement stretched all the way to the back wall.

"Nothing here, Kate," said Rory.

"I know, but there's something about this place..."

She pulled out her mobile and scrolled through the images until she came to the one of Ashling Byrne, curled up in a dark corner. She held the screen towards Rory.

"Look familiar?"

"Yes! She's in a container like this one!" he said.

"Looks like it."

"But people would be coming in and out all the time. Someone would have found her, surely?"

"I know. But it looks like the interior of a container to me," said Kate, turning to the guard. "Are there any more of these on this site?"

"No, this is the last one."

"Get on the radio, Rory. Make sure the other teams check out any shipping containers or outbuildings on the sites," said Kate.

They headed back towards the exit.

"Terrible business about Mr. Hunter," said the man.

"Did you see him often?"

"Oh yes, he was here all the time. Mostly while the show house was being finished. He'd be in supervising the decorators and all that. Then he'd bring people in to look around."

"Was he here recently?"

"Might have been. I couldn't be sure; there's a few of us rotate the shifts. There's security here twenty-four seven. Mr Hunter had his own keys anyway, so he came and went as he pleased."

"Were you here last Friday evening?"

"Last Friday... Yes, that would have been my last night on. I moved to the day shift on Monday."

"Did you see Mr Hunter on Friday, or Monday?"

"Can't say for sure. People come and go."

"Do you keep a log of cars in and out?"

"No, Sergeant. We only make a note of the delivery trucks, not the staff cars. Mr Hunter was in and out of here all the time."

In the car Rory was just finishing on the radio.

"The others have found nothing so far."

"Shit! She must be somewhere. He couldn't have had time to kill her and dispose of the body, could he?"

Kate was beginning to despair. She started the car and they set off back towards the city. The silence was soon broken by a message alert on her mobile.

"It's from Ben Tyler," she said, handing the phone to Rory. "He's unscrambled the SatNav data on the BMW. See what you can make of it."

"It looks like a map – it plots Hunter's movements since Friday."

Kate speeded up until she found a layby next to a farm gate and brought the car to a halt.

"What can you see?"

"Monday evening he left his office around five. We knew that already. Then he leaves the suburbs for what looks like the middle of nowhere. It's not a Sherwin site."

"Show me... That's not on any of our maps, is it?" she said.

"No, definitely not."

"Maybe we were wrong. He didn't use a Sherwin site. He's got her somewhere else."

"It's about half an hour away, due south..."

"Right, give me directions," said Kate, turning on the flashing blue lights.

"Call Corcoran. Tell him where we're headed. Get the

other teams to join us at that location as soon as they've done their own searches. If it's open country, we're going to need all hands on deck."

"Let's hope we're not looking for a body dump," said Rory.

33

On the rare occasions when she'd thought about dying, Ashling had imagined it to be either a sudden lightning-strike event or a gentle fading away. Her grandmother had died peacefully with all the family around her bed in the hospice. They'd taken turns to say 'I love you' and 'goodbye, Nana,' and to hold the old lady's hand. Over the course of almost an hour, her breathing had become slower and slower. Finally, there were no more inhalations. They'd all hugged and cried and even laughed together. Nana, as usual, had done things her way, going when she was ready and not a second before.

This was different, so different. Ashling knew she was dying. There was no water, no Dan, no escape. But it was neither sudden nor peaceful. It was agonising. Her stomach ached and cramped, her limbs felt numb and her mouth – dear God, her mouth! It was so dry and sandpapery. Her lips were split from screaming and her tongue felt twice the size it should be. She just wanted to sleep.

Death was coming, she knew that, but why did it have to be such a bitch?

"ARE you sure this is the right road?" said Kate. The car was bumping along a narrow rutted track through tall hedgerows flanked by forest.

"I'm reading the map, and this is it," said Rory. "There should be a clearing up ahead, if the co-ordinates are correct. Ben wouldn't make a mistake."

The headlights on full beam were only showing the winding track ahead and dark trees all around. Finally, about two miles after leaving the road, the car emerged into a flat, muddy clearing, and a field criss-crossed with furrowed tracks. In the darkness the headlights picked up a line of eerie grey structures.

"Where the hell are we?" said Kate.

"It's a ghost estate," said Rory.

A dozen incomplete houses, some only foundations, others nearing roof height, were dotted in the overgrown meadow. Over time nature had obscured the angles of the structures, giving them a post-apocalyptic look.

"This is spooky. I thought they'd all been knocked down or finished," said Kate as they climbed out of the car, leaving the headlights on to light their way.

"I thought so too. This one must have just been left to rot. Do you think it's one of Sherwin's?"

"We'll have to assume it is. Why weren't we told about it? We asked for details of all their sites."

"They probably sold this on. After the crash, vulture funds bought up a lot of ghost estates. They'll sit on it until land values come back up. One day this field will be worth big money."

"Remind me to consult you if I ever get into property," said Kate, picking her way over the uneven ground.

They split up, heading in opposite directions, each starting at the tip of the semi-circle of structures. They clambered through the skeletal buildings, stumbling over discarded blocks and unexpected voids. Within minutes they met in the middle of the semi-circle, in a house with no upper floor.

"Anything?" asked Kate.

"No. It doesn't look like anyone's been here in years," said Rory.

"Any shipping containers?"

"No, but there could be one here somewhere. Going by the last site, the builders seem to keep them hidden, to deter thieves."

"Let's look around the back," said Kate.

The two began a sweep search of the surrounding field. It was pitch dark, too far from the car to benefit from the headlights. They walked a few metres apart, moving the beams of their torches back and forth in the blackness.

"There's something over here..." shouted Rory, pointing his torch towards the tree line on the left side of the field.

They set off towards a dark rectangular shape that loomed against the tree trunks a hundred or so metres away.

"It's a container," said Rory breathlessly as they jogged across the rutted earth.

Like the houses, the container had been annexed by nature. Nettles and brambles grew to waist height along the sides. Tree branches almost covered the roof. Soon it would be completely obscured. Rory began pounding on the doors, which were secured with a chain and padlock.

"Ashling, are you in there?" he shouted. "Is anyone in there?"

There was no reply.

"We have to open it, see what's inside," said Kate.

She examined the padlock.

"It's old school, not the electronic type. We'd need bolt cutters to get through this."

"I'll radio the others," said Rory.

"No time. We'll have to improvise," said Kate. "Come on."

They ran back towards the skeleton houses.

"There must be something here we can use on that lock. See what you can find," she said.

Rory found a chisel and Kate a claw hammer.

"One of these will work, surely?" he said.

"It'll have to. Come on…"

At the container, Kate held the light while Rory wielded the chisel, which proved useless. He took to smashing the padlock with the hammer, over and over. The noise was deafening. Tiny animals could be heard scurrying away in fear. With each impact the padlock was becoming flattened and bent.

"Here, let me have a go. Hold the torch. We need to strike the right point to snap out the mechanism."

Aiming precisely for the top of the padlock where the loop joined the lock, Kate gave it an almighty wallop. She felt the impact right up to her skull.

"It's moving. Do that again," said Rory.

Two more blows and finally the padlock fell loose and open. He unhooked the lock to release the chain it had held in place. His hands were shaking and the chain was heavy and rusted but eventually it came away and slid noisily to the ground. Rory pulled open the door. Kate shone her torch into the darkness. The interior was half full, with pallets of blocks and bags of cement packed almost to the roof. A dirty tarpaulin was crumpled in a heap on the floor.

Inside, Rory squeezed himself into a space alongside the stacked pallets and moved towards the back end. Kate stood in the doorway, despair threatening to overwhelm her.

They'd never find Ashling Byrne, not alive anyway. This had been their last hope.

"This is it! It's where he held her!" called Rory. Kate slid herself through the narrow gap, the rough blocks scraping against her chest painfully. In a metre-wide space at the back, there were discarded chocolate and sandwich wrappers, scraps of duct tape and three empty water bottles. There was a strong scent of urine.

"Don't touch anything. We'll need to get the techies out. There'll be prints and trace evidence."

"He must have moved her on Monday night," said Rory.

"He could have killed her and buried her out there in the woods," said Kate, making her way through the narrow gap again, "somewhere we might never find her."

"Ssshh, what's that noise?" said Rory, joining her by the container doors.

They stood still and listened.

"Probably a fox," said Kate.

"It's not a fox."

He bent down to the tarpaulin heaped up against the pallets. Pulling on latex gloves from his pocket, he lifted the corner.

"Jesus Christ, she's here! She's under here!" he said.

Kate's heart lurched.

Was it a body?

Together they hauled the tarp away. Underneath, curled in a foetal position, they found the girl. Rory put two fingers to her neck.

"There's a pulse, but it's faint."

Kate knelt beside the comatose figure.

"She's freezing, probably hypothermic."

She took off her coat, gathered the girl in her arms and put it around her. Ashling moaned faintly and Kate felt immense relief.

"We have to warm her up and get her to a hospital."

"I'll call an ambulance," said Rory.

"No time. We'll take her. Go get the car and drive it as close as you can to this thing, and bring water. There's a bottle in the cup holder."

Rory set off running. Kate cradled the almost lifeless girl and began to massage her ice-cold face and hands.

"You're safe now, Ashling. We've got you. You're going to be alright."

The girl gave another low moan. Grateful for the response, Kate wrapped her scarf around the girl's head and neck and tried using her own body heat to warm her up. Within two minutes Rory was back. He reversed the car up close to the container doors and brought a bottle of water in.

Gently, Kate dribbled water over Ashling's cracked lips. Then she poured a little into her mouth. First it gurgled and came back out, but Kate persisted with tiny sips. Soon the girl, still unconscious, began to gulp the water back, almost choking in the process. Kate sat her more upright and kept tipping the drink gently into her. When the bottle was half empty, she stopped.

"We'll lift her into the back seat. I'll sit with her to keep her warm. You drive. Where's the nearest Emergency Department?"

"Loughlinstown. I'll ring ahead and tell them to expect us. It's going to take at least half an hour."

"Blue light it, all the way."

Between them, they lifted the comatose girl into the back seat of the car and Kate held her in a close embrace as Rory bounced the vehicle across the field.

"I can't take it any faster or we'll break the axle," he said.

"Just make it back to the road and then floor it," said Kate, "and put the heater on full blast."

34

THURSDAY APRIL 7

Kate was woken by a series of message alerts on her mobile. She was exhausted. It had been a nerve-shredding journey to the hospital, holding Ashling's still, cold form in her arms while Rory drove like a madman. Kate used her radio to call Corcoran and give him the news. By the time they reached the ambulance bay and the waiting doctors and nurses, the girl's limbs were beginning to warm. In a blur of speedy movements the medics lifted Ashling from the car, placed her on a gurney, and wheeled her through double doors marked Resus Dept. Kate and Rory were left standing, feeling useless. Having given Ashling's name, address and age to the receptionist, they made their way to the canteen. It was after nine and the place was deserted, the only offerings being vending machines. They made do with fizzy drinks and chocolate bars.

"You'd think they'd have healthy food in a hospital," said Rory, his voice low with tiredness.

"Or a twenty-four-hour canteen," said Kate.

They finished their snacks in silence.

"Do you think she'll make it?"

"She's young and fit... That should count for something."

"But she's been two days without water, or food."

"We'll just have to hope we weren't too late. Come on, let's go back and see if there's any news."

It took a while and a lot of pressure on the Emergency Department receptionist, but finally one of the doctors who'd taken Ashling away came out to see them.

"Her kidneys have all but packed up from dehydration," he said. "We've had to put her on dialysis. Hopefully that will just be a temporary measure. We're warming her up slowly. She'll be in the High Dependency Unit for a while yet, but she's stable. A few more hours and it would have been a different story."

Rory had phoned Max Egan with the news that they'd found Ashling. The boy broke down crying. He wanted to go straight to the hospital to be with her, but Rory advised him to wait until the next day. Exhausted, they'd made their way to HQ and reported back to Jim Corcoran and the other search teams, who practically applauded them into the squad room.

"Well done! You've probably saved that girl's life," said Corcoran. "CSIs are on their way out to the site. We can't risk someone getting to it before us. I know we're pretty sure David Hunter put her there, but we need to secure the evidence. Now go home and sleep. Tomorrow will be a busy one."

Now, morning had come all too soon. Kate stretched and shook herself awake. It was barely eight but the screen of her smartphone was filled with messages. Most were from colleagues, including Ben Tyler, congratulating her on finding Ashling. One message was from a number she didn't recognise.

> Marina has asked me to invite you to dinner. She would be really grateful for the opportunity to have a longer talk at a time that suits you. Please let me know when you would be free to call by one evening, hopefully soon. Kind regards, Karen.

After some deliberation Kate texted back.

> I'll be in touch soon.

The idea of another meeting with Marina Jackson was unsettling. As she showered and dressed, Kate thought back over the first encounter. It had been disturbing and emotional in a way she'd never expected, and only the urgency of the murder case had pushed it to the back of her mind.

Why on earth did she open that can of worms? There was nothing but pain to be found there.

There was a text from Greg confirming he'd visit the following weekend, which gave her heart a lift.

Driving to work she thought about the day ahead. First duty was to check on Ashling Byrne's condition, then the search for whoever killed David Hunter would be back on, in earnest. Everything they'd discovered pointed to his being a sadistic and predatory man, a violent rapist. But Kate knew the full rigours of the Garda investigation would apply to him, just as to any victim. The justice system didn't classify murder victims as worthy or unworthy of justice. But she couldn't quite silence the rebel voice in the back of her mind that said 'he got what he deserved'.

By nine o'clock the full murder team had gathered in the squad room. Corcoran called for quiet.

"You'll all know by now that Kate and Rory found the missing girl on a disused building site in the wilds of Wicklow. Everything we know points to David Hunter for this. He abducted her and left her there to die, either deliberately to keep her quiet, or unintentionally because someone killed him before he could get back to her."

"Has anyone interviewed the girl yet?" asked one detective.

"No. She was in a bad way when we found her," said Kate. "I'll check with the hospital now and see if she's well enough to be questioned."

"That's your first priority, Kate. The rest of you continue with your enquiries into Hunter – I want his coke dealer tracked down, his financials dissected, all his friends and colleagues interviewed urgently, and we need to identify his previous victims," said Corcoran. "We got side-lined in the search for Ashling Byrne, but I want Hunter's killer. Given what we now know about the man, there could be any number of people who wanted him dead."

AT THE ENTRANCE to the High Dependency Unit, a nurse stopped Kate. Showing her ID, she put the pressure on.

"I really need to ask her some questions, if she's able to talk. We believe she was the victim of an abduction and assault."

"She's very poorly... I'll have to ask her doctor if she's up to it."

"It's important; please make that clear," said Kate as the nurse hurried away.

Minutes passed. Then the door to the unit opened and a woman in full protective garb emerged. As she tore off the mask she saw Kate, who had clipped her ID onto her jacket.

"Are you the one..." the woman said, her eyes glistening with tears. "Did you find Ashling?"

Kate nodded and introduced herself, but had barely got the words out when she was enveloped in a tight hug.

"I can't thank you enough. You saved her life..." said the woman, sobbing into Kate's shoulder.

Kate gently disentangled herself and led the way to some chairs lined up along the corridor.

"You must be Ashling's mum..."

"Yes, sorry, I didn't introduce myself. I'm a bit all over the place... I'm Nora Byrne," said the woman.

"How is she?"

"She's weak, the poor love, but the doctors say she should make a full recovery."

"You must be so relieved..."

"These last few days, we've all been in bits."

"Has Ashling said anything?"

"She was awake for a little while just now, but she didn't say much, just *I'm sorry, Mum*. As if it was her fault! She's not in her right mind yet."

The woman dabbed at her eyes with a tissue and made a visible effort to regain her composure. Kate sensed the question coming before she spoke.

"Do you know... what happened to Ashling?"

"We don't know everything yet. Our investigation is on-going," said Kate.

"But do you know who took her? Have you found the person who did this to her?"

"I'm sorry, Mrs Byrne, but at the moment we can't confirm anything yet. I'm hoping Ashling can answer some questions."

"She's still pretty out of it, and she's hooked up to all sorts of drips and machines…"

"I'm waiting to speak to a doctor to see if I can have a few minutes with her."

Right on cue, the nurse returned.

"The HDU consultant is doing her rounds. She'll come and see you after she's examined Ashling," she said.

"So there's really nothing you can tell me?" Nora Byrne fixed Kate with a determined look. "My husband and sons are on their way up from Cork. A neighbour's looking after the farm. They'll want to know what happened to her…"

"We might know more when I can speak to Ashling," said Kate.

A woman in scrubs emerged from the High Dependency ward and approached Kate.

"I'm the duty consultant here. Can I help you?"

"Detective Sergeant Kate Hamilton. We're investigating the circumstances surrounding Ashling's assault. I would really like to have a few minutes to question her."

"You can have five minutes, that's all. She's on the mend, but she'll be a few more days with us. Don't tire her out."

A nurse handed Kate a plastic apron, mask and gloves, then brought her into the ward. It was quiet, apart from the low hum and beep of equipment. The long space inside was divided into glass-walled cubicles, four to each side. Ashling was in the third one on the right.

"Five minutes, Detective," said the nurse and closed the door.

"Ashling..."

The pale figure in the bed opened her eyes.

"I'm Kate, from the Serious Crimes Unit. How are you feeling?"

"Are you the one who found me?"

The girl's voice was soft. Her lips, still sore and cracked, seemed to make the effort of talking difficult.

"Yes, my partner Rory and I found you."

"I remember your voice, and the water... you gave me water... Thank you..."

"Do you think you could answer some questions?"

Careful not to displace any of the drips and tubes hooked to her body, Ashling pushed herself into a sitting position.

"I will if I can," she said, her voice a little stronger.

"What happened after you left UCD Belfield on Friday last?"

Kate had her iPhone out on record mode. Ashling took in a slow deep breath before she spoke.

"Dan picked me up and we went for drinks in a little pub, in Wicklow I think... After a while I started to feel weird, dopey and sick..."

"After the drinks?"

"Yes, but I only had two glasses of wine... The next thing I remember I was on a bed somewhere... and he was... he was *hurting* me..."

A tear rolled down Ashling's bruised cheek.

"I tried fighting him off, I really did, but he's so strong. I remember hitting him. His nose started to bleed... but it only made him worse. He punched me over and over, and he was choking me... I must have passed out."

"What do you remember next?"

"When I woke up I was in that container thing, all tied up. Every bit of me hurt. He cut me and... he... he raped me.
"

The nurse tapped on the door.

"One last thing, Ashling. Can you recognise the man who hurt you?"

Kate showed the girl a series of six pictures on her phone. She had put together the photo line-up before leaving the office.

Through swollen eyes, Ashling examined each picture. She stopped at the fourth and gulped in a deep breath before she spoke.

"That's him. That's Dan." There was a mix of terror and anger in her expression. "I hope you get the bastard."

"Don't worry, he'll never be able to hurt you again."

Kate squeezed the girl's hand gently.

"Here's my card. You can ring me anytime. I'll be back as soon as the doctors say you're up to it, to take a more detailed statement. In the meantime you just rest, and feel better soon."

The girl had identified David Hunter, without hesitation. They were right about him. The nurse opened the cubicle door and stood waiting. Kate said goodbye and left, discarding her protective gear into a bin. In the corridor the consultant she'd seen earlier stopped her.

"Did you get what you needed?" she asked.

"For the moment, yes, but I'll have to come back for a more detailed statement," said Kate.

"Give it a day or two..." The doctor paused. "I hope you

get whoever did this to her. He's done damage to that girl that'll take a long time to heal." She gave Kate a look filled with meaning. *Did she mean psychological or physical? Or both?* The consultant did not elaborate.

"He won't be hurting anyone else, I can promise you that," said Kate.

As she left the hospital, Kate couldn't help remembering the findings of the post mortem on Emily. *Internal injuries.*

35

"I want you to sit in on the interviews, Kate," said Corcoran. "We'll question Chloe Sherwin first, then her father. They've fetched up with a solicitor in tow. Interesting move for a victim's family, don't you think?"

"A bit strange, but they know we've found cocaine in the family home. Rich people have appearances to keep up. They're trying to limit reputational damage."

"Wait till they hear what we know now…"

"Are you going to tell them what Hunter was up to?"

"There's no mistaking the evidence, including that still of Ashling Byrne he posted to the Dark Web chatroom. Do you know if they did a rape kit at the hospital?"

"I asked them to when she was admitted."

"Good. The CSIs are going over the show house in Blessington, plus the storage container, and his car. Hopefully they'll find plenty to put Hunter in the frame, plus the positive ID from the girl."

"What should we tell the Sherwins?"

"Let's see what they have to say first, then we'll let them know what we've found."

"Chloe's pregnant... We need to tread carefully. The poor woman, I don't know how she'll take that sort of news."

"She's going to find out sooner or later... and she *is* still a suspect."

"I know."

Chloe Sherwin was pale and hollow-cheeked, with no obvious sign of her condition. She was with Edward Simms, the family solicitor. Jim Corcoran explained that the interview was being recorded and named all present for the tape.

"Firstly, Mrs Hunter, may I offer my condolences," said Corcoran.

Edward Simms was quick to correct him.

"It's Ms Sherwin, Detective. Chloe kept her maiden name when she married."

"My apologies. Thank you for coming in..."

The solicitor put up a hand to stop Corcoran's flow.

"Detective, before you begin your questions, I've been instructed by my client to establish certain facts. Firstly," said Simms, "is it absolutely beyond doubt that David was the victim of a violent attack?"

"It is our belief, following the post mortem on the body and an examination of the crime scene, that Mr. Hunter was unlawfully killed," said Kate.

Chloe Sherwin showed little reaction. The solicitor went on.

"Do you have any idea who may have carried out this horrendous act?"

"Our enquiries are on-going," said Corcoran.

"Has the substance that was removed from the Hunter house been analysed?"

"The results are not back from our lab yet, but a presumptive test indicated that it was a Class A drug – cocaine," said Kate.

"Before you go on, I am instructed by my client to tell you that she had no knowledge of that concealment or of the circumstances of David's death."

Corcoran had had enough.

"That will be for us to establish, Mr Simms," he said brusquely.

"May I remind you of my client's delicate condition, Detective Inspector. And that Chloe is in shock and deeply grieving her beloved husband."

Kate took over, aware that Corcoran was running out of patience. She couldn't help but feel sympathy for the young woman. Her seemingly perfect life had been shattered in the blink of an eye.

"Chloe, were there any problems in the marriage?" asked Kate.

"No. We were very happy…" said Chloe, "especially since we found out about the baby."

"Were you aware of any infidelity on your husband's part?" asked Corcoran.

Chloe looked startled but Kate wasn't sure if it was the idea of David cheating on her, or the blunt question.

"No… of course not," she said.

"We've been conducting enquiries into David's life and we have strong evidence that your husband was unfaithful," said Kate.

Chloe just stared, saying nothing.

"We have reason to believe that David was seeing other women, over the course of your marriage and before," said Corcoran.

Chloe closed her eyes and put her head down. Edward Simms took a white handkerchief from his breast pocket and handed it to her. The room went quiet.

"I know this is hard to hear, Ms Sherwin, but we've found evidence that David was not only seeing other women, he was physically and sexually violent towards some of them. In the days before his death we believe he abducted and assaulted a nineteen-year-old student. He had been seeing this girl for a few weeks," said Kate.

Chloe bowed her head and sobbed. The solicitor looked shocked.

"These allegations, if they're true, have come as a total shock to Chloe – and David is not here to defend himself."

"I want to see my dad," said Chloe through sobs.

"Just one more question," said Corcoran. "Where were you between two a.m. and eight a.m. on Tuesday morning?"

"Really, Detective, is this necessary?" said Simms, outraged.

"You know very well it is," said Corcoran.

"I was at home, in bed," Chloe said. "I'm always tired these days. I go to bed early and sleep late."

"Is there anyone who can confirm that?"

"No. It's just David and me... or it was..."

"Thank you," said Kate. "If you want to wait for your father, I'll take you to a more comfortable waiting room and get someone to bring you a drink. Do you need something to eat?"

"No... I'll have a tea, or a juice or something... I don't care."

Edward Simms stood up.

"If you're going to interview Mr Sherwin, I need to be there," he said.

Kate led the woman and her lawyer to the waiting room.

"If he asks for you, we'll come and get you," she said.

The two officers went to Corcoran's office to debrief.

"Well, what do you think?" he asked.

"I think the perfect marriage was not so perfect..." said Kate.

"She knew he was playing away?"

"Don't they say the wife always knows..." she said.

"Given his particular sexual appetites, do you think she was on the receiving end of his brutality?"

"Who knows... It's not something she's going to volunteer. Maybe for Hunter the kicks came from this secret other life. And he needed to keep her sweet," said Kate.

"But could she have killed him?"

"If she did do it, she's a bloody good actress."

"Right, now for the father. He's a different kettle of fish."

They made their way to the interview room. Tom Sherwin was pacing in the small space.

"I've been waiting for forty-five minutes," he said.

"Our apologies, Mr Sherwin. We're kind of thin on the ground, and the detective inspector and I were occupied," said Kate.

Corcoran was already annoyed.

"Let's get started then, shall we, Mr Sherwin? This interview will be video and audio recorded."

He stated the time, date and names of those present, but before he could ask a single question, Tom Sherwin spoke.

"I'd like to know how my daughter is, and to have my solicitor present."

"Chloe is fine," said Kate. "She's having a break at the moment. We've sent in a drink and offered her food, and she's got a comfortable place to rest. I'll get Mr Simms."

When Kate and the solicitor returned, Corcoran and Tom Sherwin appeared to be engaged in a silent, faintly hostile stare-off. Kate re-activated the recording.

"Detective Sergeant Kate Hamilton and solicitor Edward Simms have entered the interview room."

Simms sat beside his client, looking flustered, Kate thought.

"I'd like some time alone with Tom if you don't mind..." he said.

Corcoran was having none of it.

"As he was quick to point out, Mr Sherwin has already been waiting for a considerable time. I don't want to delay him any longer. You can have all the time you wish with your client after our interview."

Kate realised he wanted to be the one to tell Sherwin about Hunter's activities, rather than let the solicitor do it. He wanted to see the man's reactions.

Tom Sherwin nodded agreement.

"Let's get it over with," he said.

"What was your relationship like with your son-in-law?"

"He worked for me, and Chloe was married to him," he said.

"But did you like him? Were you close?" asked Kate.

There was a brief pause.

"We didn't spend a lot of time together if I'm honest, so no, we weren't particularly close."

There was an awkward silence. The detectives waited. Eventually Sherwin went on.

"He was good at his job, good at selling. We didn't have a lot in common... apart from Chloe."

"And when was the last time you saw David?" said Corcoran.

"I was in the office on Monday afternoon. I saw him then. I left around five and he was still there."

"And can you confirm your whereabouts between two and eight on Tuesday morning?"

The solicitor was going red in the face.

"Again, is this really necessary? Tom is a grieving family member, not a suspect."

"These questions are routine, Mr Simms. We are dealing with a murder," said Kate.

"I was at home in bed. My wife will confirm it. I'm not in the habit of wandering the streets in the middle of the night," said Sherwin.

"You say you were in your office on Monday," said Corcoran. "Any particular reason?"

"I make a point of being there a couple of times a week. I had a meeting with a contractor."

"What sort of contractor?"

Simms made a tutting noise.

"I can't see how this is relevant, but it was a security contractor," said Sherwin. "They've been doing a bit of work for us."

"What kind of work, exactly?"

"I cannot see how Mr Sherwin's business meetings can have any bearing on your enquiry," said Simms.

"Believe me, Mr Simms, they do," said Kate. "Our computer analysts have been examining David Hunter's devices, including his work laptop. It seems it was data-scrubbed on Monday evening last, only hours before his death," said Kate.

The solicitor looked confused. Tom Sherwin did not.

"That's not a normal working practice, is it, Mr Sherwin?" she said.

"I'm not that big on computers. It was recommended by the IT people."

"And why was that?"

Once again a tense silence descended on the room. Kate, Corcoran and even Simms all looked intently at Sherwin. Eventually, he spoke.

"One of our staff had complained about... *inappropriate* material she had glanced on another computer. I brought in a specialist cybersecurity firm to do a trawl through all the company devices. They reported back that they'd found... *questionable* files on one of the laptops. I asked them to delete those files and sanitise, or whatever they call it, that particular device and any existing backup files."

"It was David Hunter's laptop, wasn't it?"

Sherwin nodded. His solicitor looked nonplussed.

"Well, they did quite a good job of it," said Corcoran, "but our specialists are one step ahead of that game. They were able to retrieve a number of those 'questionable' files."

Sherwin and the lawyer said nothing.

"Are you aware of the content of those files?" asked Kate.

"I was given a comprehensive report, yes."

"Did you view the offending material? And did you speak to your son-in-law about it?" she said.

"I didn't view the material, I just read the report. And I didn't speak to David."

"So you were aware that he had hardcore porn and Dark Web affiliations on his laptop? How long have you known about it?" said Corcoran.

Once again, all eyes were on Tom Sherwin. Kate noticed that he looked a little grey beneath his golf tan. It gave his face a faintly yellow appearance.

"Was it at that meeting on Monday last?" pressed Corcoran.

"Maybe a week or two earlier."

"So you knew about David's activities for some time but you didn't speak to him? Those are actionable, sackable offences in any organisation, surely, offences that you should have reported to the Gardai," said Kate.

"It was... complicated."

"Because of Chloe?"

"Why else? What was I supposed to do?"

"And did you inform your daughter of what you'd discovered?" asked Kate.

"No... I didn't want to upset her, in her condition."

"If you had a 'comprehensive report' from this IT audit you'll know that not only was Hunter looking at violent pornography on the Dark Web, he was producing and uploading his own. He filmed himself carrying out acts of violent sexual abuse on a number of young women. The evidence is there in his files, and on the devices we found concealed at your daughter's home," said Corcoran.

Tom Sherwin lowered his head, his eyes closed. Simms, unable to hide his own shock and dismay, put a hand out to touch his client's shoulder.

"This is too much. I really think Tom needs a break. These revelations are shocking in the extreme," said the lawyer.

"That's the thing, though. None of this is news to Mr Sherwin, is it?" said Corcoran.

Sherwin shook his head.

"We also have very strong evidence that Hunter abducted and assaulted a young student, only nineteen years old, last Friday."

Sherwin's head shot up.

"What evidence?" asked the lawyer.

"She was found last night, on a ghost estate once owned by your company. She'd been tied up and left for dead. Thanks to our officers, to Detective Sergeant Hamilton here, she's recovering in hospital. The girl made a positive identification of Hunter."

"The bastard..." Sherwin murmured. "Does Chloe know?"

"Yes," said Kate.

"Jesus, this will destroy her..." Tom leaned his elbows on the table and put his head in his hands.

The lawyer put an arm around his shoulder.

"Once again, I must point out that Hunter is not here to mount a defence to these allegations. I want your assurance that this will remain confidential. There is no reason for these... matters to be made public. Garda HQ leaks like a sieve," said the solicitor.

"There will be no leaks from here," said Corcoran, annoyed. "However, I cannot vouch for the victim, or her friends and family."

"Will she be alright?" asked Sherwin.

"Doctors are hopeful she'll recover physically," said Kate, "but as to her mental health... she's been through a lot."

"I'd like to help her..." he said.

Simms intervened.

"I'm not sure you should be saying that, Tom. You could leave yourself open to all sorts of claims and liabilities," he said.

"David almost killed her. I don't care about liabilities. If I can help her in any way, with financial support, medical expenses or something, I will. It's common decency." Sherwin's voice cracked with emotion.

"I have some more questions," said Corcoran, and he paused to let the man gather himself. "What did you plan to do about Hunter when you found out what he'd been up to?"

"I hadn't decided. It was a nightmare – I knew I'd have to tell Chloe one day, but the pregnancy made it difficult. She's had two miscarriages over the last few years. I didn't want to put her at risk."

"But were you not afraid for her safety, living with a man like that?" asked Kate.

"Of course I was. He disgusted me. But she's never even hinted at violence, or anything untoward. She'd have told her mother if he was... hurting her. We'd have known, I'm sure of it."

"So you were going to wait, and then tell her?"

"I was trying to work out what to do."

"And now David Hunter's death has solved that problem for you," said Corcoran.

Simms almost spluttered with indignation.

"I trust you're not implying anything, Detective," he said.

"Now that we know what kind of man Hunter was, there are a number of suspects with motives to see him dead. I would be remiss if I did not include those closest to him," said Corcoran.

"Put yourself in my shoes," said Sherwin, "knowing your only child was married to this... this monster! Chloe's better off without him."

"And you're sure she knew nothing of his activities?"

"If she had the slightest inkling of that kind of thing,

she'd have booted him out and we'd have backed her up to the hilt."

"But a divorce would have been costly..." said Kate.

"Hunter didn't have two ha'pennies to rub together when he met Chloe. He brought nothing to the marriage. We'd have had a good case to argue in any court."

"Is there anything else you can tell us, any disputes David had? Issues at work, with colleagues or clients?" said Corcoran. "What about the person who complained about the stuff on his laptop?"

"She was a temp. She was only with us a few weeks. She barely knew him. She saw something amiss and she reported it to HR. Quite rightly. We took it very seriously. That's when we brought in the IT security people."

Corcoran waited.

"I don't know of anyone who'd want to harm David... but... there's a lot about him I didn't know."

"What about his finances; what can you tell us about them?" said Kate.

"He was paid a generous salary, something in the region of 100k, plus commission. He liked to spend it. The house was our wedding gift to Chloe, so they've no mortgage. He went away a lot, trips with his friends... expensive holidays, skiing, etc."

"Was he in debt, do you know?" asked Corcoran.

"No clue. You'd have to ask Chloe. She has a well-paid job and a generous trust fund. If he was in trouble she could have bailed him out. But if she did, we knew nothing about it."

"Were you aware of his drug use?"

"Of course not. How would I know?"

"Chloe never hinted..."

"No. She doesn't do drugs. She's been trying for a baby for years. She wouldn't... she just wouldn't."

Edward Simms looked pointedly at his watch.

"Tom would like to get back to his daughter. Can we wrap this up now, please?"

Kate and Corcoran exchanged a nod.

"That's all for the moment, Mr Sherwin. We'll probably need to speak to you again, and I need to confirm your alibi with your wife, as soon as possible," said Kate.

Sherwin nodded. Kate stopped the recording and brought the two men to the waiting room. Chloe looked up tearfully. Her father quickly crossed to her side and put an arm around her shoulders.

"Oh, Dad, it's so horrible! I can't bear it," she said. "They're saying David's done all these terrible things. It's not true. It can't be."

Sherwin drew his daughter into a hug, patting her back like she was still a child.

"I'm sorry, love... This is so hard for you. But the Guards say they have evidence... hard evidence. Try not to think about it now."

"It's like I didn't know him at all..." she sobbed.

"How could you? We were all in the dark."

Not quite, Mr Sherwin. You've known for a while exactly what David Hunter was up to, thought Kate.

"Would you mind giving me your wife's mobile number, please?" she said.

Tom extricated himself and did so.

"Oh God, does Mum know?" said Chloe.

"Not yet." He rubbed his palm across his eyes. "Somehow we're going to have to tell her. Come on, let's get you out of here."

Kate walked the trio down to the main exit, to where a car and driver waited. Tom Sherwin held his daughter's hand. On his other side, Edward Simms was murmuring into his client's ear. Kate caught the words 'private funeral' and 'distance the company and the family' as she offered them each her card.

"I'll be in touch, but please don't hesitate to contact me if you think of anything else."

The two men merely nodded. Chloe, her eyes glassy and red-rimmed, turned away. Kate felt a surge of sympathy for the younger woman, and a pang of worry for her unborn child. Walking back to the squad room, she reminded herself that the victim's wife was still a suspect, but instinct was telling her Chloe Sherwin was not responsible for her husband's killing.

36

C orcoran and the team were gathered around the murder wall.

"Reviewing what we've turned up so far, it's not looking great. CSIs have nothing useful from the car or the body. The killer was either damn lucky or forensically aware," he said.

Some of the squad were out on enquiries, but a couple of detectives and technical examiners were on hand.

"Let's start with the cocaine. Do we have confirmation from the lab?"

"Yes. It's high grade, about twenty grams," said one detective.

"Have you tracked down his source?" asked Kate.

"We've interviewed his friend, Brian Graham. He sources the coke, and sometimes amphetamines. They all chip in and he buys from a dealer in Coolock."

"How come Hunter kept it in his house?"

"They rotate who keeps the stash, to spread the risk. It

seems like the wives and girlfriends are either into it too, or they turn a blind eye."

"Any issues with payment or debts to the dealer?"

"No. According to this guy, that's never been an issue. These lads are not short of money. They're professionals – accountants, stockbrokers, that sort of thing. It's no bother to them to pay up. We're trying to track the dealer down but he's slippery. He may have got wind we're after him. He has minor convictions for possession, no jail time and no history of violence. The Drug Squad intel is that he caters to the top end of the market and keeps it small."

Corcoran sighed.

"So Hunter probably wasn't killed over a drug debt. Makes sense... It doesn't smell like a gangland job to me." He turned to one of the technical examiners. "Any more on his internet activity?"

"We've retrieved some other archived chats – it's more of the same. Hunter was connecting with like-minded individuals. He downloaded hundreds of videos, mostly violent rape fantasy stuff. We've got five videos he filmed and shared. He was gaining a lot of kudos among the other users. There's an appetite online for real action as opposed to the simulated stuff."

Kate felt a wave of nausea. She went to the water fountain for a drink to stifle it.

"Any progress on finding the other women he filmed?" asked Corcoran.

"Not yet, sir. It's needle-in-a-haystack stuff," said the examiner.

"Keep on it. We know Emily Sweetman and Ashling Byrne were victims, so they can be ruled out. That leaves three women – that we know of – with a strong motive... Not to mention their partners, brothers, fathers... What about his finances?"

One of the specialists spoke up.

"He took home about 5k a month between salary and commission. The car was a perk of the job, and they've no mortgage. No evidence of debt. Not even a bank loan. He cleared his credit cards every couple of months. He regularly built up a few grand in savings, but then blew it on holidays. No gambling accounts that we've found. He paid out over a grand into that online account of Ashling Byrne's, the Sugar Babies one, going back to last summer. Nothing else dodgy."

"Any business enemies? People he's crossed in the course of his work?" asked Kate.

"His co-workers are being interviewed as we speak. So far no one has reported anything significant," said Corcoran.

"Is there a chance this was a random attack?" asked Rory Gardiner.

"We can't entirely rule it out... The method is unusual. We need to check back over the last few years to see if there's anything similar on record," said Kate.

"Rory, you take that on," said Corcoran. "He was lured to the spot, otherwise why was he there at that hour of the morning? Was it his habit to drive off in the middle of the night? Any info from the wife?"

"She said he often got up before work to go to the gym, but not before five a.m.," said Kate.

"The gym – has anyone spoken to them?"

All shook their heads.

"Right. Kate, you take that," said Corcoran, "and someone go back to his rugby buddies – see if they can identify previous girlfriends. That could give us an ID on the other women Hunter abused. Show them screen grabs from the videos."

"Hunter had the camera locked off on a wide shot for most of the time. We'll have to zoom in on their faces. The image resolution won't be the best," said one of the technical examiners.

"It'll have to do."

"We only know about the rape victims he filmed. There may be others that he didn't video."

"He wasn't on our system for any offence," said Rory.

Corcoran went round the room, handing out assignments.

"Go back to UCD – see if there were complaints against him back in the day," said Corcoran, "or even rumours, or complaints that were dropped..."

"That happened a lot back then..." said one detective.

"Still does," said another.

———————

"You'll never guess what I've found?" said Rory.

"A winning Lotto ticket... the meaning of life..." Kate said wearily. A visit to Hunter's gym had turned up nothing new. His locker was empty and the staff barely remembered him.

"Alright, grumpy! Seriously, though, listen to this. There's been half a dozen similar deaths across Britain and Europe in the last two years."

"What do you mean similar?"

"I've been on to Europol Intelligence. They've just connected the dots on these killings recently, because they're scattered all over the place. The method is the same or similar, they're all men, and get this... they've all got form for sex crimes."

"What do you mean the method is similar?"

"The victim is lured to a secluded or private location, then asphyxiated. Sometimes it's a plastic bag job, other times ligature strangulation. They're ambushed, essentially."

"And are there any links between the victims?"

"They were all active on the Dark Web, on violent or child porn sites. Europol are liaising with national forces all over the continent. They're working on the theory that it's a serial killer."

"That's some theory... Have you told Corcoran?"

"I just got off the phone to Europol. I'm on my way in to him now... Come with me."

The detective inspector was intrigued.

"It's certainly worth pursuing... Get Europol to add our case to their investigation. Share what we've got so far and make sure that they keep us in the loop. I'll get on to my opposite number in Scotland Yard, see what they make of this," said Corcoran.

"But we'll carry on with the other lines of enquiry, yes?" asked Kate. The theory seemed more than a little far-fetched to her.

"Yes, interview everyone and anyone connected with Hunter. We need some concrete leads," he said.

Back in the squad room, Rory began prepping a case file for Europol. Leaving him to it, Kate studied the list of witnesses. Most had already been interviewed.

"Has anyone been out to the Sherwin offices?" she called out.

Two detectives answered yes.

"Did you speak to the girl who complained about Hunter?"

Both shook their heads.

"She was a temp. I don't think she works there anymore."

"Do we even have a name?"

The detective consulted his notes.

"Angela Stevens."

"Right – I'll take her," said Kate.

In a call to the HR manager at Sherwin's, Kate found out Angela had been sent to them by an agency.

"It wasn't our usual crowd," the manager said. "We had a flyer into the office from a new company – All-Temp Solutions. There was a good discount for the first hire, about 20% off, so when we needed someone to cover a sick leave, I gave them a call."

"Did you get a CV?"

"Yes, I have it still. She was highly qualified, a very good temp. I'd definitely use her again."

"Despite her complaint about David Hunter?" said Kate.

There was a sharp intake of breath on the other end of the line.

"Oh... you know about that..." Another pause ensued. "The girl did the right thing in reporting what she'd seen. We're absolutely clear in our policies on those matters."

"While we're on the subject, have you had complaints about Hunter in the past?"

"No."

Kate asked for Angela Stevens's resume to be emailed to her, plus contact details of the temp agency.

Fifteen minutes later she was on the way to Sherwin's office. All-Temp Solutions had turned out to be impossible to contact. The phone number was 'no longer in service' and her emails bounced back. No such company appeared in the phonebook, online or in the Companies Register.

It was business as usual in the sleek, modern offices of Sherwin Developments, with about a dozen employees in the open plan office, all working at screens. In glass display cases placed all around the room were detailed architect's models of office buildings and homes, complete with tiny landscaped gardens and plastic trees. The HR manager showed her into an office off the main floor.

"Thanks for your help. I just want to nail down a few things about this temp, Angela. What can you tell me about her?"

"She's about thirty, I'd say, long dark hair, glasses, smartly dressed, English from her accent. Quiet, a little bit mousey even... but super-efficient."

"Did she make friends here? Is there anyone I could talk to who might have gotten close to her?" asked Kate.

"I don't think she had time to make friends. She kept to herself. We had a staff member off sick and there was a backlog of work so she was very busy."

"I've been trying to track down the temp agency, with no success. Have you been in contact with them since Angela was here?"

The HR manager checked her computer.

"We haven't had any other temps from them since. I would definitely ask for Angela again, though; she was that good." She carried on scanning her screen. "That's funny..."

"What?" asked Kate.

"All-Temp Solutions never invoiced us... We don't pay the people directly. They're paid by the agency. But I can't see an invoice here."

"And you'd expect an agency to invoice fairly quickly?"

"Oh yes. It's been over a month since Angela was here. Our previous agency used to invoice weekly in advance."

"Right, and there's no one else here who might have known her a bit better?"

"I asked around when you rang, but no one spoke up."

Kate left the office, intrigued by the mystery temp. Back at HQ it took her about an hour to discover Angela Stevens's CV was a work of fiction. None of the schools or colleges cited could confirm her attendance. Previous employers and references also proved false. Kate went to Corcoran with it.

"That's a strange one... Who is this woman? Do you think she might be one of Hunter's earlier victims?" he said.

"Wouldn't he recognise her if she was?" she said.

"You'd think so. But women can change appearance very easily – hair dye, clothes, glasses..."

"That kind of fits. The HR woman said she was quiet and nondescript. 'Mousey' was her word."

"If one of his victims wanted to expose him, it's a good plan. She gets herself work in his office and reports him to HR... It's enough to ruin him, personally and professionally," said Corcoran.

"Why wouldn't she just report him to the Gardai?"

"And put herself through a trial? The legal route is still an absolute shit-show for victims, no matter what way you look at it."

"This way she ruins *his* life, and doesn't have to ruin her own..." said Kate.

"Exactly."

"It kind of makes sense. I always thought Hunter was too clever to get caught looking at porn in the office. He's gotten away with it for years. Why slip up now?"

"She only had to *say* she'd seen something on his screen.

There was every chance they'd find porn, given his appetites. If we're right, you have to hand it to her, it's a pretty clever revenge plot..."

"But who is she? And did she have anything to do with his murder?" said Kate.

"That's the question. If this woman could expose Hunter's secrets, why was that not enough?"

"Maybe she thought he'd gotten away with it, again. She reported him over a month ago and as far as anyone could tell, nothing happened. He was still living the high life, still in his job, still married..."

"So she got impatient...

"And killed him? It's a bit of a stretch... And how the hell are we going to find her? She's literally a ghost."

"Get the screen shots the techies have of his previous victims. See if anyone in Sherwin's recognises one of those women as this mysterious temp," said Corcoran.

Back in the squad room Rory was engrossed in something on his screen. Kate interrupted him to tell him about the 'ghost temp' Angela Stevens. His reaction was more eager than she'd expected.

"What if she's the serial killer?" he said.

"We were thinking more along the lines of her being a previous victim..." said Kate.

"I've been going through the files shared by Europol, and there's strong evidence the killer is a woman."

"What makes you think our mystery girl is her?"

"What makes you think she's not? Why would someone pretend to be a temp, set up a fake agency, invent a fake CV, and spend weeks working in an office for apparently no money?"

"To expose Hunter..." said Kate.

"Why not send an anonymous letter? That'd work just as well."

"Maybe... but if the intention was always to kill David Hunter, why go to all those lengths to expose him?" she said.

"Maybe killing him wasn't enough. Maybe she needed those around him to know what an absolute bastard he was," he said.

Kate mulled over the idea.

"There's a certain warped logic about it, I suppose. Take Hunter out of the picture, but justify the act by exposing him for what he was."

"Rough justice. It kind of fits with the Europol theory," said Rory. "I'll forward the files to you. Take a look."

Before getting into it, Kate forwarded the screen shots of Hunter's video victims to the HR manager at Sherwin's.

Please see if you or your colleagues recognise any of these women. Apologies for the poor quality images.

37

The case files on the other murders made for a couple of hours of reading. There were six in total – two in the UK and the others across several European countries. All the victims were asphyxiated, mostly by ligature strangulation, and two had been killed using a plastic bag. Forensic examinations had failed to find DNA or fingerprint evidence at any of the crime scenes. Locations varied from the victims' own homes to hotel rooms or cars. One murder had taken place in a club toilet in Amsterdam. Based on local police enquiries and some CCTV evidence, the killings had likely been carried out by an assailant not known to the victims, a woman. Each of the murdered men had a history of violent sexual crimes. Two had served time in prison, the others had unproven allegations against them or had been undetected. The incriminating evidence had emerged only after their deaths. Based on the victimology and methods used, Europol were alerting multiple police forces about the possibility of a serial killer working across borders.

Kate went to find Rory in the kitchen.

"Nice theory but there are massive holes in the whole idea," she said.

"It's only just been put together, and co-ordinating investigations across five countries – six if you count us – can't be easy," said Rory.

"Exactly, and who knows if the local teams are buying into this theory..."

He poured two cups of steaming coffee, and they went back to the squad room.

"Tell me where you think the idea falls down," he said.

"The choice of victims. How is this killer finding them? There must be thousands, hundreds of thousands of abusers out there, communing on the Dark Net with one another. How are these men selected? Who picks the victims? And why go all over Europe?"

"Mmm... good point. Go on."

"I've looked at witness statements, people who saw the victims with a woman just before they were killed, or saw her entering the premises where these murders took place..."

"And..."

"The descriptions... they're all different – some are tall, some short, different builds, different hair colours, even different ethnicities."

"Well, eye-witness testimony is notoriously unreliable; we all know that. What if it's not one serial killer, but a group, a killing team?" said Rory.

Kate almost laughed.

"This is getting more and more far-fetched..."

"I know, but think about it... A small team of two or three

assassins, prowling the continent, taking down rapists and child molesters."

"That's pure Hollywood, Rory. This is Dublin, not LA. And it doesn't address the issue of how they select their victims," said Kate.

"I know. That's a puzzle. Why Hunter? His activities have been kept secret for years," said Rory.

"Well, they were... until he started sharing videos on the Dark Web..."

"That could have made him a target..."

"But why him, out of all the perpetrators online?"

The two officers sipped their coffee in silence, until finally Rory put down his mug with a splash.

"It's *Ghostbusters!*" he said.

"Now you've lost me... What?"

"It's like this... You're a victim of an assault... or... you find out your husband, boyfriend, father, whatever, you find out he's a violent sexual abuser. But you don't want to go to the police, for all the usual reasons. So, you take matters into your own hands – but you don't want to get those hands dirty..."

"You call Ghostbusters," said Kate.

"Exactly. Different name, of course. It's probably Perv-Busters or something like that..." said Rory with a smile.

"It's a crazy idea..." said Kate, *but maybe Rory had something?* "OK, write it up for Corcoran, and don't mention *Ghostbusters* for God's sake. Hone it into a serious hypothesis: that this is about not one serial killer but a vigilante group or some kind of Star Chamber. See if he wants to take it to Europol. I'm going to see Ashling."

WHEN KATE GOT to the High Dependency Unit Max Egan was already at his best friend's bedside, book in hand. He looked almost as sickly as Ashling, who was asleep. This time Kate had been given just ten minutes with the patient.

"How's she doing?" she asked the boy quietly.

Max closed the book and offered Kate his seat.

"Not too bad. The doctors won't speak to me," he said softly, "but her mum says they're happy with her progress. She and I take turns sitting with Ash. Her kidneys are still not working too well, but they're hopeful that'll get better. As for everything else... well, see for yourself."

The girl stirred and opened her eyes. Max perched on the opposite side of the bed and took her hand.

"Hi, Ashling. Remember me?" said Kate.

Ashling lifted her head off the pillow and Max helped her to a semi-seated position, carefully positioning the wires and tubes that festooned her arms.

"You're the one who found me..."

Kate was pleased to hear the girl's voice was stronger. Her face looked better too, less puffy and swollen, though the bruises were still painfully vivid.

"I know you're not up to a full interview yet, but there's something I wanted you to know," said Kate. "We believe the man who abducted you was called David Hunter."

The students gave no indication that the name was familiar.

"Oh... Dan wasn't his real name, then..." said Ashling. "Have you found him? Is he locked up?"

"No... He's not under arrest..." Kate hesitated. "David Hunter was found dead in his car on Tuesday morning... We think he was murdered..."

The two stared wide-eyed at Kate. She was watching Max closely. He looked just as shocked as his friend.

"Good riddance! The bastard deserved it," he said vehemently.

"So that's why he never came back..." said Ashling, and she slumped down into the bed.

"Do you know who did it? Who killed him?" asked Max.

"Our enquiries are on-going. Ashling, I know it's been a shock but I wanted you to know that he can't ever hurt you again. And you won't have to go to court or give evidence against him. It's over," Kate went on.

"D'you hear that, Ash? It's over. You'll be out of here soon and back at college..." said Max, tears glinting in his eyes.

Ashling said thank you, the words catching in her throat. She closed her eyes as tears trickled down her battered face. Kate could see the nurse hovering outside the glass door. She said her goodbyes and left, feeling deeply sorry for the girl.

It's not over. Her body might heal... but it'll never be fully over.

"CORCORAN WANTS to sleep on my theory," said Rory, sitting on the edge of Kate's desk as she powered up her computer.

"I'm not surprised; it's a bit out there..."

"He's got a contact in Scotland Yard he wants to talk to. He says if anyone can confirm or debunk this *Avenging Angel* notion, it'll be them."

"*Avenging Angel*? That's only marginally better than *Ghostbusters*," she said.

"I like it; it's poetic! Anyway, the squad have had no joy in identifying Hunter's other victims, the women he filmed," said Rory. "UCD have no record of complaints. The rugby club mates have closed ranks. They won't say a word against their buddy."

"The old-boy network..."

"Yep. What next?"

Kate thought for a moment.

"Right, make me a list of the other murder victims across Europe, plus any email addresses or online identities they used. I have an idea."

Minutes later the two made their way to the Technical Intelligence Bureau on the top floor. Glad to see Keeva was on shift, Kate briefed her.

"See if you can find anything to connect these guys, any site or chat room where they met, any evidence that they might have been in touch with one another."

Then she explained their *Avenging Angel* theory to the computer expert.

"See if you can find anything online that backs it up," said Rory, and trotted out his *Ghostbusters* analogy. Keeva smiled.

"It's a great idea all the same."

"I'll pretend you never said that... " said Kate.

They left her to it. Finding the squad room empty, they signed off the Ops Board. It was almost seven o'clock.

"Drink?" asked Rory.

"I don't fancy a bar. Let's pick up something to eat and a couple of beers."

At her apartment, Kate and Rory talked into the night – about the case, her meeting with Marina Jackson, and, as the beer loosened their tongues, about her relationship with Greg.

"He's coming over soon, isn't he?"

"In about ten days."

"I wish I had a visiting lover... All the nice bits and none of the dreary stuff. It's like a honeymoon every two weeks!"

"Not really..."

Kate knew Rory didn't have a partner, and he rarely spoke about his love life.

"Why are you on your own? You're a catch," she said.

"God no! I don't want a partner. The gay scene is pretty full-on in this city, and it's not really my cup of tea. High camp is the order of the day, and I can't be doing with that. Anyway, I get on better with women."

"I can vouch for that, but you must have had some relationships in the past..."

"I've been in love alright, but it was a long time ago... I was just a kid, and it was disastrous."

"How come?"

"It turned out the object of my affections, another boy in school, was a bit of a psycho. He was abusive, violent."

"Oh, Rory, that's terrible."

"I was so crazy about him I put up with it for two years. Everyone could see he was a nightmare, everyone except me. Then he dumped me and I was destroyed. I ended up dropping out of school."

"You poor thing. How old were you?"

"I was seventeen when it ended. My family had to pick up the pieces. They were brilliant... but it took a long time. I had to re-sit my exams to get into college. I've never been even close to a relationship since then. Once bitten..."

"Well, you are the dark horse. How come I didn't know about this?"

"I don't talk about it much."

"Are you not lonely?"

"Not at all. I have my housemates, and I'm very close to my family. And I have good friends, like you..."

"But what about sex?"

"No thanks, love, you're alright," he laughed, and they left it at that.

As she saw him out to a waiting taxi, Rory had one last piece of advice.

"Call Marina Jackson. She reached out. You have to respond. And this time tell her who you are, OK?"

"Fine, I will," said Kate.

Drifting into a slightly tipsy sleep, she decided she had the best of both worlds – a good friend who was always there for her, and a lover who never stayed long enough to become boring. *She didn't need a family, not even a grandmother, did she?*

38

FRIDAY APRIL 8

The next morning there was a text from Keeva.

> Come and see me. I may have found
> something...

Kate and Rory headed up to the top floor.

"I haven't filed an official report yet," said Keeva, "but I wanted to let you know what I've found."

The two officers pulled up chairs.

"Firstly, I can't find any direct links between the Europol victims," she said, "or between those guys and David Hunter."

Kate nodded, disappointment rising, then Keeva went on.

"They did all lurk on the Dark Web, on the same sort of sites. It would take a lifetime to track every online interaction of six different sickos, but they were all into hardcore violent porn, or, in at least one case, child porn."

"But there's no indication that they interacted with one another?" asked Rory.

"Not that I've found... but there is something interesting. There are whispers around the benign circles of the hacking community," said Keeva.

"You mean Anonymous?" said Rory.

"I've heard of them," said Kate. "They're hackers, right?"

"Anonymous is a loose affiliation of hackers all over the world," said Keeva. "They mainly target oppressive regimes and hate sites. They're not the only group, but they're the most well-known."

"Could they be involved in this? In murder?" said Rory.

"It's not their style. They mainly hack into government or corporate websites, releasing confidential files, doxing. They take down child porn sites as well," said Keeva.

"What's doxing?" asked Kate.

"It's when you release online the private email and home addresses or phone numbers of someone," said Rory.

"So what are these whispers?" Kate asked, keen not to get bogged down in the intricacies of it all.

"There are rumours of a group – or possibly an individual; it's hard to tell – which... who take down sex offenders."

"Like those paedophile hunters? They entrap them and hand them over to the police?" said Rory.

"No. Those guys are out in the open; anyone can find them. This is a whole other level, but it could fit the bill of your *Avenging Angel*."

"Have you been able to access them directly?" asked Kate.

"No. I've just heard oblique references, hints that they're out there. If you want them to 'delete' someone, you submit irrefutable evidence of the person's wrong-doing."

"Like what?"

"Police reports, court reports, video evidence, that kind of thing, or a digital trail that proves that they're a sex offender and pose an on-going danger to women or children. They won't go after someone who's already locked up or about to be sent down."

"How does it work?"

"The rumours are that there's a kind of 'jury' that decides yay or nay. Probably not twelve people. I'd say it's fewer than that."

"And they delete... in other words, *kill* the targets," said Rory.

"Apparently," said Keeva.

"And have you been able to connect this secret group to any of the Europol victims? Or David Hunter?" asked Kate.

"No. They leave no trail. It's just whispers. I only got wind of it through certain channels I know of..."

"Hackers?" asked Rory.

"I couldn't possibly say," said Keeva, with a cheeky smile.

"Is there any way of verifying this?" asked Kate.

"I'll do some more digging, but they're well hidden..."

"If it's real, and six or seven men have been murdered by this group, they can't be that well hidden," said Kate.

As they left her office they could hear Keeva murmur "Go, Angels" under her breath.

Corcoran listened to their report with interest.

"I've been on to my friends in Scotland Yard. They're working on the serial killer theory..."

"Any suspects?" asked Kate.

"No, not yet. I'll float this idea with them."

"Keeva is scouring the net for more evidence of it. What else can we do?" asked Rory.

"If it holds water at all, then someone ratted Hunter out to these vigilantes. Look into that angle. Have you had any joy with the mystery temp?"

"No. She seems to have vanished," said Kate. "I'll submit the name for a Europe-wide background check, but it's probably as fake as everything else about Angela Stevens."

"Do you have a photo of her?"

"No, and the description I have is vague."

"It's been four days now, and we've got nowhere with this damn Hunter case," said Corcoran. "Find me something that's not vague."

Back at his desk Rory had a message from Europol. The description of Angela Stevens matched an eye-witness account of the woman who was seen at the crime scene in an Amsterdam nightclub. The murder victim, a convicted paedophile, had died by ligature strangulation in the club toilets.

"Maybe our Angela is one of the vigilante killers," he said.

"Her physical description is like a million other women on the planet – long dark hair, slim build, glasses," said Kate. "We're going to need more than that. Let's draw up a list of people who could have set David Hunter up... or put his name forward to the Ghostbusters..."

"See, now you're on board with my theory..." said Rory with a smile.

"Not completely, but if Corcoran is treating it seriously... who am I to scoff?"

It wasn't a long list, in the end.

Chloe Sherwin

Tom Sherwin
Donna Sherwin (Chloe's mother)
Hugh Sweetman
Finn Sweetman
Susan Sweetman
Max Egan
Victims 1-3 as yet unknown

Rory scheduled interviews with the Sweetmans first.

EMILY SWEETMAN'S family arrived at eleven. Kate sat in for all of the interviews. By lunchtime, as she saw the family off the premises, they'd learnt nothing new. With the coroner's inquest still months away, she still didn't have the heart to give them the more disturbing results of Emily's post mortem.

"There's no evidence whatsoever that one or all of them were involved in Hunter's murder... It seems certain they didn't know she was seeing him, or about the Sugar Babies," said Corcoran.

"What about the stuff on the Dark Web, the videos Hunter made of Emily..." said Kate.

"You're right, we can't totally rule them out. If any one of the Sweetmans saw those videos of Emily being raped, that's motive enough," said Corcoran, "but they would still have to identify Hunter, and he was clever enough to virtually obscure his identity on camera."

"I think we should move on to the Sherwins," said Kate. "Chloe has to be a suspect, and maybe even her father. He knew what David was up to; he had the evidence from the cybersecurity people."

"Has anyone interviewed the security firm?" asked Corcoran.

"Lawless and Sutton did."

"And... what was the outcome?"

Kate scrolled through the evidence reports on her computer.

"I'll look over their transcript now," she said.

It didn't take long. The two detectives had interviewed Paula Flint, owner of the specialist IT firm Cyberfixers. She confirmed that 'inappropriate' materials were found on only one device, and her team had submitted a detailed report to Sherwin's. At the CEO's request, they then 'sanitised' the laptop, the local server and the company's cloud backup. They'd also provided the firm with a USB key with copies of the offending videos, screenshots of online conversations, plus a list of the Dark Web sites 'the user' as she referred to Hunter, had visited. Detective Lawless asked why she hadn't reported him to the Gardai, but the CEO was adamant that confidentiality was key to her company's work.

"We'd have no corporate business otherwise," she said. "If a crime is unearthed, it's the responsibility of the client to take action, not ours."

Kate did an online search for the company and its CEO, but found nothing negative. Cyberfixers specialised in restoring lost files, cleaning viruses and malware, and closing off security breaches caused by hackers or systems failures.

"That's a dead end," she told Rory. "I'm fed up following useless leads. It's time we spoke to the Sherwins again. Chloe's mother confirmed Tom's alibi over the phone, but we need a face-to-face with all three. Come on, let's go. We'll go to the house. I don't want to give them time to prepare their answers or get their solicitor on board. We won't phone ahead."

"But they could refuse to speak to us..."

"If they do that, it'll speak volumes."

39

The Sherwins lived only a few miles from their daughter's house, but their home was in a whole other league. It was a grand period house, beautifully restored. It stood at the end of a winding tree-lined driveway surrounded by formal gardens. Rory was practically drooling by the time they pulled up outside the colonnaded front porch.

"I'm in totally the wrong job. I should have gone into property," he sighed.

As they stepped up to ring the bell, the front door opened abruptly. Kate and Rory held up their IDs.

"Oh, thank God you're here. I didn't know what else to do..."

Petite and in her sixties, the woman before them looked distraught.

"Mrs Sherwin?" asked Kate, puzzled.

"Yes, I'm Donna Sherwin. Come in, come in, hurry."

Through the hallway she brought them into a lavish sitting room.

"Chloe and her father – they're in Tom's study, and the door is locked. They've been arguing."

"Mrs Sherwin, did you call for Garda assistance?" asked Kate.

"Yes. There was a terrible noise… It was a gunshot, I'm sure. Now it's gone quiet and they won't let me in…"

Kate's heart thumped. She handed her partner the car keys.

"Rory, go out to the lockbox in the boot and bring me my sidearm," she said.

He left at a sprint.

"Where's your husband's study?" Kate asked.

"It's on the other side of the hall through the dining room. I can take you there."

"No, I need to get you out of here. Come with me."

Kate ushered Donna Sherwin out through the front door around the side of the house and away from the study. She called Corcoran.

"I'm at the Sherwins' home and I've got reports of shots fired."

"Intruders?"

"No. The only people here are Chloe and her parents. Mrs Sherwin raised the alarm. I'm getting her to safety now. It seems like there was an altercation between Chloe and her father in a locked room, and then a gunshot."

He agreed to dispatch an ambulance and an Armed Support Unit.

"I'm on my way. Don't do anything rash, Kate. Wait for back-up."

Donna Sherwin was trembling and pale. Kate led her to a bench in the garden, well away from the house.

"Are you sure you heard a gunshot?"

"I'm sure. Tom keeps shotguns in his study, in a locked cabinet. He used to shoot, but he hasn't in a long time, not since he got ill."

"Your husband's ill?"

"Yes... prostate cancer..."

"I'm sorry. Talk me through what happened."

"A little while ago I went to Chloe's room. She was meant to be resting but she wasn't there. She's been in a bad way since David's death... The doctors think it triggered a kind of pregnancy psychosis... but she's refusing to take the medications they prescribed, because of the baby."

"And this morning?"

"I heard raised voices from the study. I knocked on the door but it was locked and they wouldn't let me in. Tom shouted that I should go out for a while, they'd be OK, but I couldn't leave the two of them arguing like that... so I waited."

"And when did you hear the shot?"

"About ten minutes ago. I pounded on the study door, but it's quiet. I'm afraid something terrible has happened..."

"Go down the drive and wait by the roadside," said Kate. She put her arm around the woman's shoulders. "When the other Gardai get here, tell them what you've just told me, and point out to them exactly where the study is."

Rory was back. He handed Kate the Sig Sauer in its holster and a Kevlar vest.

"What'll we do while we wait?" he asked, as she strapped on the shoulder holster and fastened the vest.

"There's another vest in the car; put it on. The study is the second room off the hall on the right side of the house. Creep round that end of the building and see if you can get a visual through the window, but be careful, OK? Someone in that room fired a gun, probably a shotgun. Don't be the next target. Text me what you see."

"What are you going to do?" he asked.

"I'm going to the study door, to see if I can get a response."

"Shouldn't you wait for Armed Support?"

"They're a while away. If someone's wounded we can't stand back and do nothing."

"Shit, Kate, don't you go in there... Let me. I'm firearm certified," said Rory.

"I'm the senior officer here, and I'm trained in negotiation. I'll only go in if I have to. I've no intention of using this; it's just for show," said Kate, patting the holster.

There was no sound from the study. Kate stood to one side of the door and strained to hear anything from the Sherwins. A text vibrated on her phone, from Rory.

> Chloe is by the desk – she looks unharmed – double-barrel shotgun beside her – no sign of Tom

Kate replied.

> I'll try to get her out of there. Stay out of sight.

Wary of a shotgun blast through the door, Kate knocked lightly.

"This is DS Kate Hamilton. Can you come out, please, or let me in? I need to check you're OK."

Unable to hear anything from inside, she stepped closer and put her ear to the oak panel.

"Chloe, please open the door. I want to help you..."

A moment later she heard the sound of the chair scraping on the floor and soft footsteps approaching.

"I want to report a murder..." Chloe said, her voice calm.

Shit, what's happened in there?

"Whatever you want, I can help you, Chloe. Just open the door."

A text came in from Rory.

> She's left the gun by the chair – she's at the door

"He killed him... My father killed David, my poor baby..."

Kate took a deep breath.

Could it be true?

"Is your dad with you? I need to talk to him," she said.

"You need to take him away..."

"We will, Chloe. Just let me in..."

"Can't... You'll only try to stop me."

The footsteps retreated from the door.

What was she going to do?

"I need to talk to your father. Can you get him to come to the door?"

"You know what he said?" Chloe shouted. "He didn't want his grandchild growing up with a monster for a dad."

"That's a serious allegation, Chloe. We will investigate everything you've said... If you open the door I can take your father into custody."

"Too late..."

Another text.

> She's got the gun again.

"I'm coming in now, OK? Stand back, please, Chloe. I'm going to break down the door. I just want to help you."

Kate aimed a kick at the lock. It was an original old-fashioned door with a simple lock. The second kick splintered the wood in the frame and the door opened a few inches, but she couldn't see into the study. She drew her gun and pushed the door aside. She heard Rory coming into the dining room behind her and signalled to him to keep out of sight.

"I'm not going to hurt you. Just stay calm and we'll sort this all out."

Chloe stood behind the desk with the shotgun aimed at the floor. Next to her a chair was tipped on its side.

Where was Tom Sherwin?

"I'm coming in to you now, Chloe. I just want to check you're OK..."

"*He's* the monster... not my David," she said.

Then she turned towards Kate, the gun raised.

"Let me have the gun."

"I need it..."

"You don't need it, Chloe. I'm here now. Let me put it somewhere safe. Then I'll take your father away."

"I have to make sure..."

"Make sure of what?"

"That he's dead..."

"Who?"

"My father."

"Is he hurt?"

Chloe nodded. She lowered the shotgun slightly as if the weight was almost too much for her. Kate holstered her own gun, raised her hands and walked slowly towards the desk.

"Let me put it away... so no one else gets hurt..."

"I don't need it anymore..." said Chloe. "He's dead."

She dropped the shotgun on the desk with a loud thud, making Kate jump. She quickly slid it away from Chloe's reach. Rory came and took it out of the room. Kate finally got to see what Chloe was fixated on. She stood over her father's body, arms wrapped around herself.

"Rory, over here. It's Mr Sherwin. There's a lot of blood..." Kate said. "Apply pressure to the wound and see if he's breathing."

Kate took Chloe's arm and led her from the study, through the hall and out the front door. Two Garda cars pulled to a stop in front of the house just as they emerged.

"He killed David... he killed my David," said Chloe.

Kate handed her over to the first officer she met.

"This is Chloe Sherwin, suspect in a shooting. Caution her, secure her in one of your cars and stay with her. Use cuffs but take it gently; she's pregnant," she said.

In the study the panelling on the wall behind the desk had a metre-wide hole smashed into it and the wall was spattered with shot. It looked to Kate like the close-range shotgun blast had mostly missed the wounded man. *If he'd taken the full blast he would have been blown apart.*

Rory had placed Tom Sherwin in the recovery position. There was a massive wound in his right shoulder and a huge pool of blood. Rory was applying pressure with his bare hands to the source of all the blood.

"There's a pulse but it's weak..." he said.

"He needs to get to a hospital, and fast," said Kate.

Using her radio, Kate stood down the Armed Support Unit. The controller told her an ambulance was still ten minutes away.

"What about the air ambulance? I have a badly wounded elderly man. He's bleeding out. I don't think we can wait."

The controller said it would take even longer for the air ambulance, at least half an hour.

"Tell the others to hurry," said Kate.

Grabbing the first aid kit from the boot of her car, she ran back inside.

"No change," said Rory, both hands still pressed against the wound. "He's not losing as much blood, though, and I think he's still breathing..."

Ripping open packets, Kate bunched sterile dressings together into a wad of cotton.

"I'll take over. You listen for breath sounds," she said, and as soon as he lifted his bloodied hands, she rammed the wad of cotton onto the gaping wound.

"His breathing's shallow. I don't know how much longer..."

"Go and speak to the local Gardai," said Kate. "Once we get him evacuated they're to seal the scene. They've got Chloe. Make sure she's OK and secured."

Jim Corcoran arrived shortly after the ambulance, coming into the room just as Kate stepped back to let the paramedics work on Tom Sherwin.

"What happened here?" said Jim.

"It looks like Chloe and her father argued and she shot him with one of his own guns. She's outside under guard."

"She shot her own father?

"Yes. Going by the state of that wall, I think she mostly missed. But it's a bad wound."

"Jesus Christ, this family..." said Jim.

"She told me that her father killed David Hunter..."

"And that's why she..."

"Yes... an eye for an eye..."

"Rory says you got the gun away from her... Could you not have waited for the ASU?"

"No. I suspected someone was wounded. I took the decision to go in to preserve life."

"But you risked your own... again."

"I had no choice."

"You're going to put me in an early grave, Kate, I swear to God," he said, his expression a mixture of annoyance and relief.

As the paramedics wheeled a comatose Tom Sherwin out of the house, Corcoran went to brief the local officers. Rory was waiting by the car.

"Are you OK? That was tense," he said.

Kate leaned against the car door and took a deep breath. She could feel the adrenaline still coursing through her.

"I'm fine," she said, breathing slowly.

"What's happening now?"

"They're blue-lighting it to Elm Park. He's alive but he's lost a lot of blood," she said. "Mrs Sherwin can go in the ambulance with him. We'll head into HQ with Chloe."

Kate removed her Kevlar vest and sidearm and put them away in the boot. Her hands were covered in blood, which made her shudder, but she didn't want to go back into the house to wash them. The local guards were taping the entrance off. It was a crime scene – the fewer people in there the better.

Rory handed her a bundle of antiseptic wipes.

"I swiped them from the first aid kit, which, by the way, is still in there," he said.

"We'll requisition another one. Thanks for these; they're

a godsend," she said, scrubbing at her hands. "Our clothes are ruined."

"I know; it's soaked in. That'll be a tale for the dry cleaners."

They moved Chloe from the local Garda's custody into their own car. She was handcuffed and wrapped in a blanket. Rory fastened the seatbelt around her.

As he pulled the car around to head down the drive, Kate turned in her seat to look at the young woman. She was leaning against the window with her eyes closed.

"Are you OK, Chloe?"

She didn't answer and Kate tried again, louder. Chloe opened startled eyes.

"What's going on? Where are you taking me?" she said.

"We're going to Garda HQ. We need you to see a doctor and to talk us through what happened."

Chloe's eyes narrowed.

"I know you. You're the one... you told all those lies about David," she said, her voice suddenly venomous.

Rory looked worriedly at Kate. Kate spoke soothingly.

"Take it easy, Chloe. You've had a tough day. You should rest a little."

"You're just jealous of me and David, like all the other lying bitches... You want to take him from me. Such lies, filthy lies..." She waved her cuffed hands at Kate. "Wait till he hears what you've done to me! He'll be livid."

Kate murmured to Rory, "Don't spare the horses."

He switched on the siren and floored the accelerator.

Jim Corcoran followed the ambulance. If there was a chance Tom Sherwin had killed his son-in-law, he wanted to be right by his side when he came to... if he came to. At the Emergency Department they rushed the blood-soaked figure on the gurney past gaping onlookers. In the cubicle, a gaggle of medics descended on the wounded man, calmly and methodically working on him. A nurse pulled the curtains around the bed and waved Jim and Donna Sherwin away. He went outside to call Kate.

"How is he?" she asked.

"Can't say. They're working on him now. How's the daughter?"

"Not great. We're about fifteen minutes out from HQ. I'm hoping the on-call doctor will be waiting for us there."

"Has she said anything else?"

"Things are a little volatile."

"Are you safe? She's clearly dangerous."

"We're OK. Passenger is secured. When will you be back at base?"

"That depends on what the doctors say. I was hoping to question Sherwin when he comes round, but my guess is I won't get near him today. I'll place a Guard here and I'll be back at base in half an hour. Don't question the daughter without me."

The nurse who'd shooed Jim away came to find him.

"Are you the one who brought in Mr Sherwin?"

"Yes. I'm a DI with An Garda Siochana."

"Oh, of course, because of the gunshot wound... I wanted to let you know he's gone to theatre. His condition is serious."

"When do you think I could speak to him?"

"Not today anyway. He'll be in surgery for some time. It's a big wound, a lot of damage. If the surgery goes well you could ask again tomorrow or the day after."

Jim found Donna Sherwin in a room marked Relatives Only. Edward Simms, the family solicitor, was with her.

What was it with this family? They can't sneeze without a lawyer present.

"Mrs Sherwin, we'll need to get a statement from you later but what can you tell me now?" he said.

The lawyer replied, "She won't be making any statements at this time. She's in shock, Detective."

Donna Sherwin looked ashen, and her voice was high and shaky.

"Where have you taken Chloe?"

"Your daughter is in custody, on the way to Garda HQ. She's safe. We'll have her checked by a doctor there."

"She didn't mean to do it. She's lost her mind..."

"Donna, not now," said Simms.

Bloody lawyer...

Corcoran handed him his card.

"Keep me informed of Mr Sherwin's condition. I'll be back to talk to him as soon as he's well enough. And we'll need that statement soon, Mrs Sherwin."

"If you're going to question Chloe, I need to be present," said Simms.

"I think you'll find there's a conflict of interest here, if you're representing both the alleged assailant and the victim..." said Corcoran.

The lawyer said nothing.

"If we do question Ms Sherwin today, I'll make sure there's a duty solicitor present," said Jim, turning to leave.

"Thank you, Detective," said Simms.

"It was an accident, a terrible accident..." said Donna Sherwin pitifully.

It was a tense drive back to HQ. Kate used the radio to ask for an escort, and as soon as they hit the main roads a patrol car joined them and tailed them in. Rory could feel his hands growing clammy on the steering wheel. In the back seat, Chloe went from wailing incoherently, struggling with the restraints and kicking their seats, to slumping into a brooding silence.

In the basement car park a welcoming committee awaited them. Kate recognised the duty doctor and a social worker, and with them, two Garda constables. They handed over the prisoner with some relief.

"She has been cautioned," she said.

Quietly, she briefed the little group.

"Don't be alone with her, or leave her unattended. She's been agitated and aggressive. We believe she shot her own father little more than an hour ago. I'm worried for her safety. She's pregnant, so make sure she gets food and drink, and don't put her in a cell. Use one of the soft rooms. Let us know the minute she's fit to be interviewed."

Inside, Kate and Rory headed for the canteen. He went to the counter.

"I'll have a tea," said Kate. "I'm wired. Caffeine might tip me over the edge. I'll be on the sofas."

Rory brought their drinks over, plus a plate of chips and two forks.

"Sweet tea and starchy food is good for shock, isn't it?" he said.

"If you say so," said Kate. "God, we've so much to do... What a day..."

"Tea and grub first... We need a break," he said.

The two tucked in for a few minutes.

"Well, that wasn't what I expected at all," said Kate.

"Do you think Chloe's had a breakdown?" asked Rory.

"Her mother said she'd been diagnosed with psychosis."

"If that wasn't a psychotic episode, I don't know what is..."

"If she is psychotic, and Tom Sherwin dies, she'll get off – with the insanity defence," said Kate.

"She's certainly not rational," he said.

"If it's true that her father killed her husband... she has motive. Maybe it's all an act, this madness."

"We'll have to charge *him* with murder if he survives, and charge *her* with murder if he doesn't! This case just gets weirder..." said Rory.

"To charge him with the son-in-law's killing, we'd need evidence, and his wife has already given him an alibi, plus we've no forensics. On the other hand, there's plenty to charge Chloe for shooting him."

Corcoran arrived, bought a sandwich and coffee, and joined them in the former smoking corner.

"How's Tom Sherwin?" asked Kate.

"In surgery," said Jim. "How's Chloe?"

"She's with the doctor now, but she was pretty crazy on the way here," said Rory.

"I don't think there's any doubt she pulled the trigger on her father. Mind you, the mother says it was an accident. We have to ask Chloe what she knows about Hunter's killing..." said Jim.

"If the docs say she's unfit, we won't get to question her today," said Kate, "or maybe for some time."

"We need to talk to the father too, if he makes it," said Jim, finishing his sandwich in large bites. "Now come on, you two. There are reports to be written up."

When they'd filed their reports, Corcoran sent them

home. The doctor had refused to let him interview Chloe
Sherwin, saying her mental condition was too volatile and
she needed to be hospitalised. As Kate turned the key in the
door to her apartment, a delayed reaction hit her. She felt
suddenly shaky, cold and hyper-vigilant. Stripping off her
blood-stained clothes, she dropped them into a bin bag.
After double-checking the bathroom door was locked, she
stepped into a hot shower. No amount of washing could
dispel the sensation of warm sticky blood on her hands. She
was exhausted, but sleep proved elusive.

She'd faced down an unstable suspect with a gun, *again*.
It was little more than a year since the last time, and that
hadn't ended well. Now, jumbled flashbacks of the two
scenes haunted her night.

40
SATURDAY APRIL 9, 2011

> Hi, Kate. Is there any chance you could make dinner with Marina this weekend? She's anxious to have that chat. She can do Saturday or Sunday. Let me know if there's a time that suits. We'll work around your schedule. Best, Karen.

The text arrived just as Kate surfaced from a fitful sleep. Before she could have second thoughts, she replied.

> Sunday at six p.m. would be good for me.

Something about having a shotgun pointed at her heart made her personal anxieties seem trivial. This time she'd be honest with Marina. She owed Rosie's mother the truth. What was the worst that could happen?

Over coffee in the office, she told Rory.

"It's the right thing to do, Kate, for her and for you."

"I'm not going to think or talk about it again until Sunday night."

JIM CORCORAN BRIEFED the team on the latest developments.

"At the moment Tom Sherwin is our prime suspect for the murder of David Hunter. He was the only one on our list who knew about Hunter's activities. Now his daughter says that her father killed her husband."

"But is she a credible witness?" asked Sutton. "I heard she's been committed."

"She's been admitted voluntarily to a private hospital."

"A mental ward?" asked another officer.

"Yes, she's being assessed by psychiatrists."

"But she has had some kind of a breakdown?"

Kate answered.

"We think she argued with her father and shot him with his own legally held shotgun. When we took her into custody, she presented to us as mentally unwell."

"So, in the absence of evidence against anyone else," said Corcoran, "Tom Sherwin has to be either included or excluded as the killer. I want you all to focus on that."

"Isn't he critical?"

"That's what we're told. He survived the surgery last night, but he's not out of the woods yet."

Jim went around handing out the assignments, financial checks, CCTV trawls, door-to-door enquiries. Soon the room began to empty out.

"Try to corroborate Sherwin's alibi," he said to Kate and Rory. "Do whatever you can to prove or disprove it."

"In a couple of days Chloe went from being glued to his side, as close as any father and daughter, to accusing him of murder," said Rory.

"The question is, was it all in her mind? Did she stumble on some proof, or did he make an admission?" said Kate.

"Well, at the moment we can't talk to either of them, so let's look for the evidence."

"And do we charge her with attempted murder?" asked Rory.

"We can't, not while she's under psychiatric care."

Armed with a search warrant, Kate and Rory, along with two CSIs and two Garda constables, arrived at the Sherwin home by ten o'clock. The Technical Bureau had finished with the study area, but there was still a local patrol onsite. They confirmed Donna Sherwin had not returned to the house overnight but had stayed at her husband's side in the hospital.

Under Kate's instructions, the small group combed the entire house. It was a long and arduous task, but as the hours passed, the search yielded nothing of significance.

"We need to examine both cars, and check the SatNavs. I want to know where those cars have been since last Monday," Kate instructed the CSIs.

"This is a state-of-the-art alarm system," said Rory, peering at the control panel inside the front door.

"What good is that to us?" she asked.

"It's a sophisticated piece of kit. It probably stores data on entries and exits. It might not tell us who came or went, but it'll record when external doors were opened and closed; they're all wired."

"Brilliant. Get onto the alarm company. See if they can retrieve the data for Monday night/Tuesday morning."

She called Corcoran.

"I knew you'd get nothing from the house," he said. "If Sherwin did kill Hunter, he's had time to cover his tracks. I'm on my way to the hospital now. He's come round from the surgery. Meet me there. We'll interview him together."

———

TOM SHERWIN WAS in a private room. As luxurious as a hotel suite, it had a stunning view across Dublin Bay. He looked a lot frailer than the man they'd first met only a few days earlier. He was propped in a sitting position, hooked up to various monitors and drains, and his shoulder and chest were swathed in dressings. The moment they stepped into the room, Donna Sherwin stood up abruptly from her seat by his bed.

"Why are you here? Tom's not well enough..."

"The doctors say we can have a few minutes with your husband," said Kate.

"It's important that we speak to him," said Corcoran, "alone."

Their voices woke Tom.

"It's OK, love. You go and get a bite to eat," he said.

His voice was hoarse, but his tone firm. Donna left then, her expression unhappy.

"How are you feeling, Mr Sherwin?" asked Kate.

"Bit sore, but not too bad."

"We need to ask you about yesterday's events at the house..." said Corcoran.

"That was just a stupid accident. All my fault. I took out the shotgun to clean it, didn't realise it was loaded, Chloe went to put it away and somehow it went off. She must have got a terrible fright. Donna tells me she's been hospitalised."

"We've got reason to believe the shooting was far from an accident," said Kate. "Chloe admitted as much, at the scene."

"She's not herself. Whatever she said, I'm telling you what actually happened."

"Your daughter made certain allegations against you, Mr Sherwin," said Jim.

"As I said, she's been out of her mind with grief since David's death."

"Chloe said you killed her husband."

Tom's face showed no surprise at this. He closed his eyes and sighed.

"She's not well, and with the baby coming... we'll have to get her some serious help."

"Did you kill your son-in-law?' asked Corcoran.

"I did not," said Tom. "Now, I'm tired, so if you don't mind..."

Kate and Jim looked at one another.

What next?

"We will find out if you had a part in the murder of David Hunter," said Jim.

Tom did not flinch. They turned to leave. They were at the door when he spoke again.

"Have you ever had a dog?" he asked.

"Yes, why?" said Jim.

"We had a dog once, when Chloe was little. A stray we

found out on the road. She begged to keep it as a pet... so we took it in. We gave it a good home and she adored the creature. Then one day, while they were playing, the dog bit her. It was a nasty bite too, left quite a scar. She still loved him... wanted to keep him. But there's only one thing to do with an animal like that..."

"Mr Sherwin, would you like to make a statement..." said Kate.

"Chloe was heartbroken... but she got over it."

Tom Sherwin leant back on his pillows and closed his eyes.

———

"THIS COULD FIT in with my *Avenging Angel* theory," said Rory.

Back at HQ, Kate and Jim were briefing the team on their conversation with Tom Sherwin.

"It's the nearest thing to an admission we're going to get, but not enough to charge him. He's a clever man," said Jim.

Data from the alarm company showed that no external door in the Sherwin house had been opened during the timeframe of the killing. The SatNavs on both of the family cars indicated they'd never been near the site of Hunter's murder. Triangulation data confirmed Tom's cell-phone hadn't moved from the house during the night. Taken together, all the data supported Sherwin's alibi.

"He set up the murder," said Jim, "either by employing a contract killer, or if your theory is right, Rory, getting these online vigilantes to carry it out."

"We just need to find the evidence. Any joy from the Sherwins' computers or financials?" asked Kate.

Keeva answered.

"Nothing yet. No hidden files or incriminating emails."

"We need to look at his office computers, and all company and personal bank accounts. If Sherwin made this happen, there has to be proof somewhere..." said Jim.

41

SUNDAY APRIL 10, 2011

K ate spent the morning in bed. Exhaustion had finally caught up with her. In the afternoon she wandered along Grafton Street. She'd thrown away the bloody suit and shirt from the shooting, so it was time for some shopping. In the end she got two jackets, some smart jeans and shirts, and a couple of bright silk scarves. Several hundred euro worse off, back home, she examined her purchases. *What to wear to meet Marina?* Eventually she chose a pink shirt. *Less 'on duty' looking than a white one.* She added a patterned scarf to cover her scar, blue jeans and a navy jacket.

Looking at herself in the mirror, she tried to remember the pictures she'd seen of Rosie Jackson. At the time she'd been convinced there was a resemblance. Now she wondered if she'd imagined it. She applied makeup, wiped most of it off again, and settled for some mascara and lip-gloss.

At six o'clock she rang the doorbell at the house in Blackrock. Marina answered it herself this time.

"Sergeant Hamilton, come in, come in. It's lovely to see you again."

"Please call me Kate, Mrs Jackson."

"That would be nice, and you must call me Marina. I hope you don't mind if we eat in the kitchen. The dining room is so formal we never use it these days."

In the kitchen the table was set for two with gleaming silver and glass, and a pretty arrangement of fresh flowers in the centre.

"You sit down and I'll dish up. My lovely housekeeper made us a lasagne and salad, and there's a cheesecake for afters. Will you pour the wine?"

Kate spotted an open bottle of white on the counter and poured a tiny amount into her own glass and filled Marina's.

The food was delicious and the two chatted about the weather and other trivia as they ate. Kate managed only half her generous plateful, and refused dessert. Her stomach was churning with nerves. She helped clear away the crockery while Marina made coffee.

"Let's take these up to the sitting room," she said.

A log fire burned in the grate and soft lamps dotted around the room made it cosy. They sat in armchairs opposite each other next to the marble fireplace.

"I suppose we should get to the heart of the matter..." said Marina.

Kate could only manage a quiet 'yes'.

"I've been thinking about you since the last time. I have so many questions."

"I'll do my best to answer..."

"I've been looking at the photos of Rosie ever since you were here. I can't seem to stop. And now, when I look at your face, all I see is hers..."

What to say to that?

"I'm sorry, Kate, you must think I'm a foolish old woman..."

"I don't think that," said Kate, "and there's no need to apologise."

"What makes you say that?"

Kate took a deep breath.

"The woman I told you about, the one who died, Bernie O'Toole. She told me that your daughter... Rosie... was my mother."

"So I'm not going mad? It's not my imagination..." Marina said, and she went to the bookshelves and pulled out the album they'd looked at a week earlier. Opening the pages, she began to cry.

"You're so like her – the eyes, the colouring, and there's something about your smile..." she said.

Kate didn't know what to say.

"We won't be sure..."

"I know. I've been thinking about it every minute since I first met you. If you agree, we'll have to get our DNA tested to confirm it... but looking at you now I'm almost sure. I've been wondering and puzzling over why you came to see me and... you were born in St Mary's, weren't you? It's the only thing that makes sense."

"I think so. I didn't know about it until last year. My parents are both gone, so there's no one to ask."

"But there must be some adoption papers, surely."

"No, nothing official. Just a forged birth certificate listing the Hamiltons as my birth parents, and some bits and pieces Bernie left me."

"That's why you came to me..."

"Yes. I'm sorry it's upset you. It's all so painful..."

"It's painful, yes, it is, but I can take it... If you're Rosie's child I'm glad you found me. I have no family to speak of. If you're my granddaughter, wouldn't that be something?"

Marina was smiling and crying at the same time.

Kate struggled to keep it together.

They talked for more than an hour, Marina reminiscing about her late husband and their early family life. Kate told her about her own happy upbringing, and filled her in on Bernie O'Toole's revelations, leaving out any reference to Tim Larsson. Marina had assumed one of Rosie's twins had died soon after birth. The truth was something Kate would never willingly reveal. As she left to go home soon after nine o'clock, Marina kissed her cheek lightly.

"If it's OK with you, I'll get Karen to organise the DNA testing. She'll text you with the details. We can get someone to come to you – discreetly, of course. We'll make sure the testing is completed quickly; I don't think I could wait too long. Whatever results come back, I'm glad to know you, Kate."

The next morning Kate told Rory everything.

"That's brilliant. Now you'll know for sure."

"Hopefully, but it's still scary. She's a nice woman, but I'm not ready for a new family... not really."

"It's one little old lady. What's the harm? You don't have to move in with her! At least this way you'll finally know the truth."

42

MAY 2011

The investigation into David Hunter's murder quickly ground to a halt. Not a single shred of evidence could be found to confirm what Corcoran and Kate believed – that Tom Sherwin had ordered the murder of his son-in-law. No other lines of enquiry proved fruitful. Chloe remained under medical care, in a private clinic. No amount of pressure from Corcoran could get them access to question her. The Sherwins' solicitor, Edward Simms, reported she was still seriously ill – in his words, 'delusional'. Weeks passed with no new developments.

Europol was still keen on the idea of a cross-border serial killer, and they were also considering the *Avenging Angel* hypothesis. Some of the finest minds in cybercrime were searching for evidence of the shadowy group, with little success. There were rumours of such an organisation, but they remained within the realms of conspiracy theories and fantasy. The mystery temp, Angela Stevens, had vanished without trace, and the squad had failed to identify any of Hunter's previous victims.

A month after his death, David Hunter's funeral was a small affair in the chapel at the City Crematorium. Colleagues and rugby mates made up a crowd of fewer than forty people, including Kate and Corcoran. The dead man's sister had not travelled from Australia, but there was a wreath in her name. Tom and Donna Sherwin attended, without Chloe. There was no eulogy for the dead man and the priest's words were more generic than personal. As the coffin slid away behind dark curtains, the congregation filed up to offer condolences to the Sherwins. Kate and Corcoran joined the line.

"Sorry for your loss," said Jim, shaking hands with first Donna and then Tom, who looked grey in pallor and thin. His right arm was still in a sling. Kate murmured something similar, shook their hands, and left as the line of mourners moved on.

As they made their way to the car, Jim was clearly frustrated.

"We've got nothing on him, and yet we know he did it."

"Lots of people would say Hunter got what he deserved..."

"We're not allowed to think like that."

"I know, and I don't. I'd rather he faced justice for what he did to poor Emily and Ashling, and God knows how many others."

"Tom Sherwin looks the worse for wear..."

"He's got cancer..."

"I didn't know..."

"And the worry of Chloe, and her baby... it can't be easy."

"We're not giving up. There has to be some way of nailing Sherwin..."

"If we don't get something soon, looking at him today, I'd guess he won't be here much longer."

"What a mess. What a shitty mess."

Can you come over tonight? I've got the results. I'd like you to be here when I open them. Marina

THE DAY after the funeral Kate and Rory were poring over Sherwin company files when the text pinged into her phone. She showed Rory.

"How do you feel?" he said.

"I don't know... nervous."

"But you'll go, won't you?"

"Can't back out now."

She replied.

I'll see you around seven.

Kate presented herself at the big house in Blackrock filled with trepidation. She didn't know which outcome to fear the most – a positive familial match with Marina, or a negative result, which would leave her with more questions than answers.

Karen, Marina's assistant, opened the door and led her into the sitting room. There was a tray filled with afternoon tea treats on the coffee table. Marina came in from the conservatory.

"Thanks, Karen. You're a star. You get on home now. I've kept you late enough."

Then they were alone, and it felt awkward. Marina poured the tea and offered Kate a plate of tiny sandwiches.

"There's no playbook for this situation, is there?" she said wryly.

"No. I'm a bit at sea, if I'm honest."

"Whatever happens, I meant what I said. I'm glad to have met you."

Kate put down her cup and plate.

"Can we get it over with? I don't mean to be rude, but all of this feels a bit surreal."

"You're right. I don't know why we didn't just do it as soon as you got here."

Marina went to her handbag and brought out an envelope marked Private & Confidential.

"You look, please. I can't," she said.

The page inside was filled with technical jargon, but Kate knew enough from her work to make sense of it.

"The DNA testing shows that I share one quarter of my DNA with you," she said shakily.

43

Ashling was released from hospital after ten days. Despite her mother's pleas, she wouldn't go home to the farm. She went back to the place she shared with Max. He'd cleaned ferociously for her return, and being back in the little house felt akin to normality. Max seemed to know when to stay close and when to leave her alone. Three weeks after her abduction she went back to classes, to be greeted by hugs and cheers from fellow students. It was a bit overwhelming, but soon, to her relief, the attention died down. She threw herself into catching up on her college work. Only Max knew about the panic attacks and nightmares she still suffered. At his insistence, Ashling took up an offer of counselling from Victim Support, but it would be a long haul.

Then she got an email summoning her to an appointment with the Dean of Studies, and it sent her into a spin.

What could it be about? She'd almost caught up with her work... She just needed a bit more time.

The Dean, a soft-spoken woman she'd never met before,

asked Ashling how she was, and how her studies were going. After the small talk, she got to the reason for the meeting.

"I've got good news. We're pleased to offer you a full scholarship for the rest of your degree. A bursary has been set up, which also includes a generous living allowance. There's more than enough to cover your primary degree and further studies like a Master's or even a PhD, here or at another university. And if you choose to leave education, whatever funds remain in the trust become yours."

Ashling was speechless for a long moment.

"A bursary? A trust? But how?"

"We have been gifted a substantial amount, to be used solely for your benefit. In addition, financial provision has been made for this office to administer the funds."

"Gifted? What do you mean gifted?"

"An anonymous donor has provided a generous trust fund to cover your tuition and living expenses. It's an unusual situation, but one we're happy to deal with, especially after all you've been through."

"And you can't tell me who's done this?"

"I personally don't know who the donor is. It's all been done through legal channels. We get donations all the time from corporate bodies and our alumni, though not quite like this, and rarely for the benefit of a specific student. I know it's a lot to take in but I wouldn't worry about the source of the bequest if I were you. Just enjoy the opportunity this opens up for you."

TOM SHERWIN LIVED JUST LONG ENOUGH to see his grandchild reach her first birthday. Despite a number of interviews under caution, he never admitted to any culpability in the murder of his son-in-law. With zero evidence to support a prosecution, no charges were brought against him. Chloe's doctors signed affidavits to the effect that she was suffering a psychotic break in the days and months after losing her husband.

When finally she agreed to be interviewed by Kate and Corcoran, she claimed to have no memory of the shooting in her family home, and denied ever implicating her father in the murder of her husband. The Director of Public Prosecutions declined to pursue a charge against Chloe, given the medical evidence of her psychosis and the fact that her father insisted the shooting was accidental. Her baby girl was born by C-section soon after her release from the private mental facility where she'd spent more than five months. She named her daughter Madeleine. With the help of a live-in nanny, talking therapy and medication, Chloe slowly recovered.

In her absence, her parents had removed all trace of David from the house – photos, his clothes and personal things, all were gone. Chloe felt it was like he'd never existed. *But then her David, the man she fell in love with, had never really existed, had he?*

THE CORONER'S inquest concluded that Emily Sweetman had died accidentally by drowning. Much was made of the levels of alcohol in her blood when she went into the sea. Her video was deemed to be inconclusive proof of suicidal intent on her part. Evidence was heard of signs of violence on the girl's body, but it was judged to be a consequence of seven days' immersion in the rough dark waters between Ireland and Wales. The Sweetmans told the coroner that Emily had been quiet in the weeks before her death, but not depressed, as far as they knew. Max and Ashling were not called to give evidence. There was little media coverage. Afterwards, the family came and shook hands with the detectives.

"How are you doing?" asked Kate.

"Glad that's over," said Hugh, "and Emily's name hasn't been dragged through the mud. That's the best that we could hope for."

KATE AND MARINA took things slowly. For Kate there was a degree of natural reticence to overcome, and Marina harboured enormous guilt over the past. It made for moments of unspoken tension between the two. Both independent women, used to their own company, ironically it was their similarity that made forging a relationship difficult. They met every few weeks, in Blackrock or at restaurants in the city, but there was no getting away from the fact that they were strangers with only a tragic history that linked them.

One night, after they'd been to a piano recital at the National Concert Hall, Kate was walking Marina to her car.

"What a wonderful evening. I'll treasure these times, Kate. I don't expect to live for much longer, so every moment counts."

Where is this going?

"You're not ill, are you?" asked Kate, feeling a little alarmed.

"Nothing like that, but I am seventy-eight this year."

"That's no age these days, really."

"I'm just being practical. I'm not afraid of dying. I've been haunted by regret... for far too long, and I don't want to go to my grave carrying it... That's why there's something I want you to do for me. "

They stopped then and Marina faced her.

"I want you to find your father, Kate. Find him, and make him pay for what he did."

EPILOGUE

The woman brought only a carry-on case and a laptop bag. Dublin Airport was busy, as always, and she spent a relaxed half hour in the VIP lounge before her flight to Berlin. In the quiet confines of First Class, she even managed a short nap. At Arrivals a driver held up a sign with a name – not her real one. Soon they were en route to a discreet and exclusive city hotel. The trade fair at which her company always had a presence didn't start for another day. She would stay here only one night, and move to the conference hotel in the morning. Locking her computer and phone into the room safe, she made her way on foot to a tiny Italian restaurant a few blocks away. The others were already there. As she took her seat at the table, they raised their glasses in salute. There were four women, ranging in age from late twenties to that difficult to pinpoint stage between forty-five and sixty. One of them filled a glass and handed it to her.

"Champagne this time? What happened to our usual prosecco?"

"We took in a generous donation," said the youngest of the group, who spoke with an English accent.

"I like you better blonde," replied the newcomer with a smile. "That dark hair did you no favours, and those glasses... shocking!"

The five ordered food and more champagne. The oldest of the group then tapped her glass to still the chatter.

"Have you studied the submission?" she asked.

They all nodded.

"Time to vote."

She passed around small slips of paper and pens.

Each wrote in silence, folded the slip and put it in the centre of the table. The oldest one unfolded the slips. On each piece of paper was a black tick.

"We are unanimous. I'll be in touch to make the arrangements."

Their food arrived then, and all solemnity disappeared from the gathering. They were just five good friends, having a rare get-together and enjoying each other's company.

THE END

THANK YOU FOR READING

Did you enjoy reading *Dark Waters*? Please consider leaving a review on Amazon. Your review will help other readers to discover the novel.

ABOUT THE AUTHOR

Gaye admits to a lifelong obsession with crime, and a keen interest in psychology and social history. She credits her parents, who were avid readers, with her love of fiction. When she graduated from Enid Blyton to Agatha Christie at age nine, so began a life of crime... reading.

She enjoyed an award-winning career as a TV Producer/Director working for the BBC, ITV and RTE. She's always written in her spare time, and during lockdown, when her husband built himself a workshop at the end of the garden, she seized control (peacefully) and renamed it her writing cabin. The result was *Blood Mothers*.

Now a full-time writer, she has three adult children and one adorable granddaughter. She lives in Dublin with her husband, *to whom she now owes a workshop*, two of her grown up kids and two rescue dogs who are not at all grown up, but make for great company at the bottom of the garden.

ALSO BY GAYE MAGUIRE

The DS Kate Hamilton Crime Thriller Series

Blood Mothers

Dark Waters